"TA... ...HIS VO... ...HUSKY, LIKE A WHISPER ACROSS A FOOTBALL FIELD.

The gunman stepped out of his hiding place in the shower. He stood in the semi-darkened room, hidden by the shadow of the door, watching me. He was huge, much taller than I had guessed, over six feet. Everything about him was dark. Black hair, long and unruly, curling around his collar; dark, faded black jeans and a leather jacket; a black T-shirt and dark black boots. The gun hung at his side, not forgotten, but no longer pointed in my direction.

"I know all about you, Maggie Reid," he said. "I made it my business to know. I know where you live. I know where you work, and I know what you do when you think no one is watching you." My heart was stuck in my throat. What had he seen? Where had he been hiding and watching? And for how long?

He walked over and squatted down in front of the chair where I sat. He put his hands on each armrest, pinning me back.

"You know why you want to help me?" he said. "Because bad things will happen to everyone you care about if I don't find Vernell Spivey. If he isn't already dead, he could wind up dead. I'm not the only one looking for him, you know. I'm just the guy who's going to find him and straighten a few things out. The others are going to kill him."

A small smile crossed his face, but there was no warmth behind it.

Also by Nancy Bartholomew

Your Cheatin' Heart

NANCY BARTHOLOMEW

STAND BY YOUR MAN

HarperTorch
An Imprint of HarperCollins*Publishers*

This is a work of fiction. Names, characters, places, and incidents are products of the author's imagination or are used fictitiously and are not to be construed as real. Any resemblance to actual events, locales, organizations, or persons, living or dead, is entirely coincidental.

HARPERTORCH
An Imprint of HarperCollins*Publishers*
10 East 53rd Street
New York, New York 10022-5299

Copyright © 2001 by Nancy Bartholomew
ISBN: 0-06-101410-9

First HarperTorch paperback printing: May 2001

HarperCollins ®, HarperTorch™, and ❦ ™ are trademarks of HarperCollins Publishers Inc.

Printed in the United States of America

Visit HarperTorch on the World Wide Web at www.harpercollins.com

10 9 8 7 6 5 4 3 2 1

For my brother, John—
the one who keeps the music and wisdom
alive in our family,
and to his beautiful family:
Vicky, Jimmy, and Emily.
I love you.

Acknowledgments

My books couldn't happen without the support and encouragement of my family. My boys are all the world to me and I want to thank them once again for eating lots of noodles! Thanks to my husband for being the first reader, no matter that he hasn't gotten to put his briefcase down or loosen his tie!

Thanks also to my incredible editor, Jeffery McGraw, who sees the vision and pushes me forward. And to my agent, Donald Maass, for keeping my feet on the ground and my fingers on the keyboard. I would also like to thank my critique group for their unflagging support.

Now for the real scoop . . . Thank you, Town and Country Cloggers: Miss Patsy, Susan, Caroline, Kenny, Christine, and the gang! And Wendy, thanks for pretending to be my publicist and for giving so much of your time, energy, and love!

One

The first time I laid eyes on Detective Marshall J. Weathers of the Greensboro Police Department's Homicide Unit, I heard Mama's voice echoing in my head. "It's the fire that'll burn you, sweetie, not the smoke." Marshall Weathers was pure fire, from his icy blue eyes and handsome tanned face right down to his tight, faded jeans. But trying to bring the two of us together was like trying to put two angry porcupines in a Coke bottle—a sticky proposition on the best of days.

It was no different when my ex-husband, Vernell, disappeared. Marshall Weathers was the first person I knew to turn to, but he should've been the last. Despite his handsome ways and that thick cowboy mustache of his, I figured Marshall Weathers was just a lowlife snake in the grass.

I jammed a quarter in the meter across the street from the police station, knowing full well that I shouldn't go see the man, but where else could I go? Vernell Spivey, North Carolina's self-proclaimed King of the Satellite Dish and Mobile Home Kingdom, had been missing for two days. His bank accounts were as dry as his liquor cabinet, and I was worried half out of my mind. So I figured it didn't matter that Marshall Weathers had promised to call. So what if it had been two months? So what if I remembered the way he held me out on the dance floor, with a look that promised forever and a touch that said tonight? This was an emergency.

"Detective Weathers," the receptionist said into her little headset, "a woman is here to see you. Says her name is Maggie Reid. Says she knows you."

Why did they always make it sound like you were a liar? I stalked over to the waiting area, picked up *Guns and Ammo Magazine*, and held it in front of me, my face flaming nearly as red as my hair.

He'd accused me of murdering my brother-in-law a mere two weeks before he two-stepped me around the floor at the Golden Stallion, the club where I sing with the house band. He'd kissed me that night and disappeared. So, what the hell was that? Now Vernell was gone. A smarter woman would've seen the trend, but not me. I'm an optimist. I figure one day God'll make a model that doesn't rust out and holds true to its promises.

I closed my eyes for a short second, feeling his lips on mine, smelling his cologne, and remembering the way his arms had squeezed me close to him. My heart started to pound and I could feel my face turning redder at the thought of what might have happened if only I'd had half a chance.

"If you're napping, I can come back," a deep voice said. I hadn't heard him coming.

I jumped up, threw the magazine down on the coffee table, and got ready to launch right in. All right, so he hadn't called. He didn't need to think I gave a good fig about it.

"I need to report someone missing," I said.

He had the nerve to just stand there, smiling and staring at me in that way of his. I was having trouble looking at him, but I wasn't going to give him the satisfaction of breaking off first, either. He wasn't going to best Maggie Reid.

"All right, Maggie," he said finally, "let's talk."

He turned and walked off, with me following behind and studying the back of his neck. What had I done to lose this one? One minute he was holding me in his arms, the next he had vanished. And don't go thinking I didn't want to call him, because I surely did, but pride kept watch over my impulses, holding me back from a short waltz with foolish desire. I wasn't going to chase him like a silly schoolgirl. Whatever was keeping him away from me could just remain a mystery. My days of chasing after scoundrels were over, that is, just as soon as I found out what happened to Vernell Spivey.

Marshall Weathers led us right past the hallway where his office was and on to a small interview room. I stared up at the one-way mirror and back at him.

"Well," I said, "this is certainly familiar. Are you thinking perhaps Vernell is dead and I killed him? 'Cause if you are . . ."

I was geared up for a confrontation, but Weathers just chuckled and held up his hand like a traffic cop.

"Maggie, they're painting my office. I don't have anyplace else to go." He walked around the big metal desk that occupied half the room and sat down in a chair. "Now, what's this about you killing Vernell?"

"I didn't!" I shrieked. "What makes you think I'd do a thing like that?"

He was laughing to himself. "I don't, Maggie. You're the one who brought it up." When he saw that I was serious, he stopped. "Okay, Mag, sit down and tell me what's going on."

I slid into the chair across from him and to my complete surprise and consternation, lost my cool and began to cry.

"Vernell has been gone for two days," I said, tears sliding down my cheeks. "I don't keep tabs on him usually, but what with him and Jolene getting divorced, and Sheila moving back in with me, well, I just figured it was better if I checked on him."

Marshall was listening, leaning back in his chair, tipping it up off the ground like always. He had rolled up the sleeves of his white dress shirt and was tapping a pen on his thigh.

"He's been drinking pretty steadily, too," I added. "So, when his manager at the mobile home lot called and said Vernell hadn't been in for two days and he needed his signature on the paychecks, I went over to his house." I looked up at Marshall. "I figured he might've been drinking so much he'd gotten sick, but he wasn't there. His truck was gone too."

Marshall started to say something, but I kept on going. "I know what you're thinking. He might've just run off for a couple of days. Well, I thought that too. So, I went over and signed the checks. I can do that with the mobile home lot, on account of Sheila and me owning almost half of it." I rushed on: "But the checks all bounced. Vernell's gone and so is his money. The bank said he withdrew almost everything two days ago. I've got to cover it, too, or we'll be arrested for bad check writing. I can't cover that kind of expense!"

Marshall Weathers was frowning. He reached inside his shirt pocket, pulled out a little notepad, and scribbled something on it.

"What bank does he use, Maggie?"

"Wachovia," I said, "on Church Street." I watched him writing more on the tiny pad. "Vernell didn't run off. He wouldn't do us that way, ex-wife or not. I think something bad's happened to Vernell. I want you to find him."

Marshall looked up at me, his eyes softening. He reached into his back pocket, pulled out his handkerchief and handed it to me.

"Maggie, have you thought that he might be very depressed over his second marriage ending? That he might've wanted to hurt himself?"

I thought about the Vernell Spivey I knew. When Jolene and Vernell first split and he saw her for the woman she was, even right after she went to prison, maybe then he could've felt suicidal, but not longer than ten minutes. Vernell was too pitiful to kill himself. And he had enough hope in him to know another woman would come along.

"Nope. Vernell's not the type," I answered.

Marshall's eyes hardened a little as he asked his next question. "Did it occur to you that he drained his accounts and ran off? I mean, face it, Maggie, the man's not exactly reliable. He ran out on you. What makes you think he hasn't done it again?"

That stung. I sat in silence for a moment, my throat closing with pain and not trusting my voice to speak.

"Vernell Spivey is many things," I said slowly. "And true, his zipper flies up and down like a flag on the opening day of a Boy Scout jamboree, but he wouldn't leave his little girl, even if she is almost grown. Vernell doesn't get in trouble because he's mean. He gets in trouble because he's stupid and believes the best about women, even when the evidence lies to the contrary." I looked Marshall squarely in the eyes and continued. "Sheila's birthday was yesterday and Vernell missed it. He's never done that. He'd never do that."

Marshall Weathers slowly closed the notebook and put it back in his pocket. He sighed and ran his hand through his hair. He was putting off saying what was on his mind.

"Maggie, my guess is that Vernell's fine. I know you don't think so, but most times, the simplest explanations are the best. I think he's run off, but I'm going to see what I can find out. It would help if you could go over to his house and see if you can find anything at all that might give me some more information."

I nodded. "Will you do the missing persons thing?" I asked. "You know, tell everybody to look out for him? Let other departments know?"

He sighed again. "Honey, I don't think it'll do a lot of good, but of course I will. But I'm betting he's holed up in a hotel room somewhere, drinking. I don't think he wants to be found."

I stood up and stared down at him. "Thank you," I said, "I'll be in touch." I said it with all the dignity I could muster. I said it when I wanted to ask him a thousand other questions. Then I turned to leave.

"Maggie?" His voice rolled over my shoulder, a plea, not a command.

I turned around, waiting, my hand still clutching the door handle.

"I know you're wondering . . ."

I was. I was *so* wondering, but the doorknob suddenly lurched in my hand. I turned back, reacting to the movement, and felt my world dissolve into a fiery explosion of red, black, and pain.

Two

I grabbed my nose, the world went starry and black, and I was propelled backward into the desk.

A voice said, "Oh, man!"

Marshall Weathers was suddenly right there, grabbing my shoulders and pushing me right back into the chair I'd just come from.

"She's bleeding," the door pusher said. "I'll get some paper towels and ice. Oh, man! I'm sorry." My attacker was a female, a sumo wrestler, if the strength of her pushing was any indication.

My hands were covering my face. I could feel blood seeping through my fingers as my nose started to swell. Great. This was all I needed.

"Maggie," Weathers said, "just lean back." His hands tenderly brushed my curls out away from my face. "Do you think it's broken?"

"It can't be," I wailed. "I've gotta sing for a living!"

Marshall slipped his arm around my shoulders and pulled my head to his chest.

"Shhh," he said softly, "it'll be all right."

I wanted to cry, partly because I hurt so bad and partly because it took a broken nose for him to take me in his arms again, but I was cried out. Telling Marshall about Vernell and hearing the reality of the situation had drained me.

The door swung open, cautiously this time, and the pusher stepped back into the room. I looked up and took in the fresh-scrubbed, young, blonde officer, carrying a roll of paper towels and a bucket of ice.

"I'm so sorry," she said again.

"Me, too," I said, before I could remember my manners. "But I'll be fine."

She was staring at Marshall Weathers the same way I had when I first met him. I could tell right then and there that she was smitten. Marshall smiled up at her, took the towels and ice from her hands, then said, "Thanks, Trace."

She blushed. "I was just coming to see if we're still on for tonight," she said softly.

Weathers looked at me, then back at her. "Um, yeah, sure."

"Five thirty okay?" she asked.

He nodded and I jumped up out of my seat, a paper towel jammed against my nose.

"I'm fine," I muttered through the thick cloth. "And I have to go. Right now. I'm late."

"Maggie, wait," Marshall said.

I favored him with my nicest glance, considering that all he could see was eyes and a blob of white towel. I wasn't Einstein, but I wasn't stupid, either. "Let me know as soon as you find out about Vernell," I said. "Be sweet."

"Be sweet." That's southern for "curl up and die, you idiot!" A true southern woman never betrays her temper. Instead, she kills you with kindness. She lowers her voice almost to a whisper, looks you straight in the eye, and wishes you to stay as sweet as you are. It's her eyes that tell you the true story. Marshall Weathers was a Southerner. He knew exactly what I was saying.

I walked off through the Homicide Unit, weaving through the gray partition walls, heading for the lobby and the outside exit. People glanced up, then just as quickly looked away. I was guessing they didn't want to think too hard about what had happened to the Reba McEntire look-alike who had only minutes before strolled past with Marshall Weathers.

I wasted no time walking to my aging white VW Beetle and taking off. I drove through Greensboro's rush-hour traffic, heading for College Hills and my tiny Victorian bungalow. I hardly noticed the five-minute trip home or the beautiful fall colors that accented the tree-lined streets; I was too busy thinking. Besides, my nose ached and I just knew I was going to have two black eyes.

What was I going to tell Sheila? She was probably home, waiting for me. I hadn't let her in on how worried I was about her daddy, but now I was going to have to tell her.

When Vernell left us two years ago for Jolene, the Dish Girl in his satellite dish commercials, Sheila was just turning fifteen. I was a beautician and co-owned the Curly-Que Beauty Salon, and while it wasn't enough to keep us in luxury, it did afford me the little cottage off Mendenhall Street. Sheila hated the house, said it was a dump, but I loved it. It was full of character. It was just like me, waiting to be rediscovered and loved.

Sheila couldn't see that. No, she took up with a dope dealer down the street and eventually ran off to live in her father's pressed-cement, nouveau riche mansion in snobby New Irving Park. Time won out, though. Money can't buy a mother's love, especially when your stepmother is a greedy schemer bent on separating you from your father and his money. Poor Sheila.

I thought about Vernell for a minute. After his brother died, Vernell had started back drinking the hard stuff on a daily basis. I remembered sitting on a sidewalk curb one night, Vernell sick and crying beside me, and realizing that for all his restless meandering, Vernell truly loved me. He just couldn't live up to it. And try as I might, I couldn't hate him for that. Vernell was a just a junkyard dog trying to live indoors.

I drove down the alleyway and up into my small stamp of a backyard, trudged up the steps, and unlocked the door that opened into my bedroom, a converted sleeping porch. Sheila was lying across the bed, her head on her arms, wailing. From the sound of it, she'd turned up the volume as she heard my key fit into the lock.

She raised up slowly onto her elbows, her stick-straight red hair spilling around her freckled, tear-swollen face. She was a mess, but she stopped in midcry when she saw my face.

"It's not nearly as bad as it looks," I said.

"Oh my God! Who did that to you?" She drew her lanky frame up into a lotus position in the middle of Mama's yellow wedding-ring quilt. She was using her affected New York accent.

"Pride," I said, knowing she wouldn't let it go at that.

"Pride? You know somebody named Pride?"

I slung my purse down onto the dresser and looked into the mirror. My nose stood out between my green eyes like a Mercedes on a sucker lot. The skin around my eyes was puffy and starting to glow red and a bit purple. I touched it gently and winced. It hurt, but it wasn't broken.

"It was an accident. I ran into a door at the police department."

Sheila started to smile. "I knew you'd go see him," she said. "And after you gave me that big lecture on waiting for the boy to call you!"

That was when I knew for certain my concern for Vernell hadn't spilled over onto Sheila.

"You didn't go to school today, did you?" I asked, not quite ready to broach the Vernell subject.

Sheila's eyes narrowed and her face flushed the telltale way it does when she's done wrong.

"Did the headmaster call you?"

Sheila attends the Irving Park Country Day School because her father insists. He sees it as yet another way of clawing up into Greensboro society. I try to tell him that money can't buy breeding, but he wants his picture sprawled across the newspaper's society page, hobnobbing with the la-de-dahs at the Heart Ball.

"I had cramps," she said, sliding back down onto the bed. "I just couldn't make myself go."

Self-discipline was another one of Sheila's "opportunities for growth." She'd learned about this in her psychology class and now every time I tried to call her onto the carpet for slacking off, she'd call it a "growth opportunity" and say she was "working on it." I'd about had it with Sheila's personal growth.

"Well," I said, "it's probably for the best anyhow. We've got a problem. Your daddy's missing along with almost all of his money. I'm going to need your help."

The pretense fell away from Sheila. She sat up, started at me for a minute, and then decided I was serious.

"What happened? Where is he? Is he all right?"

I went over to her, sat down and looked straight into her eyes. "Sheila, we don't know. No one knows, but everyone's looking for him."

Sheila's face went still and pale. I could see her working to control her emotions, and it wasn't going well. She bit her bottom lip, but her chin quivered.

"Did someone hurt him?"

I reached out a hand and stroked her arm. "I don't know, honey. I'm going to find out."

"Do you think he left?"

I wasn't going to lie or sugarcoat the truth. "Some folks think so. I don't. Your dad's got his shortcomings, but he wouldn't leave you."

Sheila folded up like a hinged chair, drawing her legs up to her chest, wrapping her arms around them and laying her head on top of her knees. Her hair spilled around her like a sheet of silky satin. She sighed, her thin shoulders moving with each breath. I stretched out my hand and touched her, letting my fingers rest gently on her arm, a reminder that I was still there with her. After a minute she raised her head and it was my Sheila, back again, strong and tough.

"Okay," she said, her voice clear. "Let's go get Daddy!"

I smiled at her. "I think we should start with his castle."

"Oh, most definitely," she said. "Daddy's house is a mess. I'm sure we'll find tons of sh . . . um, clues, there."

She was up and moving, grabbing her small leather backpack purse and looking back at me with her usual air of impatience.

"So, like, are you coming or what?"

Mama said once, "You can't skin a rattlesnake with a toothbrush." She was cautioning me about not studying for a test in high school, but it clearly applied here. Sheila was loaded for bear, all right, and ready to go find her daddy, but what did we know about tracking down a missing person?

I thought about Detective Marshall J. Weathers and had a pang of regret. I needed his help and expertise. It would've been nice to know I could count on him, or to feel we were working together to find Vernell, but this was the same man who'd promised to call and vanished. Now he'd said he'd help me, but what kind of guarantee was that? Maybe it meant he'd file a report and forget about it. Maybe it meant less than that. Maybe it was all talk. No, Sheila and I were on our own, tracking down a man who'd cheated on me, left me, and still, in his heart of hearts, loved me.

Three

$\mathcal{F}$ate has a funny way of slapping you in the face. I don't
say that on account of Tracy the police cadet whopping me
with a thick, steel door. I'm just making the observation.
Every time I think I'm in control and in charge of my life,
something happens. Vernell's house was just another reminder.

Who knew Vernell would amount to something? I guess I
thought we wouldn't starve when I ran off with him, pregnant and in love and barely as old as my Sheila is now. But I
never thought he'd parlay an empty plot of land into a few
million dollars' worth of hype and commotion. Vernell
Spivey, The Mobile Home King. Then, Vernell Spivey, The
King of the Satellite Dish.

I thought about it every time I pulled my VW up into his
driveway. Don't get me wrong, I don't regret his leaving and
I sure don't miss his money.

"Mama," Sheila said, her voice sharpening to get my attention. "Let's go!" Sheila, never slow to move unless it involved chores or homework, set off for the front door, her

key in hand. As she moved through the early evening darkness, motion lights flashed on, lighting her way and bathing the concrete castle in a warm golden glow. By the time I reached Sheila's side, she was disarming Vernell's security system, punching her birth date into the keypad and hitting the light switch. The huge crystal chandelier lit up like a birthday cake. The marble foyer was empty and I realized I'd been holding my breath, half expecting to find Vernell's body on the cold floor.

Vernell's mansion looked just as it always did, uninviting and overdecorated. Come to think of it, it looked just like Vernell's ex-wife, Jolene. I chuckled silently and moved past Sheila.

"I'll take the downstairs," I said. "Why don't you look around upstairs?"

"Gotcha," she said, moving at warp speed to the sweeping staircase. "Remember, don't touch too much. In fact, I think I have a pair of gloves that came in my hair dye box. You want them?"

I looked up at her and choked off a laugh. Her face was set in a hard line of determination. She was going to find her daddy.

"No, baby," I said. "I'll be careful. Why don't you use them? Anyways, there's bound to be some of those yellow rubber things under the sink." Jolene would never have risked chipping a nail on something as mundane as a dish. In fact, I doubted she ever washed so much as a saucer. But there would be gloves in place, just for show, just in case she had to act like the little homemaker in front of company. Too bad the girl was doing time in Raleigh, otherwise I'd know she was somehow behind Vernell's sudden disappearance.

Sheila reached out and hit a switch, plunging the house into almost total darkness.

"What did you do that for?"

"Mama," she whispered, her disembodied voice floating out into the air above my head, "don't you watch TV? We don't want to be seen." She didn't say by what or by whom, and I let her have it her way. If it made her feel better to be in charge, well, it certainly wasn't hurting anything.

"There's a flashlight under the sink in the kitchen," she said. "I've got one in my bedside table. We'll use those."

I followed a dim light that glowed from the stovetop in the kitchen and used it as a beacon to find my way. Vernell's kitchen was a mess. Dishes lay out on the countertops; pots crusted with dried food sat in the sink. Vernell's housekeeping habits had not changed with his new status. An empty fifth of Wild Turkey sat out in the middle of the kitchen table, an overturned silver tumbler next to it. I sighed and touched the bottle. Poor Vernell—his drinking was the one thing holding him back.

I walked out of the kitchen and down the hallway that led to the three-car garage. Vernell's home office was on the right, tucked away like a turtle in its shell. I stepped inside the room and flicked the flashlight around the room. A black velvet Jesus jumped out at me from the far wall, his eyes glowing. My heart flew up to my throat and I made myself count to three to calm down.

When Vernell's brother, Jimmy, died, Vernell had a vision. Jimmy appeared to him and told him, "If you paint it, they will buy." Immediately afterward, Vernell started painting Jesus on all of his satellite dishes. He did a pretty good job of it, too. Black backgrounds and gold trim around Jesus's head and arms. When Vernell got finished, it appeared that Jesus was beckoning from outer space. Jimmy must've known something about retail, because those dishes sold like hotcakes.

I moved toward the desk, slipped into Vernell's chair, and settled in for some serious snooping. Vernell was a packrat and I just knew that somewhere, under all the piles of papers and envelopes, I would find the piece of information that would unlock the entire puzzle.

Vernell owed money to everyone, and apparently hadn't been paying his bills on time. There were second and third notices from the mortgage company, the utility companies, almost every store in town, and every major credit card company. Vernell was no better at paying his bills rich than he was at paying them poor. There was even a letter from the attorney for VanScoy Mobile Homes, offering to buy Vernell out for half a million dollars. But Vernell had scrawled "better in the red than VanScoy dead" across the top of the page, crumpled it up and stuffed it in the middle of a pile of mail.

I was working away, tossing irrelevant papers onto a pile on the floor, when I heard the squeak of the floorboard behind me.

"Find anything, sweetie?" I called absently, not turning to look at her.

"Maybe that's what I should be asking you," a deep voice whispered. "Now don't move and keep those pretty little hands out where I can see them."

"Wait just a minute," I started, then stopped as a cold ring of metal bit into the back of my neck. Whoever he was, he obviously had a gun and the odds were now in his favor. In the same instant I thought of Sheila, blissfully rummaging through her father's belongings on the second floor. What if this man took Vernell, or hurt him? What if he was here to get us?

My heart started banging away in my chest and I felt lightheaded for a second. How had he gotten in? I would've sworn that Sheila had locked the door. Had he been here all along, waiting?

"Whatever you say," I said. "But there's no call for gunplay."

"Who's playing?" he answered, his voice harsh and clipped.

The gun slipped a little, trailing an icy path down my neck, slipping just beneath the collar of my shirt. It wasn't an accident. This man was in complete control.

"Where's Vernell Spivey?" he asked.

"If I knew where my ex-husband was, would I be here? And if he owes you money, take a number." My hands were shaking but I managed to keep my voice from cracking. My brain was working overtime. Who was this guy? If he hadn't taken Vernell, then what did he want? What was he doing here? And better yet, how could I get rid of him?

The gunman laughed softly. "I don't care who he owes or how much he had or hasn't got. I'm just doing my job." I stiffened as the gun nuzzled the back of my ear.

"Does your boss know you're over here threatening Vernell's wife?"

The laugh again, throaty and cruel. "The people that pay me don't care how I get the job done. They want results. So how about you tell me everything you know about your ex and his business."

"Mama?"

Sheila's voice broke through the darkness. She was heading for the office. In a minute my daughter would come face to face with an armed gunman.

"All right," I said, staring at Vernell's cluttered desk, not daring to turn around. "Let me get rid of my daughter and I'll tell you everything you want to know. Just don't drag her into this." *Please, God, don't let him get to my baby.*

"Mama, are you in the office or where?"

"Just hide and let me get her to leave. Please. There's a bathroom right beside that Jesus picture. Get in there. Please!"

"Mama!"

I heard his voice, moving behind me toward the bathroom. "You try anything at all," he said, "and your kid'll have automatic ventilation." The door opened just as Sheila made it to the edge of Vernell's office. I was praying he made it in time.

"Were you talking to someone?"

I looked up at her, my eyes flickering over toward Jesus. My chest was tight and I wanted to cry, but I had to get her away from the gunman.

I sighed and frowned, bending forward ever so slightly. "Yeah, I guess I was talking to myself. I can't make heads or tails out of his financial stuff without my reading glasses."

"Well, put 'em on!"

I stared up at her, my "nice" face on. "That's just it, baby.

I left them back at the house. Be a sweetie and go get them for me? Please? And why don't you stop at Wendy's on your way back and pick us up something good?"

Food did it every time for Sheila. "I don't have any money," she said, her hand automatically reaching out toward the Bank of Mom.

"My purse is on the front seat. Make sure you get a dessert too."

"No way!" Sheila frowned. "Mom, at your age weight gain is very hard to take off."

"Will you just go?"

Sheila looked hurt. "No problem. You don't need to, like, go postal." She flounced off, her footsteps dying away through the garage, the security sensor beeping as she opened the door and walked out to my car. A moment later she was back.

"I've got something in my contact," she announced and headed straight for the bathroom door.

"Wait! Don't go in there!"

Sheila stopped dead in her tracks, whirled around and favored me with a one-eyed glare. "Is it hormones, Mama, or PMS? Whatever it is, you are not holding up well under the stress. My psychology teacher says . . ."

"Sheila, I don't give a rat's tail what your teacher says." I could feel my head starting to spin and little dots flashed before my eyes. I was going to have a heart attack or go crazy, one. "I just want you to go get my glasses! Time is of the essence here! Let me look at your eye."

Sheila turned sullen. "No, I'll do it myself." She walked straight into the bathroom, flicking on the light as she entered. My voice choked on her name. He had us both now. I waited for him to confront her, to march her out at gunpoint, but there was only the sound of Sheila running water and muttering under her breath.

In a few minutes she switched out the bathroom light and returned to the study. She glared at me with both eyes, humphed, and marched out of the room. I listened as she crossed the garage floor, opened the door again, and walked outside. This time I heard her slam my car door and a moment later the engine caught and Sheila peeled off out of the driveway. So much for her advice about keeping a low profile.

There was a sound from the darkened bathroom. The gunman was stepping out of his hiding place in the shower. He stood in the semidarkened room, hidden by the shadow of the door, watching me.

"Good job," he whispered and stepped out of the bathroom. He was huge, much taller than I had guessed, over six feet. Everything about him was dark. Black hair, long and unruly, curling around his collar, dark, faded black jeans and a leather jacket, a black T-shirt, and dark black boots. His eyes were obsidian pools that were staring as hard at me as I was at him. But I was memorizing him for the cops, assuming I would live long enough to tell them: tall, dark complexion, and built like he worked out, over and over again.

The gun hung at his side, not forgotten, but no longer pointed in my direction. A scar ran from the corner of his left eye and down along the top edge of his cheek. It was the only spot of light on his face.

"Talk to me," he said, his voice again thick and husky, like a whisper across a football field.

I leaned back in my chair, swallowed, and tried to think up a wild goose chase to send him on.

"Have you talked to Jolene, his other ex-wife?" I asked. He was looking me over, studying me, his face unreadable.

"She's in Raeford. Why would I talk to her?" He hadn't moved from his spot by Jesus. *So, he knows about Jolene. What else does he know?*

"Maybe she hired someone."

This brought him a step closer. I wanted to shrink down in the chair but I forced myself to look back at him, right down into those huge black eyes.

"You watch too much TV," he said, and smiled softly. For a moment he almost looked friendly, but the smile vanished. "Jolene doesn't have money, or access, or any friends crazy enough to take a whack at her ex-husband. Maybe we should ask Sheila when she gets back."

My heart started banging against my chest. My palms were sweating. Bastard!

"All right. All I know is that Vernell vanished two days ago, without any belongings but his truck. He took all the money he could grab and didn't do anything to let me know where he was going." I never looked away even though I couldn't stand the intensity of his gaze. "Would I be here if I knew where Vernell was?"

"Maybe he sent you back to get something he needs?"

He walked over and squatted down in front of the chair where I sat. He put his hands on each armrest, pinning me back and keeping me from leaving. A small smile crossed his face again, but this time there was no warmth behind it. I knew in that one instant, that this man expected to get what he wanted and would stay in my face or on my back until I gave him everything he was looking for.

"I don't know," I said softly. "Vernell's missing. That's all I know. I'm his ex-wife, for Pete's sake!"

He frowned and reached a finger out to touch my cheek. I winced. "Ouch!"

"Sorry," he said softly. "You need to put some ice on that. What in the hell happened to you?"

I glared back at him. For all I knew, this man was going to kill me. What did black eyes matter? "I ran into a door," I answered.

"Uh-huh." He didn't seem to believe me.

He dropped his hand down onto the arm that rested in my lap and I froze. His face was now mere inches from my own. My skin prickled with adrenaline, my face was starting to flush. All I wanted to do was run, or maybe not run. Something in the way he moved made him both terrifying and mesmerizing in the same instant.

"I know all about you, Maggie Reid," he said. "I made it my business to know. I know where you live. I know where you work, and I know what you do when you think no one is watching you." My heart was stuck in my throat. How did he know anything about me? What had he seen? Where had he been hiding and watching? And for how long?

"Vernell will contact you," he said. "Because I know he still loves you. Wherever he is, Vernell will try and get word to you. Now here's the easy part." His voice had a hypnotic quality that drew me in as it swirled around me. "When Vernell calls, I want you to let me know immediately. I want you to set up a meeting with him." He leaned back slowly and focused on my face.

"You know why you want to help me? Because bad things will happen to everyone you care about if I don't find Vernell Spivey. If he isn't already dead, he could wind up dead. I'm not the only one looking for him, you know. I'm just the guy who's going to find him and straighten a few things out. The others are going to kill him."

Another jolt of alarm shot through me. What kind of trouble was Vernell in?

"What has Vernell done?" I asked.

"He's left a very important person in a very embarrassing position," he said.

I raised my eyebrow and gave him a dose of my mama. "Now why should I believe one word of what you're saying? Vernell Spivey wouldn't run out on anyone!"

The stranger laughed again and gave me a "wake up and smell the coffee" look.

"Okay," I admitted, "he ran out on me, but that doesn't mean he'd welch on a deal. Vernell's an upstanding businessman. He'll turn up, and when he does he's gonna be mad as hell that you bothered me!"

I leaned forward like I was going to get out of my chair, but he stopped me. There was no going through this man.

"Why, you're a little wild thing, huh?" he said, but he laughed as he spoke, like he found my situation amusing.

I tossed my head and forced myself to stare back at him. I wanted to cry, or scream, or do any one of a thousand things, but I wouldn't. "I'm not afraid of you, you know. You can walk around like a big man when you're carrying a gun, but if you meant to kill me, I'd be dead by now."

"You think so, do you?" he asked softly. His face was eye level with mine and he was watching me. "And you're not afraid, not even the least little bit?" He moved closer and I backed as far as I could go into the chair. "You know me that well, do you?"

I couldn't move. He was coming closer and closer and I just couldn't move. That's when he leaned in and kissed me, his hand sliding around my neck and pulling me closer to him, crushing my lips against his. I started to squirm, trying to push away, but he held me fast. He wanted the control, I knew that. This was no kiss of passion. I felt myself spinning, caught up in the sensations that swirled around me: the way he smelled like old wood, the way his leather jacket was warm butter on my skin, the way my heart jumped into my throat, and the way my body started to respond, against my will, to his touch.

He stopped as suddenly as he'd started, rocking back on his heels and smiling a smug little grin like now we both knew something.

"Scared now?" he said.

"Don't you ever do that again!" I said, working to catch my breath.

He laughed, knowing how my body had responded, knowing I was powerless to stop him. He rose up onto his feet and towered over me. "I'll be watching you, Maggie Reid. Find Vernell for me, and I might be able to help him out. I'm the only guy not looking to shoot him on sight."

Oh, right, like I believed that! Did he think he could just burst in here, hold me at gunpoint, and then expect me to believe every word he said? "Do you think I'd trust anything you said or did?"

He jammed the gun in his pocket and cocked his head slightly to the left. "Let's hope you do, Maggie Reid, because Vernell Spivey's life depends on it."

He turned around and walked out the door, out into the garage and into the cool evening air. A moment later, in the distance, I heard the roar of a motorcycle starting up and taking off down Vernell's quiet little street.

I brought my fingers up to my lips, touching the skin that

still tingled from the rough feel of his kiss. I stood there for a few minutes, thinking. What in the hell had just happened here? And why hadn't I made one move, in the moments he'd been gone, to call the cops?

Four

Sheila came rushing back into the house half an hour later. Her hair was windblown from my convertible and her eyes were huge.

"Mama," she said, her voice breathless with anxiety, "we've gotta lock these doors! Some guy is watching the house!"

"What?" I moved over to the window, staring outside at the well-lit driveway. I didn't see anything.

"Yeah, Mama, and he's not doing a real good job of hiding, either. When I got to the top of the street, there he was, leaning against his motorcycle and just staring back down here!"

I tried not to react. I bet this was just what he expected her to do, see him and warn me. Just his way of letting me know he was going to be on the two of us like ugly on an ape.

"It was probably just some guy smoking a cigarette. Your imagination's in overdrive, Sheila."

"You didn't see this guy, Mama. He's tall, and built like a

WCW wrestler." Sheila's eyes were huge. "He was wearing nothing but black, even his hair was black. Mama, I swear to God he's watching us!"

"He wasn't wearing a helmet?" I asked.

Sheila gave an impatient shake. "No, Mama, his helmet was on the seat of his bike. It was one of those helmets with a dark windshield over the face. I'm telling you, I know he's dangerous. Once, in this movie, you know, this guy that looked just like him took this socialite captive. And she didn't want him to touch her, but he did anyway and man, Mama!"

"Sheila, stop! You are letting your imagination get the better of you. Now let's stay on task. We don't have time to fool around with strangers on motorcycles and other non-sense such as that." I looked around Vernell's office. "I don't think we're going to find a thing here. We might as well go on home."

Sheila shrugged. "Good idea, maybe that man's still up there. You'll understand me completely when you see him. I'm telling you, he's watching us."

I put my hand on her shoulder. "Honey, it's good that you've got your eyes open, because there is a slight chance that whoever is responsible for your daddy disappearing may come sniffing around us." Sheila's eyes were as big as silver dollars. "I mean, honey, Daddy did make a pile of money, at least on paper, and sometimes people get a little crazy when money's involved."

"Oh my God!" Sheila shrieked. "I could be a kidnapped debutante! I could get shoved in a trunk and . . ."

"Sheila! Enough! You're not even a debutante. I'm just saying be careful."

Sheila pouted. "Well, Daddy said I was going to make my debut this year."

I kept my mouth shut. Vernell probably meant to show-case Sheila on one of his mobile home commercials. I could hardly see Vernell descending the staircase at the Greens-boro Country Club, dressed in his blue polyester leisure suit, escorting Sheila to her debut. No way. Besides, debuts were nothing but glorified selling blocks for young women from high-dollar families. I mean, look at the symbolism. White dresses, proud fathers. It was nothing but a meat market and nothing for my little girl.

"Come on, honey," I said. "Set the alarm and let's go home. For all I know, Vernell's been found and was only on a spur-of-the-moment vacation."

"Yeah, right," she muttered, "and I'm a computer nerd."

"Sheila!"

"All right, all right!"

We walked out through the garage and Sheila hit a switch on her remote control keychain.

"The system is armed," a disembodied voice said. "Step away from the house and resume your business."

"Where did your daddy find that thing?" I asked Sheila, but she was already sitting in the driver's seat. *Great,* I thought, *now I get to risk life and limb twice in one night.*

"Mama, I'm telling you, there was a man on a motorcycle right up here." Sheila pointed to a street lamp at the head of Vernell's cul-de-sac. I looked at the empty spot. It was only the kind of place where someone would stand if he wanted to be obvious. He was warning me. A thrill of fear ran circles around my stomach and crawled up my neck. Until now, Vernell's little sojourns into trouble hadn't been more than harmless accidents. With the arrival of an armed gunman, Vernell had stepped into a category five hurricane of bad karma.

"He's gone," she said, throwing the car into first and peeling out of Vernell's pricey neighborhood. In a few moments Sheila was whizzing across Greensboro, traveling down Battleground Avenue like it was an obstacle course and running yellow lights just as they turned red.

"Sheila, slow down!" I grabbed the sides of my seat as Sheila rushed the split between busy Battleground and Lawndale Avenue. The strip of road, crammed with restaurants and stores, was deluged by suburbanites, all looking to ease the burden of soccer practice and overtime with fast food and video games. My little VW would be no match for a chunky Suburban.

Sheila ignored me, reaching over to switch the radio from my favorite country station to her favorite alternative rock station. I leaned back and tried to breathe. One of the boys in our band, Harmonica Jack, is a big proponent of breathing as a way to nirvana. It wasn't working. To complicate the matter further, a motorcycle wove slowly in and out of traffic, following us about a football field away.

Sheila cranked up the volume, and a woman started moaning about love. Sheila sang along as if she actually knew something about angst. I shook my head and kept my eye on the moon of a mirror that clung to the passenger-side door. Sheila's purse chirped and she fumbled around inside it, all the while driving, singing and running yet another yellow light. I checked; the motorcycle was still with us. It had to be him. He was just the type to dart through red lights.

"Yeah?" Sheila said into the microsized receiver. Irving Park Country Day School apparently failed to instill cellphone etiquette into its students.

"No way!" This was followed by: "You didn't! What did he say? He does?" Sheila's voice softened. True love was apparently waiting in some distant corner of the city. Her tone changed. "No," she sighed. "I can't. We're worried sick about my dad. He's gone off somewhere. I'd better stick close to home. Maybe when he gets back." Her voice trailed off.

I was watching the motorcycle creep up, then fall back, trying to think of what to do next. Sheila's conversation drifted into my consciousness as if on a time delay.

"I think you should," I said suddenly.

Sheila looked over at me, her eyebrow raised. "Should what, Mama?"

"Spend the night with Ashley. That's who it is, isn't it? And that's what she's asking, isn't it?" I looked in the mirror again. "Might take your mind off things a little, and you have a phone. I can always reach you. Besides, nothing's gonna happen tonight. Go on."

Sheila mulled it over, then completely blew it and ran a red light, narrowly missing a blue Lincoln. This accomplished two things: We lost the motorcycle and Sheila was startled into letting me take control.

"That's it!" I said. "You go spend the night with Ashley and get a grip. Your daddy's probably fine. There's nothing you can do in a state like this. Tell her we'll be there in three minutes."

Before Sheila could come up with a good reason to protest, I had yanked her out of the car and deposited her on Ashley's doorstep. Ashley lived in one of the huge old mansions that rimmed Fisher Park. The streets were fairly dark. The house was a fortress of security and Dobermans. There was no better place to leave Sheila. Besides, if push came to shove, Ashley's mother had a black belt.

I jumped into the driver's seat of my little car and pulled back out onto Elm Street, slipping under the huge shadow cast by the First Presbyterian Church. I knew what I'd find if I went home. My new friend would be waiting. There was really only one option left.

Five

I heard Harmonica Jack before I saw him. Jack lives in a converted warehouse on the edge of Greensboro's business district, teetering on the line that divides the gleaming, multistoried office buildings and funky antique shops from the broken-paned abandoned shells of older, once useful warehouses.

I pulled off Elm Street, turned down the narrow alley to Jack's parking lot, and stopped in front of the loading dock Jack uses for a front door and living-room window. I cut the engine and heard the gentle lisp of his harmonica float out into the crisp fall evening. He was playing something slow and sweet and incredibly sad. For a moment I couldn't move, but he saw me, stopped playing, and began to walk toward the car.

His wiry, blond hair stood out in spikes from his head, as if taking off in different directions. He was wearing a faded green-plaid flannel shirt and jeans. Even fully clothed, Jack looked too thin. And he was barefooted. It's being barely sixty degrees, he was begging for a cold.

"Didn't your mama teach you no better?" I called out, pointing to his feet as he stepped closer to the car.

"My mama figured I'd get cold at some point and take care of myself," he said. He peered in the window at me, squinting in the glow of the streetlight that illuminated his tiny parking lot.

"What happened to you?" he asked. "Maggie, your nose is all puffy and it looks like your eyes are turning kind of black."

I tried it one more time. "I ran into a door at the police station," I said wearily.

Jack leaned back, cocked his head to one side, and sighed. "I knew you'd get up with him somehow. I just never figured him for the type to use violence."

I leaned my head against the steering wheel. "He didn't," I moaned.

Jack pulled open the car door and patted my shoulder. "Those doors can take their toll on you, can't they?" he said. "Yep. Gotta keep your eye on 'em. You never know when they'll take it into their heads to attack! Come on inside. I've got just the thing for a door whuppin'."

I didn't even bother to try and explain further. Sooner or later, Jack would pull the whole tale out of me. He always did, after a lengthy session of New Age breathing and transcendental meditation to realign my karma. Jack seems to think I'm uptight. On the other hand, I figure he's spent a little too much time smelling incense and assuming convoluted yoga positions. But he's trustworthy, and he's my friend. He's also a good seven years younger than me. I only mention that on account of sometimes he seems to get ideas, and I have to remind him that a relationship between the two of us would never work.

Jack pulled me up onto the loading dock and into his living room before hitting the door opener that brought the rusty metal bay door sliding down on its hinges. He wandered over to the counter in his tiny kitchen, pulled two wineglasses down from a rack, and grabbed a half-full bottle of red wine from a cupboard.

"There's more to this than meets the eyes," he said, chuckling to himself. "Come on over here."

We walked across the echoing loft, crossing the wooden floor to his living room area.

"Have a seat," he said, motioning to his battered old sofa. He put the wine and glasses down on the coffee table then walked over to the tiny potbellied stove that pumped out heat like a furnace. He fiddled with a knob on the front of the stove, then, when it satisfied him, moved back over to his place next to me on the couch.

"You're in trouble again, aren't you?" he asked. He reached past me for the wine and started to pour it into the glasses. He moved slowly, as if we were having a casual conversation, without a care in the world.

There's something about Jack. Something that makes me tell him the unvarnished truth, something warm that makes me want to curl up inside his confidence. And something else, I just can't quite put my finger on it. It's a feeling I get, every now and again, like there's something I'm missing about him. I don't know. I just know now isn't the time to go looking for trouble.

I looked at the ceiling, then reached for my wineglass. "Jack, I'm in a load of trouble, I think." I looked over at him. "I can't go home tonight, and maybe not for a while. Do you think I could . . . I mean, I don't mean, but what I need is . . ."

"Maggie," Jack said, "of course you're staying here. What about Sheila, she coming too?"

I guess sweetness turns me to mush. I spilled it all right then and there: how Vernell was missing; how Marshall did me, and finally, I told him about the Shadow.

"Something's bad wrong, Jack," I finished. "You believe me, don't you?"

Jack set his wineglass down on the coffee table and reached over to take my hand.

"Of course I do, Maggie. Why wouldn't I?"

I sighed and curled my fingers around his. His hand was warm and dry, his grip gentle, yet strong. He believed me, I knew that much.

"We need a plan, huh?" he said.

I nodded and reached for my wineglass, staring out the windows that flanked Jack's stove. Something had moved in the parking lot. I stared harder, trying to isolate the area where I'd seen movement, then shook myself. Maybe it was only a dog, looking for food in the trash can.

"So?" Jack said.

"So . . . what?"

"Don't we need a plan? Don't we need to start talking to people Vernell knows, see if we can find out what's up?" Jack was twirling his wineglass slowly between his fingers.

I saw a flash of dark out of the corner of my eye again. "There's something out there," I said. "Look!"

Jack turned and peered through the window. The parking lot was empty. The streetlight cast a perfect moon of yellow light onto my Beetle. Nothing moved. He stood and walked over to the window, staring hard into the night, then glancing back at me.

"Maybe it was the wind," he said softly.

The "wind" chose that moment to begin banging on Jack's loading-dock door.

"Maggie," Detective Marshall J. Weathers said, "I know you're in there. Please open the door."

Jack sighed and shook his head, then looked at me. "Well?"

I stood up and nodded, facing the huge cargo-bay door. Jack punched the garage-door remote and the heavy metal began to rumble.

The fact that Marshall Weathers had tracked me down to Jack's house was not at all unusual. At one time he had made it his business to know the ins and outs of my life. He knew I'd come to Jack. So that part didn't bother me. What bothered me was that he'd said "Please open the door." *Please*. That sent a little tingle of alarm moving through my body. Marshall Weathers knew something and it wasn't good. Why else would he be so nice? Nice wasn't usually his style.

The door rose with creaking uncertainty, catching on the cogs and hesitating as it shook its way open. Marshall stood there, still wearing his suit, frowning.

He ignored Jack and stepped onto the ancient wood floor of the warehouse. He looked instead at me, his frown softening.

"Maggie, I'm afraid I have some bad news." My stomach flipped over and a cry tightened my throat. "They've just found Vernell's truck out at the airport. Honey, I'm sorry, but there's a body inside and the description fits Vernell. I'm on my way out now."

I stood there in stunned silence, tears welling up in my eyes and spilling over. Jack stepped up to my side and rested his hand on my shoulder.

"You want me to come look, don't you?" I asked. My voice wouldn't raise any louder than a whisper.

Marshall nodded. "If you think you could."

I stepped toward him, unaware of how I moved because it all seemed like someone else's bad dream. Vernell was dead?

My mind flashed on Vernell holding Sheila and dancing around the delivery room in the seconds after she was born, smiling, tears rolling down his thin cheeks. Then I saw him out in the backyard at our first house, holding a green garden hose up in the air, his thumb over the nozzle. The water shot up, arcing and falling down around him and three-year-old Sheila, and they laughed and laughed as the sun hit the water and created a rainbow.

Not Vernell. Not that Vernell.

I didn't say a word to Jack. I forgot about him. I couldn't hold more than Vernell in my head. I didn't realize he'd let go of my arm or that Marshall had taken it, until Marshall was helping me into his unmarked squad car. What I was aware of was the growing pain in my chest, the way my heart brimmed with a sadness so utterly deep that it filled my lungs and took my breath away. Vernell.

Marshall stuck a blue light up on the roof and took off. It takes fifteen minutes to cross town and hit the airport. Marshall made it in less than ten. We didn't speak. I stared out the passenger-side window, wishing it would rain, and surprised that it didn't. Somehow rain would've been appropriate. Mama used to say rain was how God washed away his disappointment. I just knew it would take more than my tears to grieve for Vernell.

We raced across lonely Bryan Boulevard, streaking from one streetlight to the next, passing through gray-white spots of light that became a strobe of pain-filled awareness.

When we pulled up into the airport and took the turn to extended-stay parking, the dark night was suddenly filled with explosions of blue flashing lights. The entire deck was sealed off, with officers directing cars away and sealing off the crime scene area. My heart was beating in my throat and I was aware of not being able to catch my breath.

Weathers paused briefly, rolled down his window, and spoke to the patrol officer. I didn't listen. I was staring straight ahead at Vernell's shiny white pickup. They had set giant lamps up beside the truck and several technicians seemed to be hovering, along with a blonde in a flappy black trenchcoat. She looked over at our car, pushed a frizzy lock of hair out of her eyes and motioned impatiently.

Marshall Weathers slapped the car into drive and pulled neatly to the side, away from the crime scene tape, just on the shadowy edge of the parking deck.

"Okay, Maggie," he said, his voice soft, "wait here. I want to check it out first. I'll come back and get you when we're ready."

He pushed the door open and stepped out into the light. I sat there, numbly watching him take twenty steps before something in me churned and I was out of the car, following him. I had to know. I had to know now, when he knew, before another minute passed.

Weathers had reached the blonde. Her dark eyes flashed from his face to mine, frowning as she clocked an intruder. She jerked her head in my direction. Weathers whipped around and started toward me.

"Maggie, you need to wait."

"No I don't."

"Detective, who is this?" She was a tall, thickset woman who wore stockings and running shoes. I caught a glimpse of a paisley polyester shirt-dress peaking out from the all-business black trenchcoat. She'd missed a button at the collar, making her neckline look loose and rumpled. I figured she was that ambiguous age between forty-five and sixty. Her hands were big, clutching a metal clipboard.

"I'm Maggie Reid," I said, sticking out my hand, forcing her to acknowledge me. "That's my ex-husband's truck you're examining."

She took my hand and softened. I revised her age downward as I stepped close enough to realize she was tired, not old.

"I'm Kay Edwards," she said, "medical examiner for Guilford County."

"I want to see him," I said. I didn't feel anything but cold inside. My feelings had retreated to a box, contained for later.

Kay Edwards looked past me to Marshall Weathers. He moved his head to the left, as if he were passing the decision on to her.

"All right, Mrs. Reid," she said, and I didn't correct her. "If you can walk up to the truck without touching him or anything else, we'll go."

Marshall stepped toward me, standing close, hovering. I held my head up, took a deep breath, and started toward the truck. If I prayed, it wasn't conscious. Instead, I probably did what I always do when I'm in a fix: summon Mama and her strength.

The technicians backed away. Vernell's passenger-side door hung open, the seat pulled up and away to reveal a pair of legs, curled up and shoved down behind the seats in the tiny rear cab. Vernell's workboots, untied. Vernell's blue twill workpants, the ones he wore when he wanted to prove to his employees that he was still just good ol' Vernell.

My body went still as the medical examiner led me closer, pulling a white sheet away from the upper half of the body.

"Is this your husband, Mrs. Reid?" she asked.

"Yes," I whispered, a sob catching in my throat. There

was blood everywhere. Blood and stuff I don't want to mention. Someone had shot Vernell at point-blank range, must have, the back half of his head was missing and his face was almost unrecognizable. His skin was a waxy yellow and he looked dirty. I forced myself to examine him. I was making him dead in my mind, making myself accept the reality by studying him dead. Then I saw it.

"Maybe it is," I said, my voice rasping out like a stranger's. "Except, Vernell has a mustache and it's missing."

Of course, my brain was telling me that mustaches don't disappear, but I couldn't quite put it together that a body in Vernell's clothing, minus a mustache, could possibly not be Vernell.

"Does your husband have any identifying marks on his body?" Dr. Edwards asked.

"Just the eagle tattoo on his chest," I said.

Edwards leaned into the backseat of the cab and gently unbuttoned the man's shirt. She motioned me closer. I stepped in and peered over her shoulder. I sighed, turned, and threw up, right there on the concrete.

Six

Cops have a way of taking care of you and backing off, all at the same time. When I threw up, Marshall Weathers whipped a square of white handkerchief from his pocket, handed it to me, and went right into his interrogation.

"You have no idea who that is?" he asked. "You've never seen him before? Think. Never?"

Cameras were flashing again, zooming in on the victim's naked chest. He didn't so much as have one curly hair on it, and there was definitely no tattoo. I was awash with relief and horror. Who was this man and where was Vernell? Furthermore, why was he wearing Vernell's clothes? Was Vernell wearing his?

Dr. Edwards pulled Marshall aside, talking in a low, urgent undertone that I couldn't quite catch. They seemed to have forgotten me, so I sidled closer.

"That would put the time of death somewhere between twenty-four and thirty-six hours ago," I heard her say. Weathers muttered something to which Dr. Edwards replied, "Maybe a thirty-eight. I don't know yet."

If another officer hadn't walked up, I might've gone home with more information, but as soon as the officer arrived, they noticed me.

"Maggie, I'm sorry," Weathers said. "I'll have someone take you back. I'll catch up with you later." I was in the way. "Will Sheila be home when you get in?" His way of seeing where I'd be and when.

"No, she's staying with a friend for the night. She won't be home until after school tomorrow."

"Well," he said slowly, "I'll catch up with you if I need to. I've got to get back to this here." He nodded toward the truck. Sixteen minutes later I was standing on Jack's loading dock, dumped without a backward glance by a tall, bald-headed cop who seemed to spend more time on his cell phone talking to his girlfriend than he did listening to his radio calls.

I raised my hand to bang on the metal door but it began to groan open. Jack had been waiting. His eyes were soft with concern and he reached out to pull me inside before I could move to walk.

"Maggie, I'm so sorry," he whispered, pulling me into his arms and hugging me. He stroked my hair and held me so tight, I almost hated to tell him.

"It wasn't him," I said. "It was his truck, but it wasn't him."

Jack pushed back and looked at me. "Well, who was it?" He hit the switch to close the garage door and walked me over to the sofa. The cool October night had chilled the warehouse, and the only warm spot seemed to be the area in front of the wood stove.

"I have no idea who it was. He looked a lot like Vernell, what was left of him." The images of the bloody body came flooding back, and along with it a wave of nausea. I sank onto the sofa and gripped my head with both hands, as if that would do any good.

"Jack, it was so horrible."

He poured a glass of wine and handed it to me. "I know, honey. Just lean back and breathe, let the feelings evaporate."

I sighed. Here we went with Jack's New Age breathing techniques. Next thing I knew he'd be handing me a fistful of herbal tablets and telling me to imagine world peace. Sad thing was, most of Jack's ideas actually worked.

So I leaned back against the sofa, closed my eyes, and envisioned a better world. The breathing helped, but I had to open my eyes. All I could see when I closed them was the body in the backseat of Vernell's pickup.

"Vernell's gonna be mad as hell when he sees his truck," I said. I sat back up and took a swig of wine, a big swig. "I figure that's a hell of a way to go joyriding!"

Jack just stared at me, his brown eyes unchanging. Then he shook his head. "You think someone stole Vernell's truck and left a body in it?"

I didn't need Jack to say another word, because the next dreadful thought crowded in on top of it. "What if they killed Vernell?" I whispered. Whoever had been in the truck with the dead man had certainly killed him. What if he'd killed Vernell too?

Jack just shook his head again. "There's another possibility, Maggie," he said slowly. "And I don't think it's one you'll want to hear." I gulped down another hefty portion of wine and looked at him.

"What if Vernell killed that man?"

The possibility lay between us like a heavy stone. I wanted to be angry with him, but I just couldn't do it. He was right. I could hear it, coming from him, my friend. I just didn't know what I was going to do if the police started talking that way. It was a possibility, but I knew Vernell. I didn't think him capable of making that large a commitment. After all, dead is dead, and Vernell Spivey likes his options open. No, Vernell Spivey couldn't knowingly kill anybody. Impossible.

I closed my eyes again and leaned back against the sofa. I wasn't exactly envisioning world peace, I was just too tired to do anything else. A sudden wave of fatigue had settled in my bones and it made all thought and memory disappear.

Jack let me stay that way for a few minutes. I heard him

get up and throw another log into the wood stove, then twist some knobs to adjust it. The longer I sat, the heavier I felt.

"Come on, Maggie," Jack whispered. The now empty wineglass was tugged from my hand. He reached for me, pulling me up and out of my stupor. "Let's go to bed," he said. "You can think on this in the morning."

I wanted to fight it. I muttered, "Let me sleep here." But he didn't listen.

"Come on."

He led me up the twisting, wrought-iron steps to his bedroom. We stepped out into a room filled with a huge waterbed and a thousand candles. A giant window took up the far end of the room, with a tiny balcony off of it. The lights of downtown Greensboro twinkled in the near distance, cut by the leaves of an aging oak tree.

"Okay," he said, pulling out a drawer and rummaging through it, "you can have the 'I Love Rodeo' T-shirt or, lemme see, there's a 'Take This Job and Shove It' tee that's broke in right nice. Which do you fancy?"

I stood there, numbly staring at the two T-shirts, unable to make even that small decision.

"You look like a rodeo," he said, shoving the shirt in my direction. "I get first call on the bathroom. You go on and get changed." He entered the bathroom and closed the door.

I stared after him as I fumbled with the buttons on my shirt. That was Jack for you. Mama would've called him a gentleman. He was, the gentlest man I knew. This wasn't the first time I'd stayed with Jack. I'd done it before, when the chips were down and I couldn't stay in my own home. He'd taken me in, slept with me in his bed, and never laid a hand on me. With another man I might've worried, but Jack wasn't like most men. He'd walked out of the Golden Stallion on many a night with one cutie or another. It wasn't that Jack didn't like women, quite the contrary. Jack loved women. He just didn't take advantage of them.

I pulled the T-shirt over my head and dropped my jeans to the floor. I was stepping out of them as he emerged from the bathroom. His shirt was off and his hair looked a little wilder for it.

I passed him, slipping into the tiny bathroom, where I found my guest toothbrush in its holder, just as it had been the last time I'd come to stay three months ago. I could hear him bustling around the room and knew what he was doing. By the time I stepped out into the darkened room, he had lit some of the candles and was already lying in bed. Naked. Jack always slept naked, said it made his dreams more vivid because he wasn't confined by clothing.

I took a deep breath and gently rolled into the waterbed, pulling the pile of quilts on top of me and trying to use them as a buffer between us. Just because Jack was a gentleman didn't mean he wasn't prey to temptation.

Jack rolled to face me, watching.

"Still uptight, huh, Maggie?"

I wedged the covers a little tighter. "Jack, just because sleeping with a naked man makes me uncomfortable, it doesn't mean I'm uptight. Besides, I'm too old for you."

He half-propped himself up on his elbow and grinned. Then he reached out his finger and twirled it around a strand of my hair.

"You're a pretty woman, Maggie. Don't underestimate yourself. I kinda like my women a little older, gives 'em an edge on the competition, to my way of thinking."

Suddenly the room seemed much warmer and I felt my face flush. Jack was enjoying my discomfort.

"Go to sleep, sweetheart," he said. "I'm not gonna bite you. Not yet, that is." He turned to blow out the candles, chuckling to himself. Then he gave the bed one good hard bounce that sent me rolling into him. I squeaked and pulled back, he laughed, and suddenly it all hit me funny too. We laughed and laughed, until I remembered Vernell and fell silent.

"Come 'ere, Maggie," Jack said, pulling me into him. "Get comfortable and go to sleep. When you're feeling this bad, sometimes it's nice just to feel another human being up next to you. Kinda keeps the universe in perspective, so to speak."

He was right. It did feel good to sleep with someone's arms around me, even if he wasn't Marshall Weathers. Lying there I remembered another night, three months ago, when I'd done the same for Jack. We had a strange relationship, unlike any I'd ever had before. The other men I knew couldn't sleep naked with a woman, not without getting ideas and feeling they had a point to prove.

I nestled in closer, the quilt still wrapped around my body, feeling Jack's arm, skin-on-skin against mine. Vernell was missing. Marshall didn't love me. And a stranger on a motorcycle was stalking me. Somehow, with the moonlight streaming in through the window and Jack beside me, everything seemed temporarily smaller and I could drift off to sleep. It wasn't world peace, but it was a temporary truce in the chaos of my life.

Seven

I stirred at dawn, sensing movement in the room. Jack was standing by the window, fully dressed and staring out at Greensboro by first light. He wore faded boot-cut jeans and a dark navy blue shirt. In the half-light of morning I studied him. Jack's mother was dying and he wore the sadness of her leaving like a heavy cloak. His shoulders bowed under the weight of losing his confidante.

"Are you going to see her?" I asked, my voice startling him.

He turned back to me, shaking off the mantle of sorrow and trying to smile. "Mornings are tough on her," he said. "I like to help her get started."

I thought of Evelyn, her short white hair framing her face like a wispy halo, so frail she could barely walk unassisted, yet hanging in, refusing to leave her son and the world she loved so much.

"Want me to come with you?"

He smiled. "Sleep, Maggie. I'll leave you some coffee."

I snuggled down deeper under the thick quilts, my eyelids

heavy with fatigue. I heard his footsteps dying away as he descended the winding iron stairs, then listened as he made coffee for the morning. I tried to sleep, but found myself following Jack's movements around the kitchen. The awareness of yesterday came rushing back in flashes, and as it did I realized there would be no more sleep.

I lay floating on the warm surface of the waterbed, chilled by the reality of my situation. Mama had a way of summing up life when it got to its roughest going. She'd say: "Sugar, life is like a winding mountain railroad. It's the quality of the track that determines the ride." Vernell's track never ran true, while mine seemed to hit the brick wall of unpleasant reality with increasing regularity.

As I listened, the loading-bay door swung up and Jack left for his morning ritual with his mother. I stayed under the covers for all of another five minutes before I jumped out, ready to start my own day. Jack's shower was slow to warm up, but once it did, I stood under the spray and thought about my first move.

By the time I'd finished dressing and coated my developing black eyes with makeup, I had a plan. It was still early. I could slip into my bungalow, take some clothes and supplies, then head out on my search for Vernell. If I got there early enough, the Shadow might miss me.

When I stepped out onto the loading-bay platform, my hair was still wet, hanging around my shoulders in thick, spiral curls that matched the steam from my coffee cup. I had purpose and intent. Marshall Weathers apparently felt the same way. He was perched on the hood of my car, a thick Styrofoam coffee cup clutched in his left hand. My breath caught in my throat as he brought the cup to his lips, took a swallow and slowly brought his hand back down away from his mouth. The way that man moved sent a shiver up my spine. I just wanted to be his coffee cup.

He watched me walk down the concrete steps and cross the parking lot to my car, all without speaking. I saw no sign of his unmarked sedan. His tan leather cowboy boots were spotted with the dew that clung to the grass that sprouted between the pieces of broken asphalt of the lot. The suit was gone, in its place a pair of faded blue jeans, another crisp white shirt, and a navy blue blazer.

"We need to talk," he said, as I drew closer.

"You found Vernell?" My heartbeat quickened.

"No, but I'm working on it." His icy blue eyes never left my face. He was searching for something inside me, I could tell that much. I just didn't know what he wanted.

He took another swallow of coffee and stood up. "Let's walk a little bit."

I raised an eyebrow. This was new behavior. Weathers wasn't the type for strolls.

He took off, as if he had a destination in mind, barely waiting to see that I'd joined him. We left the parking lot and turned out onto Elm Street, moving south toward the railroad tracks. The early morning rush had started and cars passed us, heading into the main business district, moving quickly away from Jack's fringe neighborhood, unwilling to linger among the closed antique shops and funky nightspots.

Weathers kept moving too, toward a little triangle-shaped park that lay just in front of the train tracks, tucked behind the front row of buildings and the encroaching neighborhood of aging Victorians. The park was seldom used, even in the daytime, because of its proximity to Lee Street and the people who wandered the neighborhood looking for handouts or a bench to sleep off a drunk.

Weathers walked toward a bench that faced the entrance to the park. It was the only one of the few benches a cop would've taken. It backed up to a brick wall and had a view of all three park entrances and exits. There was no way to sneak up on it. No surprises possible here.

He motioned for me to sit down, then sat next to me, but further away, so he could face me as he spoke. I sat there waiting, but he didn't say a word. Instead he was watching me, then looking away, paying exaggerated attention to the park and the train tracks.

Mama says any man'll eventually get around to making his point and it doesn't do to rush him. "A man holds counsel with himself, Maggie," she said, "and only comes to you when he thinks he's drawn a conclusion." Mama always saw it as her job to help Daddy "interpret" his conclusion to her way of thinking.

Marshall finally turned to face me, drew in his breath and exhaled for a long, silent moment. "I wanted to call you, but I couldn't," he said. "The timing wasn't right, Maggie. It wasn't you. It was me."

I sat there, staring at my hands. I wasn't sure I wanted to see the look in his eyes, or read a lie on his face. I've heard every excuse a man can give in life. I didn't want to look up and realize this was just another one.

He must've sensed that, because he reached over and laid one strong hand on top of my two. I looked up finally and saw him watching me. I had a hundred other questions lined up for him, but I couldn't make the words come out.

"Maggie, I'm divorced," he said. "When I met you, it hadn't been final for more than a month. I just wasn't ready for a woman like you. You're not the type for something casual. And right now, that's all I have to offer."

He looked at me as he spoke, straight into my eyes, and on through. When I looked back at him, all I could see was a wall.

"That doesn't mean I'm not attracted to you, or that I wouldn't want to spend more time with you. It's me; that's all. I'm not ready and I don't want to hurt you."

Of course, he couldn't see that he was hurting me now. What was he saying, that girls like Tracy were what he was looking for? What was I, yesterday's cornbread?

"I understand," I said, and stood up in front of him. "You don't owe me an explanation. It was just one of those things."

I was holding my head up, like maybe I could keep the rush of tears from climbing uphill from my heart to my eyes, but it wasn't working. I turned away and he snatched my hand and tugged me back. He stood up and pulled me into him, so close now that I could feel his breath on my hair.

"You don't understand. It matters to me. I don't want to see you hurt."

I looked up at him, the top of my head just touching his chin. He reached up with one hand and stroked the side of my cheek. His fingers were rough but gentle as he cupped my chin and leaned down to kiss me. His lips brushed mine, soft at first, then more insistent.

"It matters to me," he said again, and pulled me the rest of the way into his arms. We stood like that, in the crisp early morning, in the park by Jack's house and I felt as if the entire world had vanished, leaving us alone, together.

Of course, the world had to intrude, crashing back in like a drunken stranger with the shrill ring of Marshall's cell phone.

"Weathers."

He listened, cocking his head and squinting his eyes almost shut. He too, was trying to salvage the moment, his arm still encircling my waist, his hand stroking my back.

"You're sure?" Weathers barked. His hand tightened, then froze. "See if you can find a more solid link. Any family?" He listened. "All right, I'll take that. You get on this other." He touched a button and slid the phone back into his pocket. The Weathers of a moment ago had vanished. The cop was back and it wasn't good news.

"Is it Vernell?" I asked. I took a step backward, out of his arms, out where I could read him and know.

"Not directly," he said. He drew the words out so that they began to take on the opposite meaning. Directly. Somehow I knew he felt Vernell was involved directly.

"We've got an I.D. on the man in the truck. His name's Nosmo King. You know him?"

I frowned. Why would I know him?

"No. Should I?"

Weathers turned and nodded in the direction of Jack's warehouse. Our moment in the park was over. He meant for us to start walking, and the pace he set was a quick one.

"He's trouble. He's a money man for the Redneck Mafia. You ever hear of them?"

It felt like an accusation instead of a question. His tone and manner had changed, making me wonder what else he knew.

"Why don't you quit running around the barn and tell me what's really going on?"

Weathers cut down the alley that ran up to Jack's warehouse. His unmarked sedan was parked beside a scraggly clump of mimosa trees. He stepped just short of the bumper and looked at me.

"Nosmo's a real predictable guy. He ate breakfast at Tex and Shirley's three days ago, just like he always does. Had two eggs over easy, grits and gravy, dry toast and black coffee. Then, after breakfast, Nosmo did something completely unpredictable: He left the restaurant and disappeared off the face of the earth." Marshall's electric blue eyes darkened. "His breakfast partner that morning was none other than your ex-husband, Vernell."

My head spun and I couldn't put the pieces together. What had Vernell been doing talking to Nosmo King? The possibilities were endless and none of them were good.

"So what happens now?" I asked.

Marshall's hand was on the door handle. He was already thinking three moves ahead. In his mind, he was a million miles away.

"I'm going to see Nosmo's widow," he pronounced calmly, "and then I'm going to find out how Vernell and Mr. King came to hook up."

I thought about the stranger in Vernell's house. Could the Redneck Mafia be looking for Vernell? Was that who the stranger was working for? I shook myself and looked at Weathers. I thought about telling him, but for some reason held back. If the stranger worked for the Redneck Mafia, Weathers would find out sooner than I could. And what did I have to tell him anyway? A dark-haired stranger held a gun on me and then kissed me? And how would I explain not telling Weathers earlier? I needed more proof before I started raising a fuss about someone who could turn out to be perfectly harmless.

My stomach did a little flip, remembering the feel of his lips on mine, the way his eyes had seen right down inside my soul, as if he could read my mind. No, that guy wasn't harmless. It was my Pure T. Stubborn nature that held me back. I would tell Weathers when I was good and ready.

Eight

My little cottage sits on a small side street between two college campuses. It is over a hundred years old, drafty as your granny's drawers in a hurricane, and totally mine. I parked my ancient Beetle a good two blocks away, behind the YMCA parking lot, and snuck up on my own house.

I looked up and down the street for a motorcycle and saw none, but that didn't mean I wasn't cautious. I slipped down the alley, looked both ways before I crossed my dot of a backyard, then darted up the stairs to the door that opened into my converted sleeping porch–bedroom. I had the door open and was inside the house in seconds, the thrill of victory quickly shattered by the reality of defeat. My bed had been slept in and my house smelled like coffee. Freshly brewed coffee.

"Sheila?" I called softly.

The Shadow stepped into the doorway of my bedroom, one of my coffee mugs in hand, and a huge grin on his face.

"Just like I thought," he said. "Those eyes blackened right up." He sipped his coffee, all the while studying me. "It's not bad, though, what you did with the makeup. From the stage they might not even be able to tell. Guess it's the sunlight, huh? Kind of shows up everything."

I spun around and grabbed the doorknob. My heart thudded against my chest and my palms were sweating.

He didn't move from the doorway. "Have a nice day," he said slowly. "When Sheila gets in I'll tell her you were by."

That got me. I turned back and glared at him. "Get out of my house. I'm calling the police!"

He shook his head. His dark black hair reflected the sunlight that streamed in through my bedroom windows. His eyes twinkled. He was getting just the reaction he wanted. He slouched against the doorjamb, studying me over the rim of his coffee mug. He stopped smiling and the light went out of his eyes.

"Call them," he said. "But if you do, Vernell's a dead man."

"How do I know he isn't dead already?" I said. "Where is he?"

He shrugged his shoulders. "Your guess is as good as mine. I'm just telling you what the others will do if they find him, especially with the police in on it. You get them all wrapped up in this and I'll guaran-damn-tee you that they'll kill him first and ask questions later. You don't want to go calling the police or raising a bunch of senseless hell. You need my help."

"I need your help? I do not need help from you. What I need is to call the cops and get you out of my house!" I tried to look like I meant business, like I wasn't terrified, but he didn't seem to take me seriously.

He half-turned away from me, heading back into my kitchen. "You need all the help you can get. Now, come on," he said, "the coffee's fresh and I was about to rustle up some breakfast. You hungry?"

"No," I lied, sounding for all the world like a surly teenager. I hung back, trying to make up my mind. For some reason, I didn't think he was going to hurt me. You don't cook breakfast for someone you intend to kill—at least that's how I saw it.

"I want you out of my house," I said, moving reluctantly toward the kitchen. "This is breaking and entering, you know."

He chuckled. "As easy to pop as your house is, it oughta be called trick or treat." He laughed again, highly amused with his own cleverness. "How do you take your coffee?"

"Black."

"Figures," he said. "Wouldn't want any cream and sugar to lighten you up."

"Now listen here," I said, "I'm about over this act of yours. You cannot break into someone's house, eat their food, and threaten them without repercussions."

He spun back around and smirked. "Didn't figure you for the type to use uptown, big words. Repercussions, huh? Well, let me tell you something, Vernell's the one facing repercussions. You're just lucky I'm helping you out. I know more about him and the trouble he's in than the cops will ever know."

"You are not helping me out!" I crossed the kitchen floor, took my skillet out of his hand, and shoved him aside. "Move! If anyone cooks here, it's me." He took a step backward and frowned. "And another thing," I said. "I don't break bread with strangers. Who are you? I think you at least owe me that much."

I crossed my arms, holding the skillet against my side. I hadn't ruled out using it for knocking some sense into him, but if he was telling the truth and could help me find Vernell, then I'd be a fool to run him off. I stared at him, trying not to look at his mouth, trying not to remember the way he'd kissed me and the way I'd reacted.

He reached one hand back into his jeans pocket, pulled out his wallet, and flipped it open for me to see. Inside was a picture and a card identifying him as Anthony Carlucci, licensed private investigator.

I looked at the picture and then I looked at him. The picture didn't do his dark eyes any justice, but it was him. His hair was longer now, and he had a serious case of five o'clock shadow, but it was definitely him.

"You can call me Tony," he said, and stood there, staring me down in my own home.

I looked away at the carton of eggs sitting on the countertop. He had really been intent on cooking breakfast in my kitchen. Next to the stove sat my coffeepot, full of strong, black liquid. I inhaled and half-closed my eyes, then sighed and turned my attention back to Carlucci. Well, at least he was somewhat domesticated.

"You didn't start the grits water?" I said, pulling out another pot.

"Hashbrowns," he answered.

"Grits," I said. "My house, my food, my rules."

He smiled and stepped over to the coffeepot, grabbing a new mug as he went. "Here," he said, pouring the steaming coffee into the cup. "You haven't had enough to be thinking straight."

I slammed the skillet down on the stove and cut the fire on underneath it. "Who hired you?" I asked. I reached past him, pulled open the refrigerator door, and grabbed the bacon. Mama always said, "If you fill a man's stomach, you'll dull his senses." Mama never argued with Daddy when he was hungry, and Daddy never won an argument.

"I can't say. It's confidential."

Tony was leaning against the counter, uncomfortably close. He was slightly taller than Marshall Weathers, and larger, but without an ounce of flesh that wasn't muscle. Even without looking at him, I could feel him there. It was as if he radiated heat and something else that I couldn't quite put a name to.

"Man or woman?" I asked.

"Can't say," he answered.

I threw four strips of bacon into the hot skillet and listened to it sizzle against the burning surface.

"Why are you looking for Vernell?"

" 'Cause I got paid to look for him."

"By who? You can tell me that," I said. "What harm can that do?"

He shrugged. "I don't like to violate my code of ethics."

The bacon hissed and popped. "Yeah," I said, "like you have one. You work for the Redneck Mafia, don't you?"

That stopped him cold. He reached out, grabbed my arm and turned me toward him. "What do you know about that?" he asked. His eyes darkened and the look in them frightened me, but I wasn't going to let him know that.

"Nosmo King a friend of yours?" I said, letting my voice drop down to a near whisper. His grip on my arm tightened and I winced.

"How do you know about them?" he growled.

"The bacon's burning," I said, and jerked my arm away. I turned my attention back to the stove, knowing he wouldn't let it drop.

"Maggie, answer me. You can't drop a name like that and then stop talking. It's too dangerous."

"Who do you work for?" I shot back.

It was a standoff. I pulled the bacon out of the pan and slipped in the eggs. Over easy. I wouldn't look at him and he wasn't volunteering a thing. I poured grits into the boiling water and stirred them. The words *Redneck Mafia* and *Nosmo King* sure seemed to hit a nerve.

By the time the eggs were ready and the grits almost done, I had a plan. Mama always said, "A critter'll always come to sugar, long before he'll lick salt."

"Breakfast is on," I said. I pasted a stupid smile on my face and gestured toward my dining room. "You go sit down, let me tend to things."

Apparently he'd taken lessons in the same school of common sense. "Let me help you."

"I wouldn't dream of it," I purred. "You're a guest." *Like hell,* I thought, but swallowed it.

Tony picked up the coffeepot, filled our mugs, and then carried them into the dining room. Butter wouldn't have melted in his mouth.

I set his plate of food down in front of him, then added a huge bowl of grits. I just couldn't help myself. Then I went back for my plate.

"Umm, umm," I heard him moan from the dining room.

"You know, Maggie, where I come from, we don't eat grits, but these are delicious!"

I know a liar when I hear one. I stuck my head around the corner and stared at him. He was shoveling plain grits into his mouth as fast as possible, ignoring the bowl of red eye gravy, and ignoring the pepper. What was wrong with him? It could only be one thing. He had Yankee written all over him.

"Glad you like 'em," I said, breezing past him to my seat. "Where I come from, grits just ain't no good without gravy and pepper, but I'm so happy to see you love them plain. What a tribute!"

Tony shot a longing glance at the redeye gravy, realizing his error, and knowing he couldn't switch over now.

We would've continued like this for I don't know how long, but Sheila saved me. The front door latch clicked, the door swung open, and my teenaged daughter faced down Tony Carlucci with a haughty glare.

"What are you doing here?" she demanded. "Mama, that's him! That's the guy that was watching Daddy's house!"

Sheila marched through the living room and straight up to the dining-room table. She was wearing a little plaid miniskirt, black knee-highs, and pigtails. She looked like a Catholic schoolgirl.

"Baby, this is Mr. Carlucci," I said. "He's a private investigator looking for your dad."

"No you're not," Sheila sneered. "Private investigators don't wear black leather jackets and ride motorcycles."

"Sheila, where are your manners? And why aren't you in school?"

Sheila gave me a pitying look. "Mama, I am trying to save your life!"

"Cutting school again, huh?" Carlucci said, grinning.

"Shut up!"

"Sheila!" I swung back to face Carlucci. "How do you know she cuts school?"

"Doesn't everybody?" he answered.

"Well, I didn't."

Now Tony and Sheila both favored me with a pitying glance.

"I just stopped by to pick up a book I forgot," Sheila said, taking my side. "I do not cut school!"

"Stand by it if you want," Carlucci said, still smirking. "But I bet you wouldn't want your mama to check up on you." Sheila's face said all I needed to hear. I'd deal with her later.

Carlucci's plate was nearly clean. "I guess you'll be going now, huh?" I said, snatching the plate away. "I know you're busy with your investigation."

Sheila had stalked off to her room and was rooting around in search of something. I doubted it was a textbook. In this one instance, I figured Tony was right: Sheila had planned on cutting school and not getting caught.

"I'm not so busy that I can't help you do the dishes," he said. "My mother raised me right and I've got all day." He leaned back in his chair and stretched his long legs out in front of me. When he smiled, as he was doing now, without the smirk, he seemed almost human.

"You're not from around here, are you?" I asked.

"Philadelphia," he said. "South Philly." He shifted in his chair and I stared at his shoes. He wore motorcycle boots, rounded toe, black, scuffed leather. His arms were crossed, the muscles cording like thick bundles of wire. I thought I caught a glimpse of a tattoo peeking out from his shirtsleeve, but when he moved, it vanished.

"Mama!" Sheila said, sticking her head into the dining room. "I'm leaving." Her backpack was slung across her shoulder and she was moving fast toward the front door.

"You *are* going straight to school?" I asked, ignoring the smirk that had returned to Carlucci's face.

"Bye, Mama!"

"I'll be talking to the attendance officer later," I warned.

Sheila spun around, glowered at Carlucci, and took a deep breath. "You see what you've done?" she asked him. "Making my mama doubt me!" She straightened her shoulders and looked right at me. "Mama, in psychology class they say that if you let someone come between you, it's called splitting. Mr. Carlucci is trying to split us. He should know better than to try and corrupt our relationship!"

She was gone without another word, stomping off down the front porch steps. I went to the living-room window and watched her hop into a car full of her girlfriends. She was gesturing wildly, obviously filling them in on the ruination of her day and the realization that now she had to report to school. Carlucci was right. I kept my eyes on the street in front of the house, not wanting to turn around and face him.

I heard him get up and take the dishes out to the kitchen. Then the water started in the sink. The domesticated biker–private eye was cleaning up. First he threatened my family, then he invaded my home, and now he was doing my dishes. What in the hell was going on?

I stayed there for a few minutes, just staring out the window at the college students walking by and the cars that jockeyed for a parking place within a mile of the campus. It all looked so normal, but my world was going crazy a piece at a time.

I didn't hear the water cut off. I was lost in thought, figuring out how I was going to get to the bottom of things, when I heard Carlucci's voice behind me.

"I said it was a woman."

I didn't turn around. I didn't want to give him the satisfaction.

"A woman what?" I said finally.

"That hired me. That's all I'm gonna tell you. I shouldn't even have told you that much, but I'm starting to feel sorry for you. You got a teenager out running the streets, a husband leading a life you don't even know the half of—"

"Ex-husband," I snapped.

Carlucci ignored me and went on. "—no money and two black eyes. Somebody oughta take pity on you."

That got me to turn around, but he was watching the street, his eyes narrowed to wary slits. I opened my mouth to tell him he didn't need to feel sorry for me, but how could I? Everything he'd said was apparently true.

"I don't need your pity," I said. "What I need is something to go on. How can I help you or Vernell or my family if no one will tell me anything? Why don't you just shoot straight? Tell me what it is you're trying to say about Vernell."

Carlucci stared at me until I felt myself go cold with worry. His eyes flickered past me, out onto the street, and then back.

"Don't you ever wonder how Vernell can just start up a new business? Don't you ever ask him where the money comes from?"

"He started up the satellite dish company with the money he got from the mobile home business. It was going well."

Carlucci shook his head. "A mobile home business, a satellite dish company, a mansion, three vehicles, money, money, money. It don't grow on trees."

Carlucci was looking back out at the street. "I'm gonna tell you one thing, and I shouldn't probably, but it's time you grew up. There's a motel on Battleground Avenue, the Twilight Motel. It's been there for years, next to the Your House Diner. Why don't you go there sometime and drive around the back of the place?" He glanced over at me. "You might take it into your pretty little head to wonder how come it's so full of Volvos and Mercedes in the middle of the day."

Carlucci smiled softly. "Of course, you wouldn't be that type, would you?"

"What type?"

He didn't answer. Instead his shoulders tightened and he was frowning at something outside.

"Looks like your bad day's about to take a downward turn," he said.

I looked to see what he meant and found Marshall Weathers climbing out of his unmarked car. If anyone would get the straight facts out of Carlucci, it would be Weathers. I moved to the door, turned the lock, and swung the door wide open.

"We'll see who knows what now," I said, looking back at Carlucci. But he was gone, and the slamming of the back door was my only answer.

Nine

Marshall Weathers was in a foul mood and maybe that's why I didn't tell him anything. Maybe if he'd made it easy, I would've told him about Carlucci, but as it was, I didn't get a chance. At least, that's how I chose to see it.

"I thought you might be here," he said. "I need your signature on a search warrant so we can go through the books and other stuff in Vernell's offices." He was whipping out the papers as he spoke.

"Come inside," I said. The curtains fluttered across the street and I knew the unmarked patrol car, with its antennae and state plates, was drawing the attention of my neighbors. It wasn't the first time they'd seen police cars in front of the house, but I didn't want them to start speculating on my lifestyle.

Weathers stepped into the living room and sniffed. He smelled breakfast. He looked past me at the dining-room table and I saw his eyebrow twitch. The radar was on. Two coffee mugs sat out on the table. Two crumpled napkins.

"Company?" he asked.

There was something in the tone of his voice, a hint of sarcasm or suspicion that I didn't like one little bit.

"Sheila. I always make her breakfast," I lied. I don't know why I did it, except I didn't like the insinuation.

"I thought you said she stayed at her friend's house and was going to school from there." He had me and we both knew it, but I couldn't bring myself to admit it.

"She forgot her science book." My neck was starting to flush red, spreading across my chest, burning its way up to my ears. I never was a good liar, but pride made me continue to try. "You know young'uns," I said, "always hungry."

He looked at me, his eyes zeroing in on my neck. He took his time folding up the search warrant and pushing it slowly into his jacket pocket.

"Yep," he said at last, "I know young'uns, and I know Sheila. She just don't strike me as the breakfast type." Before I could argue, he turned away. "Guess you learn stuff about folks every day. Next time I see you, maybe you'll catch me up on why Sheila drinks black coffee instead of juice. And how come she's started carrying pieces of motorcycle chain around with her."

I looked back at the table and saw Carlucci's mug. It was half full. My mug was easy to tell. It had a lipstick-stained rim. A few pieces of metal lay next to Carlucci's mug. I hadn't noticed them. Weathers was out the door and down the sidewalk without a backward glance.

"Damn," I said, "damn, damn, damn!" I'd lied to Weathers for no other reason than stubborn pride and he'd caught me. "Okay," I said out loud, "it's time to make a move. Forget those stupid men!" I grabbed the cordless phone from its stand by the front door and punched in the number I knew by heart. It was time to call in backup. It was time for brains over brawn. In short, it was time to do the job myself, without relying on a Prince Charming.

"Curly-Que Salon and House of Beauty," a familiar voice rasped.

"Bonnie," I said, "what are you doing?"

There was a snort, and then the sound of a long exhale as Bonnie blew out a stream of cigarette smoke.

"Honey, what the hell do you think I'm doing? I'm doing hair, that's what. I know you've been gone from here a while, but I didn't figure singing would make you forget about the business totally. What am I doing!" She laughed again, her deep voice rumbling through the phone. "You must be having one hell of a time if you can't remember your partner's occupation!"

"Bonnie," I said, breaking in before she took off again, "I need you."

That was all it took. "All right, sugar, what you got going on? I reckon Velmina can take over my customers for a while. You need me now?"

Bonnie never asks why. When Vernell walked out and left us, Bonnie never asked the obvious questions, the ones everyone else asked over and over. She's raising six young'uns on her own, she doesn't have to ask why. Why doesn't matter when you've got to go on. When I told her I wanted to take a leave of absence from our shop and go be a country singer, Bonnie smiled and said, "Go for it, girl!"

"I'm coming to get you," I said. "Vernell's gone, his money's gone, and I've gotta find him."

Bonnie started to say something and stifled herself. I figured it ran along the lines of "don't look for something what needs to stay lost."

"Come on then, honey. I'm just puttin' the blue rinse on Neva Jean. Chances are the old bat won't know whether it's me or Velmina what does her comb-out. I'm good to go."

Fifteen minutes later, I rounded the corner onto Exchange Place, drove slowly down the short side street, and found a parking place in between the bail bondsman's office and the karate studio, directly across from the intensive parole offices and down from the IRS building. The way Bonnie and I figured it, we were in a prime location.

The Curly-Que was humming with the midmorning bluehairs, all in for their rinse and sets. Bonnie met me at the door, spun me around, and shoved me away from the front desk.

"Get out! Neva Jean sees you and that'll be the end of it! You know how she is! She only wants you to do her. I've finally got her to where she'll let me do it. Don't spoil things."

"But I thought Velmina was doing her comb-out. How'd that happen?"

Bonnie sighed, closed the door to the salon and squinted into the bright sunlight. "Neva dozes off in the chair. What she don't know won't hurt her. Besides, Velmina's almost a spitting double for me."

I looked at Bonnie. She was fifty, had brassy blond hair cut short, and never wore makeup. Velmina was twenty-three, made up like a Barbie doll, and a good six sizes smaller than Bonnie. Denial is a wonderful thing.

As we made our way through the downtown traffic, I caught Bonnie up on the details of Vernell's disappearance, the death of Nosmo King, and the arrival of Tony Carlucci.

When I'd finished, Bonnie leaned back in her seat, and looked over at me with a big smile on her face.

"Man," she said, "some people just have all the luck. Look at you. Your husband leaves you, you become a country and western singer, meet a hunk of a detective, and get stalked by another hunk, all courtesy of your low-life, scuzzball husband!" She shook her head. "Honey, I just don't know how you do it. Rodney walked out on me and all I got were the kids and a pile of bills."

It was edging up on eleven A.M. I was flying up Battleground Avenue heading for the older strip of businesses that housed the Twilight Motel and the Your House Diner.

"You know why he wants you to look in the parking lot, don't you?"

Bonnie was staring at me with this curious half-smile that she seems to wear most of the time. To some folks, it might seem she was being smug. To me, it merely meant she was about to say something I wouldn't want to hear, and was trying to cushion bad news with a smile.

"No, why?"

"Baby, the Twilight Motel is centrally located to Irving Park. Them tennis ladies drop their kids at the preschool and then they're right over here taking lessons from the pro, or whoever else is the flavor of the month. Sugar, they rent these rooms by the half-day or the hour. See what I'm saying?"

I did. And so help me, I thought of Vernell in the same breath. This would've been where Vernell took his skunk of a girlfriend back when we were still married. Centrally located, all right. The Twilight Motel was also less than a mile away from the Satellite Kingdom, Vernell's newest endeavor.

I pulled into the parking lot and followed the narrow driveway around to the back. Carlucci was right. Three Volvo station wagons sat in front of motel room doors. The rest of the lot was taken up with pickup trucks and assorted other cars, but it was the upscale models that stood out.

"All right," I said, swinging back around to the front, "here's where we get creative."

I pulled right up to the motel office and stopped the car under a portico. The way I saw it, there was nothing to do but hit the situation head on. I got out of the car, with Bonnie right behind me, and walked into the fifties-time-warp of an office. A pimple-faced young man, somewhere in his early twenties, was behind the counter, his black hair slicked to the side of his head. His lips were too thick for his face, making him look somewhat like a fish.

He slid a pad across the desk to me and smirked. "You want it by the hour or the day, ladies?"

I reached into my purse, pulled out my wallet, and stuck my fingers down into a side slot. Vernell's picture, the worse for wear, and about ten years old, came sliding out.

"Do you know this man?" I asked. I stared hard at the kid, trying to look important or official, but he snickered.

"Yeah, right," he said. "Lady, we work the same as the government here: Don't ask, don't tell. Just like I'd do for you two."

He leered at Bonnie and that was all it took. She reached

across the counter, snatched the boy up by his shirt collar, and yanked him halfway across the registration desk. She had a cigarette leaning out of the left side of her mouth, and for a moment, I thought the guy was in danger of being branded.

"Listen here, you little punk," she rasped, smoke billowing out into the boy's face. "This ain't the movies and we ain't playing. I've got young'uns at home older than you and I can whip their asses with one hand tied behind my back." The guy wanted to struggle, but Bonnie uses her hands and arms all day long. There was no prying loose from her grip.

I reached back into my wallet and pulled out a twenty-dollar bill. I stepped behind Bonnie and waved it where the kid could see me. He coughed, eyed the money, and looked back at Bonnie.

"All right, all right," he whined, "turn loose of me!"

"Do you know that man?" Bonnie asked, drawing out each word so that it seemed to slap Junior right between the eyes.

I pulled out another bill and added it to the twenty.

"Yes, I do," he said. Bonnie released him with a shove and he fell back, grabbing at his collar.

"Start talking," Bonnie said.

"Mr. Smith's been coming in here semi-regular for the past few months. He used to come in all the time, a couple of years ago, with this knockout, but now he's got him a new one."

I slid a twenty across the counter and it was gone instantly. "Keep talking," I said.

"What do you want to know?"

"When was the last time he was in, and who was he with?"

Bonnie blew smoke across the counter and glared at the boy.

"He was here, um"—the kid looked at the ceiling, thinking—"Friday." The day Vernell vanished.

"You're sure?" I said, my heart beating hard against my chest.

"Yep," he said slowly. "It was payday. And it must've been his too, on account of he tipped me fifty bucks." The kid eyed me like maybe I was going to cough up a fifty.

"Who was the woman?" I asked.

"I don't know," the kid said, shaking his head impatiently. "They don't introduce them to me, they just rent the rooms. Ain't you never done it before? The man gets the room while the woman waits in the car."

"Don't get smart, boy," Bonnie said, stepping a little closer to the counter.

"All's I could tell was, she didn't look like the one he used to bring. This one was closer to Mr. Smith's age." I thought about Jolene the Dish Girl, twenty-four, bleached white-blond, and stacked.

"What color hair? What did she look like?"

The clerk thought a moment. "Um, brown hair, you know, dark hair. Kinda cut short, maybe curly. Had a pretty smile. That's all I could tell."

A Mercedes pulled up behind my VW under the portico. An older businessman stepped out of the driver's side door and started toward us.

"Are you done?" the clerk said.

"You ever seen that woman come in here with another guy?" Bonnie asked.

"Nah," the kid answered. "And she wasn't pro material, either."

Bonnie nodded, satisfied. "Just wondering," she muttered to me. "I just can't figure how Vernell keeps coming up with pretty women, as dog-butt ugly as he is!"

We reached the door at the same moment the businessman did. He held the door and I walked out, but Bonnie stopped, looking from him to the young woman waiting in his car.

"Go on back to work, you old fool," she said. "You got a wife and young'uns, don't you?"

The man's face reddened and he walked right on past her, into the office. Bonnie stepped out into the driveway and glared at the blonde in the Mercedes.

"Hussy," she said. "Rodney would've loved this place. Would've saved him taking his pickup out to High Rock Lake and fooling around in the broad daylight!"

I wasn't listening. I was thinking. Vernell had been coming to the Twilight Motel for the past few months with a woman. Vernell, single again, had no need of a motel. He had a mansion. For some reason, this woman wouldn't come to Vernell's stone palace. Why?

I slid into the car and cranked the engine. Bonnie was still going on about Rodney leaving her and his history of seducing women. Rodney, never too proud to show his ass when he was drinking, apparently showed it off regularly to the bass fishermen of High Rock Lake. The idea of getting sweaty on the underside of Rodney while lying on the bedliner of a pickup truck did nothing for me, but Bonnie seemed to think Rodney never lacked for partners.

"Bonnie," I said, "Vernell's new honey must be married to someone he knows or someone who lives in the neighborhood. Why else would she come here every Friday?"

Bonnie, in the middle of her monologue about Rodney, stopped talking and stared at me.

"Guess that's why they pay you the big bucks," she said.

"Of course." Bonnie looked out the window as I pulled out into traffic. "Guess we're going to the Satellite Kingdom, huh?" she said.

"Why?"

Bonnie snorted. "On account of that's where he met up with his last honey," she said. "Men ain't free thinkers, you know. They're creatures of habit. Betcha five dollars she's the new receptionist. That's how Rodney got his out at the dealership. Just you wait and see."

We headed north on Battleground, homing in on the Satellite Kingdom. Bonnie was humming to herself now, something that sounded like "Faded Love."

"Bonnie," I said, not looking over at her. "What do you think it means when a man tells you he doesn't want to get involved and then kisses you?"

Bonnie snorted. "Baby, just let me tell you one damn

thing: Men are like fish. You can't just plop your line in the water and think they're gonna see it for what it is and run with it."

She was looking at me now, I could feel it. I focused on the traffic, which in a town where everyone feels entitled to having it their way, is a good idea. Vernell's kingdom was straight ahead, just outside of the main business drag, across from Wal-Mart and next to a lot where a guy sat in a truck and sold rocks to wealthy gardeners.

"Naw, a man's gotta mouth the bait a little," she said. "I take it we're discussing your detective fella." I nodded ever so slightly. "Honey, he's a big 'un. Them kind slip up, try and take the bait off your hook, then run if you ain't watchin'. You gotta wait 'em out. Don't go yanking on the line and trying to reel him in. He's got a lot of fight in him. You can tell that, just by the way he walks."

I couldn't let that one go. "How can you tell what a man's gonna do by the way he walks?"

"Your boy walks slow like he's prowling," she said. "Remember, I've met him. He came into the shop when Jimmy got hisself murdered. Thought he could get to you by going through me. Huh!" she snorted. "Yeah, right, like I'd talk about you to the po-lice." Bonnie reached in her purse for a cigarette, remembered I didn't like smoking in the car, and dropped the pack back into the leather pouch. "That detective can't keep his eyes off of you, that's another sign. You got him, but you gotta give him room to run."

I had no idea what Bonnie was going on about. The way I had it figured, it was hopeless. My head knew this, but my heart and a few other parts of my anatomy didn't want to throw in the towel quite yet.

I pulled into the gravel lot of the Satellite Kingdom and stopped in front of the doublewide Vernell used for a sales office.

"Now here's where the rubber meets the road," Bonnie said, and opened the car door. "Five dollars says it's the receptionist." And with that she marched up the stairs and into the building.

By the time I reached the door, Bonnie was stomping out. "Clever ruse, that Vernell has," was all she said as she walked past me and down the steps. She was fumbling with a cigarette and a lighter and apparently had no intentions of returning. "Just make it snappy. I need to get back to the shop as soon as possible. They can't keep the place going more than an hour without me there to watch 'em." She gave me a sharp glance and touched my arm. "I mean, unless you need me to whip that one inside into shape." She looked back toward the door and shook her head. "There's more to all this than meets the eye, honey."

I had no idea what she was talking about and Bonnie wasn't sticking around to explain. She walked off across the parking lot, headed for the car and her smoke break.

I pulled open the glass door and stepped inside. The receptionist looked up and smiled, her gray hair piled neatly on top of her head.

"Can I help you?"

"You're new," I said.

The woman adjusted her thin framed glasses, pushing them back up her nose and squinting through them to see me better. Her face was a maze of wrinkles and laugh lines. She was the double for Vernell's grandmother.

"Oh dear," she sighed, "now just tell me you're someone important and I'm supposed to know you." She shook her head. "I told Bess I didn't need a job, but she had to have it her way."

"Bess who?" I asked.

The woman stood up from behind the desk and walked around to stand in front of me.

"Bess King, my daughter. She's the one told me I needed something to do now that Guthrie's gone. She said Mr. Spivey needed help, and here I am." She smiled and I couldn't help smiling back, but inside my heart had skipped a beat. Bess King. Nosmo King.

"Don't mind me," she said, "I wander on." She stuck out her hand. "I'm Eugenia Price. Welcome to the Satellite Kingdom. I'd be glad to help you with all your satellite needs but as you can see, I don't know a thing about new-fangled technology. Our salesmen are, um"—she looked around—"out in the field today."

Out in the field, indeed. With Vernell gone, and pay-checks missing, it meant the sales team hadn't shown for work.

"How about Andy Little?" I asked. Eugenia Price looked puzzled. "The manager."

"Oh yeah, him." She shook her head. "I think he's in the field, too." Eugenia was looking around, her gaze flitting back and forth from one vacant office to another. "I just started Thursday. To tell you the truth, I'm just not the one to help."

"Don't worry about it, Mrs. Price. I reckon you don't know, but I'm Mr. Spivey's ex-wife and I'm worried about him." There was suspicion in Eugenia Price's eyes now. *Concern* and *ex* don't always run together.

"He's missing," I said. "He hasn't been seen since Friday. He and I are co-owners of his other business, the Mobile Home Kingdom. I'm just plain scared something's happened."

Eugenia's eyes widened. She folded her arms, her fingers running up and down the silky material of her sleeves, as if she were trying to warm up.

"Missing?" she repeated.

I nodded. "You know, if your daughter is a friend of Vernell's, she might know where he is."

Eugenia shook her head slightly. "Oh, I don't think so. Vernell Spivey is the last thing on her mind. Bess's husband died this week." Eugenia's face seemed to crumple a little as pain slowly filled her eyes. "I was only here this morning to tell the boss man I can't stay." She looked around the empty trailer. "I guess there's no point in waiting around anymore. I was supposed to start at twelve, but I can't stay. Bess has got so much on her."

"I'm sorry for your loss," I said automatically.

Eugenia Price's head went up. "Oh, sugar," she said, "that weren't no loss. Nosmo King was the meanest man alive.

I've been after Bess for years to leave him. I'm only sorry he died and left things in such a mess. No will. No instructions. And her with them two kids and Nosmo's gas station to run."

I could see Bonnie outside leaning on the hood of my car, a cigarette in hand and a scowl on her face.

"That's terrible," I said.

Eugenia nodded. "Yeah, but at least she won't be hurting for money. That gas station is a gold mine. Sits right out at the corner of Summit Avenue and Wendover. I never knew there was so much money in gasoline!"

Eugenia shook herself and looked back at me. "I'm sorry, here you are worried about your husband, and I'm running on about my own worries."

I smiled again. "Vernell'll turn up," I said, "he always does. You know," I said, "I think I may've seen your Bess around here before. She have short brown hair, kinda curly, and a real pretty smile?"

Eugenia Price smiled. "That's her," she said. "Prettiest smile in Guilford County, I always say."

Ten

There was a crown on the sign in front of King's Gas and Go, but that was the only thing golden or regal about the place. The gas station was packed tight into a corner that had to see traffic all day and night long. In years gone by, Summit Avenue had been the hub of the cotton mill village that took up the southeastern edge of town. But now the mill was closed and the houses and businesses that had flourished with mill money were falling into disrepair.

Fast-food restaurants and used car lots had moved in. Summit Avenue was now a stopping point in a journey to somewhere else. Folks just didn't stick around to find out what was going to happen next, because something bad was always happening next on Summit Avenue. The cops had even set up a field station there so they wouldn't have so far to go between calls. At night, Summit became a drug-dealing, whore-peddling, one-stop-shopping opportunity. By day it merely looked dirty and hung over.

King's Gas and Go had been celebrating. Grimy red and white triangles like dragon's teeth spun their way down a thick white tape, framing the entrance to a new car wash that sat on a little hill to the right of the station. Nosmo King had packed every bit of his corner lot with money-making opportunities, leaving his customers to fend for themselves when it came to parking and maneuvering their way off of the tiny lot and back into oncoming traffic.

I pulled my VW up to the pump and took the opportunity to fill it up while I studied my approach. Bonnie was back at the salon, so I couldn't rely on her to bulldoze her way inside and run the interrogation. Anyway, this situation probably called for a softer approach. Nosmo King was dead, but the station still stayed open. I figured whoever was running it had to be a minor peon, but still, they might know something. I looked up at the dirty white building. The bay doors were open and an ancient pickup sat high atop a lift receiving some kind of care. The front window was mirrored with tinted glass making it impossible to see inside. On the whole, you couldn't tell that the owner had just been murdered.

Mama always said, "A potato's just a potato, until you start peeling." I figured that was true of King's Gas and Go too. I walked across the tiny lot and pulled open the tinted glass door. A bell tinkled and the dark-haired woman behind the cash register looked up for a second, then went back to poring over a huge black notebook.

My heart started beating faster, my skin prickled, and I just knew it had to be her. Dark hair, kind of curly. I walked down the aisle, looking at the potted meat and saltine crackers. I stepped to the window and pretended to study the rows of trophies that stood on display.

They were huge gold and silver monuments, the kind they give out to sports teams when they win championships, only these weren't sporting trophies. They were made out, in most cases, to Bess King. Grand Champion, Maggie Valley Clog-off, 1999; First Place, Georgia Nationals, Town and Country Cloggers. There wasn't a second place among them, and there were enough to completely fill the ledge. I began to peel the potato.

"Those trophies," I said, stepping up to the counter, "they're amazing. What is clogging?"

The woman looked up and favored me with a faint smile. Her eyes were red-rimmed, and she looked as if she'd maybe been standing in the same spot for days. Her white cotton shirt was rumpled and stained with blue ink marks. Her hair fell in ringlets around her face. The little lines that women get in their late thirties had deepened with fatigue, and she looked almost relieved to see a stranger.

"You on pump one?" she asked softly. I turned and looked out the window. I was the only one at the pumps.

"Yep," I answered. She wasn't going to talk to me.

"Okay, that's eight dollars even," she said. "That gets you a free car wash. Here's your token."

She slid the brass coin across to me and I picked it up and turned to go.

"Oh, you wanted to know about the trophies, didn't you?"

I spun back around. "Yeah. I've heard of clogging, but I'm not sure I know what it is."

Bess King ran her hand through her hair and sighed. "Clogging is a form of dance, brought over to the Appalachians by our English and Irish ancestors. It looks a little like tap dancing."

I pointed to the biggest trophy, the Grand Champion, 1999. "Is that yours?" I asked.

"Yeah. Clogging's what keeps me going," she said. "You've probably seen my team, the Town and Country Cloggers? We dance all over Greensboro."

The potato was unraveling. "Hmm," I said, pretending to think, "I don't know." I looked up at her, as if an idea was slowly dawning in my head. "You dance to country music, don't you?" She nodded. "You know, I sing for the house band out at the Golden Stallion. How come y'all haven't been there to dance?"

Bess King grinned quickly. "Haven't been asked," she said. "It's not like we charge a whole lot, either. We dance for donations, we dance for food, sometimes, we just flat-out dance!" Her eyes sparkled, and for an instant I saw why Vernell had been drawn to her. She looked alive and happy. But the curtain of fatigue and pain quickly dropped back into place.

"My name's Maggie Reid," I said, and watched her reaction. Her head shot back up, and her eyes studied me, a startled expression on her face.

"Maggie Reid?"

Vernell had told her about me. I could see that as plain as day. I decided to hit it head on.

"Vernell's my ex-husband," I said. "Your husband was found in his car last night."

Bess King made no more pretense of looking at the papers in front of her. "You're Vernell's ex?" she asked.

"That's why I'm here. I need to find him."

Bess's eyes narrowed. "Why did you come to me? What makes you think I'd know where he is?"

I hated to do it. She seemed like a nice woman under an incredible amount of strain, but I didn't know her. What if she'd done something with Vernell? What if she were lying to me and hiding him? Worse yet, what if she'd killed her husband?

"I'm coming to you because you were the last one to see him, Friday morning, at the Twilight Motel." I said it hard, like maybe she had some explaining to do.

Bess King's face crumpled. "Go away," she said softly.

"Where's Vernell?" I demanded. "Your husband's dead. You were fooling around with Vernell, and now he's gone. So far, honey, you're looking like the missing link."

Through the door leading out to the bay, I could hear the sound of the impact wrench, loosening tires. She wasn't alone on the lot. If she needed reinforcements, all she had to do was call out.

"You don't know anything," Bess said, her voice tight and angry. "Vernell Spivey is the kindest man to ever walk the face of this earth. If it weren't for him . . ." Her voice trailed off and tears filled her eyes. "If it weren't for him, my life would've stayed the living hell it's been since I met Nosmo King."

I stepped back toward the counter. Her hand jumped instinctively to a shelf just beneath the cash register. She was reaching for a gun.

"Hey," I said, softly, raising my hands, palms up. "I don't think you understand. I'm just worried about Vernell." I smiled a little. "I guess I'm like his second big sister nowadays. I worry about him. His daughter is worried sick about her daddy. Vernell didn't make payroll this week, and that's just not like him." I edged a little closer. "I just want to know if you've seen him, but I guess you haven't."

I dropped my hands slowly and looked at her. "I don't know what you and Vernell had going on, and frankly, I don't really care. If you're good to him, that's fine. But you gotta admit, finding your husband dead in Vernell's car looks bad for you and Vernell."

Bess stood there, watching me, tears slowly rolling down her cheeks.

"I was hoping you'd be able to help me, or at least talk to me woman to woman, but I guess you're not the kind, and I'm sorry for it."

With that I started to walk away. My hand was actually on the door handle when she called out.

"Wait! I just didn't . . ." Her voice trailed off and I turned back. "I wasn't sure I should talk to you, that's all. I wasn't sure how you'd feel, or what you'd think."

"All right," I said. "Let's talk."

Bess closed her thick notebook with a sigh. "I'm trying to make heads or tails of what's going on with this place," she said. "I need to know if I can cover the funeral, but I guess that's a joke. From the looks of it, I could buy Nosmo his own cemetery. Who knew a gas station in this part of town could make that much money?" She looked past me, out at the pumps. "Shoot! Look at that! Now that's just what I don't need. That man's turning into a real pest." A familiar unmarked sedan was pulling into the parking lot. Marshall Weathers was rolling in on us like a thick fog. If he found the two of us talking, there'd be no telling what he'd think.

"Well, he sure doesn't need to find me here," I muttered.

Maybe he wouldn't notice my car. Old white VWs were common. Maybe if I slipped out the side door and drove around to the car wash, he'd come and go.

"Listen," I said, "I'll go wash the car and check back. If he's gone we'll talk, if not, I'll ride back by in a few minutes."

Weathers was getting out of his car, staring right at me, as if he could see my face through the tinted windows. I turned and fled just as he stepped up onto the stoop and put his hand on the door.

I could hear the bell on the door tinkle as I made a quick dash to my car. I slunk down into the driver's seat, started her up, and pulled up the incline and around back, out of Weathers's sight, to the car wash entrance. I pushed my token into the slot, hit the button, and lined the car up with the automatic tracks.

The lights came on, water started squirting out from every possible surface of the interior walls, and the brushes began to whir. I reached up to crank the handle and close the sunroof as the car began moving forward. I turned and turned, moving the panel slowly forward, but just as the hood touched the front water jets, the handle came off in my hands.

"*No!*" I yelled. I tried furiously to reattach the handle, but there was nothing for it. The screw was stripped. I was headed into a deluxe hot wash and wax with my sunroof open a good four inches.

I reached up and tugged on the panel. It groaned and moved slowly forward, one inch. There was no budging it after that. The water moved slowly up the hood of the car, smacking into the windshield, suds foaming up like billowy clouds. I reached into the glove compartment, hoping for a map or something to cover the opening, but remembered too late that I'd cleaned the entire car out only a few days before. I leaned back and moaned. There was nothing I could do. Not one thing. I was about to have the complete works, all three minutes' worth, wash, wax, and dry.

Water started streaming through the opening in the sunroof, hitting my hair and raining down across my face.

"Oh man," I sighed, "is it my karma? Have I ticked somebody off?"

That was when the hot wax light sprang on and little squirts of slippery thick liquid began hitting my head. I learned something then. When hot moist air hits the cooler interior air of, say, a car, it begins to form a cloud. A misty fog thickened as I rolled forward, covering my windshield and the side windows.

The fuzzy sweater I'd thrown on as I left the house began to clump up and resemble a wet alley cat. Little beads of wax stuck to it, clinging like sequins. There was nothing to do but sit and wait for the blow dryer to begin its job.

A huge gust of wind from the dryer blew through the sunroof, whipping my hair into a red tangle. The cloud began to clear and I could see the light at the end of the tunnel. I was almost through. With a final blast of air, the car wash pushed me out into the late afternoon sunlight, leaving me poised at the top of the little hill, overlooking the parking lot. At my angle I couldn't tell if Weathers was gone.

But that wasn't really the issue. As I started to roll forward, down the hill, water that had been blown back into the sunroof's housing came rushing forward, like a waterfall, raining down right on top of my head.

I screamed, slamming on the brakes instinctively. The car stopped at the bottom of the hill as the last gush of water escaped and covered me. Another cloud billowed up, and I leaned forward to rest my head on the steering wheel.

"Why me?" I muttered. "I was only trying to help."

I sat there for a moment, remembered Weathers, and sat up. But of course, it was too late. He and Bess King had left the Gas and Go office and moved outside to see what kind of idiot would run her car through the car wash with an open sunroof. Bess's eyes were wide-open dinner plates. Marshall Weathers, on the other hand, was smirking.

He left the curb and sauntered up to the driver's side. "I was wondering how you did your hair," he said. "You know, so it always has that wild look about it. I never dreamed the lengths a woman could go to for beauty."

I opened my mouth to say something smart, but he stopped me. "I'm sorry," he said, "I couldn't help it. Tell you what," he said. "I don't live too far from here. Give me a minute to finish up, and we'll go to my place. I reckon I can help you clean out your car before you start mildewing." He peered up at the roof. "Reckon I can take a look at your sunroof too. I mean, it is broken, isn't it? You didn't just elect to do the wash-and-dry job on yourself, did you?"

He didn't wait for an answer, just turned his smirky self back around and walked over to Bess. I wanted to tell him to go jump in a lake, but a chill was starting to set in, and the way I figured it, this was no time to get huffy.

The mechanic had wandered outside to take a look at the cause of the commotion, and while Marshall Weathers talked to Bess, he stood staring at me. He was a thin rat of a man, with greasy coveralls and thickset eyebrows. When I looked right back at him, he began to smile. The guy was actually trying to come on to a woman who had just been hot-waxed. I couldn't believe it. I winked and pulled one lock of my hair straight out from my head. It stuck there, and I believe that's what finally convinced the guy that I was not his type. He turned away, an ill-at-ease smile in place, and walked back into the garage.

Of course, Marshall Weathers turned back around just in time to see me pull out another strand of hair and stick out my tongue at the retreating mechanic. It was just one of those days.

Eleven

$\mathcal{M}$arshall Weathers was a liar. I figured this as I followed him out of the gas station and away from town on Wendover Avenue. He couldn't live nearby. I didn't figure him for a city boy and we were definitely in urban territory. He'd driven east for approximately three minutes when he abruptly split off onto a narrow road that ran alongside a roller rink. It seemed we'd gone for less than a mile when the paved road ended. We were five minutes from busy Summit Avenue and yet, he had me running down a gravel and dirt lane, out into pure pastureland.

"What is this?" I muttered. "Another cop trick? Drive me out into the country where I can't get away, then interrogate me?" My imagination ran wild. I had to admit the idea of being alone with Marshall Weathers wasn't totally unappealing. In fact, if I recalled the way he kissed me just a few hours before, I could downright anticipate it. However, at the same time, my sweater began to shrink up over my belly button, and my entire body began to itch. It had to be the detergent and hot wax. Human bodies weren't made for the harsh chemicals of a car wash.

We were running alongside a horse farm. Split-rail fences with barbed wire kept a few beautiful bays penned inside a green pasture. Weathers abruptly made a turn into a dirt driveway and slowed to a crawl as we passed two log outbuildings that had to be over two hundred years old. The driveway was lined with cedars that formed a shady tunnel. The trees ended and we drove out into the brilliant sunlight of the clear October afternoon. Marshall's car rolled to a stop in front of a small white farmhouse.

I drew in my breath and slowly exhaled. It was perfect. It was the farmhouse I'd always wanted. Yellow and white gingham curtains fluttered from the kitchen window. Bright yellow chrysanthemums and pumpkins edged their way up the back stoop steps. The roof was red tin, and the woodwork was such a shiny white that I figured he'd painted the place within the past month.

I jumped out of the car and walked toward the front of his house. It sat on the peak of a rise overlooking acres of tobacco fields. It had to be his home place, a farm that had gradually been surrounded by the growing city. I stared at the front porch, lost for a moment in the idea of what it must be to live in this place, to walk outside every morning, coffee cup in hand, and sit, watching the day begin. The air was still and silent, with only a breeze kicking up now and then.

When I remembered to look for Weathers, I found him watching me, leaning back against the hood of his car and smiling to himself.

"Now that's quite a picture," he said slowly. For a second I thought he meant the view from the hilltop, but no, he meant me. I looked down at myself. My jeans were soaked, my sweater was a balled up mass of fiber, and my hair was drying into a solid mass of red tangles. I shivered and he moved.

"Come on," he said. "You're gonna get sick standing out here, and besides that, you might harden up and not be able to move." He reached me and touched my shoulder.

"It's beautiful," I said. "I had no idea this was out here." I turned a little away from him and looked back at the valley. His hand stayed on my shoulder, warm and firm.

"I like it right much," he said. "Now come on inside."

I followed him up the steps, across the wide blue-gray porch and through the thick front door into the house. I squinted, waiting as my eyes adjusted to the inside. We were in a wide foyer. A big mahogany sideboard took up the far wall, holding the day's mail and a worn Braves cap, his cap, I thought. Marshall walked past me, leading me down the center hallway, past the wide staircase with its worn-smooth steps, and into the kitchen. It was a woman's kitchen.

I stood there, taking in the gleaming vintage white appliances, the spotless black and white checkered linoleum floor, and the cast-iron skillets that hung in a neat row along the far wall. A red towel hung from the oven door. The teakettle had a little bird on the spout. African violets bloomed along the windowsill and jars of home-canned vegetables lined the open shelves next to the refrigerator. My heart fell. Here was the kitchen of my dreams and it was most certainly *her* kitchen.

"Sit down," he said, indicating a chair at the light pine kitchen table. "Want some coffee or tea? It'd warm you up."

He wasn't waiting for me to answer him. He was filling the teakettle with water, his back to me.

"I'm fine. No thank you."

"Suit yourself." He went on bustling about his kitchen, opening the refrigerator, reaching in for milk, then walking across the room to the pantry and pulling out bags that crackled and boxes that opened with a soft popping sound.

I sat there and felt good and sorry for myself. Marshall Weathers probably still carried a torch for his wife. What was I thinking, hoping we could have a relationship? I watched him make the coffee, carefully measuring it into the carafe, pouring steaming water in a thin stream through the filter.

He still loved her. He wasn't ready for anything serious. Hell, he'd told me that. What was I thinking?

Marshall walked toward me, setting a plate of cookies down in front of me. They looked homemade. I figured she brought them over to him, feeling sorry maybe. I decided her name was Wanda. Wanda Weathers. She was a big-haired, big-boned woman who sang in the choir every Sunday. She wore fake eyelashes on New Year's Eve and didn't like to spoil her makeup by fooling around. I figured her for a cross-stitcher, sewing away on cold winter evenings.

"You don't look right," he said, materializing in front of me, a steaming mug in his hand. "Too bad you're not hungry." He sat down across from me and shoved the cookies in my direction. "Sure you won't have any?"

"I don't think so," I said, my voice almost frosted. "I'm watching my figure."

"Uh-huh," he said, his eyes wandering up and down my torso. "Looks fine to me."

"Nope," I said firmly, "no cookies."

Marshall Weathers shook his head ruefully. "Too bad, my Aunt Lou made these. Won the county fair one year with this very recipe."

Aunt Lou? His aunt made the cookies? I snuck another peek and felt my stomach rumble. I hadn't even stopped for lunch after I'd dropped Bonnie back at the salon. Now I'd denied myself cookies.

I scratched at my stomach, then behind my ears. I was about to lose my mind sitting right here in Wanda Weathers's kitchen.

Marshall lowered his mug and frowned, then leaned closer. "Maggie, you're breaking out in a rash."

I looked down at my stomach. Flat red splotches had sprung up everywhere.

"Hold on," he said, jumping up. He was moving across the room, opening cabinets and grabbing at stuff. But he'd opened the Pandora's box to my ailment and I was too busy scratching to pay attention to the particulars.

"Hurry up," I called.

Marshall crossed the room with two pink pills and a glass

of water. "Take this," he said. "It's an antihistamine. It'll help the itching."

He didn't need to finish the sentence. As soon as he handed me the pills, I downed them.

"Might make you a tad sleepy," he said, "but that's better than clawin' yourself half to death."

I didn't care. I was in agony. He grabbed my hands, pulled me up, and started back down the hall.

"What you need is to get those clothes off and take a shower. Those chemicals are probably irritating your skin."

He was all business. Not rushing, but not his usual slowed-down self, either. I was up the stairs in no time, headed to the right and into a huge open room anchored by a large antique bed. A family heirloom, I guessed.

"Oh God," I moaned. "I'm going nuts! It's burning!"

"Okay, come on now, calm down." He spoke quietly, all the while leading me forward into a white-tiled bathroom. A claw-footed tub stood against the far wall of the room, surrounded by a white shower curtain. Marshall leaned over, turned on the taps and turned back to me.

"Maggie," he said, "I don't mean a thing by what I'm about to do." And with one fluid movement he leaned toward me, grabbed the bottom of my sweater and pulled it off over my head. He reached for the button on my jeans, popped it efficiently and pushed the wet denim down around my ankles.

He straightened, looked me in the eyes, and reached his hands around behind my back. My bra slid down my arms and onto the floor. My panties followed them, and before I could really put it all together, I was in the shower. Alone.

"Are you all right?" he asked. He was moving around the room and I heard a cabinet door open and close. "I'm getting you something for the itching. Hang on."

The water ran over my skin, quenching some of the fire, but not enough. I moaned and he crossed the room instantly. "Maggie? You all right?"

"No," I said, my voice sinking about as low as my spirits.

"I itch everywhere. I look like Bozo the Clown, and now you've seen me naked and looking like a critter in a freak show." A sob caught in my throat, and my voice trailed off as I indulged in even more self-pity. I would have wallowed in my situation, but the burning seemed suddenly worse and I shrieked.

"Maggie?" his voice was louder, closer to the curtain and filled with concern.

"I'm on fire!" I was losing it. The itching was unbearable. I couldn't stop myself from clawing at my body. "Make it stop!" I yelled. "Help me, Marshall. Do something! Get me something! Oh God, it hurts!"

I could hear him rustle around outside the shower. I heard a clunk as something metallic hit the floor. A few seconds later the curtain opened. Marshall Weathers stepped into the tub behind me, completely naked, holding a box of baking soda in his hand.

"Turn back around and don't move," he whispered. "I'm putting baking soda on you," he said. "Old family remedy." His hands moved softly over my skin, caressing my back, and touching me like a cooling breeze. I sighed as his fingers moved down my arms.

"Feels better right off, doesn't it?" he said, his tone neutral but his voice a thready giveaway. Marshall Weathers wasn't feeling a bit like Harmonica Jack.

He stopped for a second, grabbed the box and poured more baking soda into his hand. When he turned back, he slipped his arms around my waist and began rubbing the powder onto my stomach. The water sluiced down my belly, melting the baking soda into a slippery liquid as his fingers moved across my torso. It was heaven. Wherever his fingers touched, the burning stopped and the pain eased.

I felt him edge closer and closed my eyes. I could see his body, captured in the brief second when he'd opened the curtain. What had looked fine in jeans looked downright magnificent without clothes. I wouldn't look back over my shoulder again. Instead, I stuck my face under the spray and tried to remind myself that this was nakedness for medicinal purposes. I tried to picture Harmonica Jack telling me that "parts were parts," or Marshall saying just a second ago "I don't mean nothing by this." But when he touched me I felt my pulse quicken and my breath catch in my throat. As his hands drifted lightly across my shoulders, I tried to pretend he still wore his clothes, but I was failing miserably. I was itching, but I wasn't brain dead.

"Okay, turn around," he said softly. His hands rested gently on my waist as I turned to face him. The burning fire in my skin was subsiding but another one was just catching, and it was far more dangerous.

He doesn't mean a thing by this, remember. I stood in front of him, completely naked, trying not to let him know how I felt, or what his hands were doing to my self-control.

I couldn't find a safe place to rest my eyes. If I looked at his face, he'd read me, he'd know what I was thinking, and worse, he'd know what I wanted. I looked at his chest, but it was smooth and corded with muscle. Nope, couldn't look there. And when I dropped my eyes, I stopped breathing. Magnificent didn't seem to accurately describe Marshall Weathers.

"Are you all right?" he asked.

"I'm fine," I said, raising my head and looking into his eyes.

He laughed. "Your face is red," he said. "I don't think it's the rash." He reached behind me and pulled a bottle of shampoo out of the metal holder that clung to the showerhead. "Lean back a little," he said, "let's see if we can get some of that goo out of your head."

"I can do it," I said.

Marshall looked at me, his blue eyes darkening. "I know you can," he said, and calmly poured the shampoo into the palm of his hand. "Close your eyes."

I wanted to relax. I wanted to lean into him, but I didn't. His fingers massaged my scalp and I tried once again to convince myself that Marshall Weathers didn't want me. His body wanted me, there was no doubt about that, but the man inside that body didn't want a relationship.

His hands were strong and moved slowly, kneading my

scalp. I must've sighed, because he chuckled. "See, that isn't so bad, is it?"

I moaned softly and felt him shiver.

"You're cold, aren't you?" I whispered. "Here I am, under the water, and you're standing out there."

He was rinsing my hair, the last bit of soap running down the drain in a soapy swirl.

"Come here," I said, and pulled him closer. "Warm up."

That was all it took. It was time for the tables to turn and for me to take charge. The way I figured it, Marshall Weathers was at war with himself, and that was his problem, but there were two people in this shower and one of them was absolutely clear about what she wanted.

I reached for the soap and turned back around to grin at him.

When I touched his chest, his eyes closed. I ran my fingers over his skin, discovering. His hands tightened around the small of my back, pulling me into him. His eyes opened and he stared deep into my eyes.

"Maggie," he said, softly, "I do want you."

He pushed away, pulling himself from my grasp and bringing me up tight against him. His lips found mine, then began moving, behind my ear, down the side of my neck, his tongue exploring and sending a spasm of delight and desire throughout my body.

"Not here," he whispered.

He straightened and looked at me, his blue eyes burning into mine. And then he smiled. He reached behind me, turned off the shower and grabbed two towels from the rack outside. He wrapped one towel around me, using the other one to dry my hair. The burning in my skin was gone, the pink spots fading. But I was only aware of the heat that coursed through my body. I wanted more. I wanted it right then. Why was he torturing me?

He took his time drying himself off, watching me, teasing me as the towel reached all the body parts I wanted to feel against my skin. He was enjoying himself. He stepped out of the tub and turned back.

"Come here."

I stepped to the edge of the tub and he took me in his arms, picking me up as easily as a child and carrying me to his quilt-covered bed. He pulled the towel away, his eyes moving across my body, just looking. Then he came toward me, moving onto the bed and lying on his side next to me. He stretched out his hand and ran his index finger in a line down the center of my body, igniting it with his touch.

He held me deep inside his arms, his lips whispering re-assurances, until he felt me go limp against him and relax. A wave of pleasure and relaxation washed over me and I felt . . . well, I started to feel sleepy. I yawned and he laughed softly.

"I wondered when that medicine was gonna start slowing you down," he murmured. "Relax, honey, it's all right. I'm right here."

He pulled the thick quilt up around us and pulled me up onto his chest. My head rested on his shoulder, listening to the strong beat of his heart. I lay there wrapped in his arms, fighting sleep until at last I had to give in. The last thing I remember was the feel of his lips as he softly kissed my hair, and the scent of him, warm and comforting in the early evening.

Twelve

I woke up to the sound of a dresser drawer sliding out. I opened my eyes, letting them adjust to the darkness. Marshall stood across the room, pulling on a black T-shirt and tucking it into the waistband of black and gray camouflage pants. As I watched, he reached into a drawer, drew out a thick equipment belt and strapped it to his waist. Next he pulled out a piece of black leather, with Velcro straps, attached it to his thigh, then jammed an ugly black gun down into the holster.

"Marshall?"

He turned, surprised by the sound of my voice. "Hey, I was going to let you sleep."

"What are you doing? Why are you dressed like that?" In the darkened room, he seemed menacing and not at all like the man who'd taken me into his bed.

He looked down at his outfit, as if suddenly aware of how he must have appeared to me.

"I've got a call-out," he said. "I have to leave. I thought

you'd probably sleep through it or I would've tried to wake you up."

I sat up in bed, pulling the quilt up over my breasts. "What's a call-out?"

Marshall sat down on the side of the bed next to me and began pulling on heavy black combat boots.

"I'm part of the Special Response Team," he said. "It's a SWAT team. We get called in if there's trouble, the kind of trouble a normal patrol couldn't handle. If I get paged, I have to go."

He stood up, reached under the bed, and pulled out a black duffel bag. He unzipped it, moved some things aside, then pulled out a rifle case and unzipped that. The gun he took from that case was a nasty-looking weapon that he seemed to be examining.

"I don't know when I'll be back," he said. His face was impassive and his tone removed. He zipped the gun back into its case, closed the bag, and stood looking down at me. "I'll call you later."

I'll call you later? That was that? Now that I was awake I wasn't trusted to wait for him in Wanda's sanctuary? Was that how things went with him?

I tossed back my head, sat straight up, and glared at him in the darkness. "That's all right," I said, my tone every bit as cool as his. "I need to get home and see about Sheila anyway."

In the darkened room the clock on his bedside table glowed a red 8:45. Sheila was working at the bagel shop. My whereabouts were probably not too high on her list. She was at the age where she never expected anything to go wrong, and everything to always turn out right.

"Okay," he said, moving away from the bed, "I've gotta go. They're waiting for me. Just close up when you leave, the door'll lock behind you."

Almost as an afterthought, he crossed the room and leaned down to brush my lips lightly. "I'll call you," he said.

Then he was gone, clunking down the steps, walking

through the empty house and out the back door. As I listened I heard the sound of his car starting up, and then the crunch of gravel as he left me. That was that. Almost no sign that we'd shared anything at all.

I pushed the quilt aside, stepped out onto the cold wooden floor, and began looking for my clothes. As I gathered them up, the phone on the bedside table rang. I stopped, staring at it. The tape in his answering machine clicked on, playing his message, then preparing to record. After the beep, a familiar female voice began to speak.

"Marsh," Tracy the door buster said softly, "did you leave yet? I'll try and get you on your cell. I'm just going to meet you over there," she said. "Don't worry about coming to get the van, I've got it."

I could've cried. Marshall Weathers wasn't going to a call-out. He was keeping a date with Tracy. Dressing up like a commando was probably just his way of distracting me, giving me a good excuse for why he had to leave. After all, he couldn't have known his afternoon would turn out like it had.

Now, wait a minute, girl, maybe she's on the team and they're responding together, I thought. But just as quickly, I tossed the idea aside. A green rookie on a SWAT team? I couldn't see it. No, she was meeting him and they were taking her van somewhere. Probably to a drive-in movie, that looked like his speed. Yep, he'd be out on a date with Tracy, the girl voted most unlikely to fall asleep when *he* touched *her*.

"I don't believe this," I muttered to myself. "What is it with me? Do I have a sign over my head that says sucker?" Mama used to talk about women like me, women who attracted all the wrong men. She'd say we had "bad picker" genes. But I'd thought Marshall was different.

I sat back down on the bed and pulled on my still-damp jeans, looking around the empty room. I thought he would be the one, the final one to break through every other bad experience I'd ever had. Instead, I'd overlooked my family and put my heart out on the line with disastrous results. Just like I'd done with Vernell, and Digger Bailey before him.

My sweater was a total loss. Instead I took the white dress shirt he'd worn and left lying on the bathroom floor along with the rest of his clothes. It smelled like him, like leather and his cologne. I had no one to blame but myself. Marshall Weathers was hurt and running like hell. He'd as much as told me so, and I'd ignored it. I'd seen right past the shield, right on down into his heart, and I knew he needed someone like me. Too bad he didn't know that. Too bad he thought he needed a hotcake like Tracy.

"Nothin' for it, girl," I said aloud. "Get on with your life." No sense to throw good love after bad. That's when I remembered Vernell. Here I was moping around and Vernell could be in danger or worse. I shook myself, walked down the steps, out of Marshall's house and across the backyard to my car.

I did turn around once and looked out over his valley. A light twinkled from the window of another farmhouse and I imagined a woman moving around her kitchen, putting the dinner dishes away and preparing for another day with her family. For some reason, that only made the sadness in my heart that much more unbearable.

"Kick it, girl!" I said to myself. "Kick that mood right on out of your heart."

I slid into the car. The seat squished. Cold water seeped through my pants, chilling my legs and reminding me how I'd come to be in this mess in the first place. I cranked the engine, pulled on the headlights, and started off down the drive. I tried to focus on Vernell. By the time I reached Summit Avenue, I'd succeeded, mostly.

I rolled into King's Gas and Go, but it was closed. The office was dark, with only the sparkle of Bess King's trophies to add any luster to the flat windows. There wouldn't be any talking to her tonight. I sighed and drove on home. But as I turned into my back alley and pulled up in the backyard, I could see that things weren't right. Every light in my house was on.

The house was so well lit that I almost missed the two figures sitting on the back steps, but my headlights trapped them for one brief moment before I shut off the car. Tony Carlucci and Sheila were sitting on the back steps, side by side.

I jumped out of the car, crossed the yard, and stood right in front of them, a tiny thrill of fear leaping across my skin as I saw my baby sitting with Carlucci.

"Are you okay, baby?" I asked Sheila, not wanting to alarm her with my concern.

"Totally," she answered, her face unreadable. "But like, what the hell happened to you?"

Carlucci was laughing, a gut laugh that lit up his face and eyes. His eyes roved the length of my body, taking in the wet jeans, the rumpled man's shirt, and my disheveled hair.

"It's a long story, honey. My sunroof broke."

Sheila's eyebrow rose. She looked up at the starlit sky and back down at me. "It didn't rain, Mama. What really happened?"

I sighed and put a hand on my hip. "It really is a long story," I said.

Sheila and Tony looked at each other and smirked. Somehow, the man who had been her mortal enemy this morning was now sharing a joke with my daughter.

"We got time," Tony said.

"Shut up."

"Mama!" Sheila said. "That's not nice."

How had the tables turned? What in the world was going on between these two?

"We were just worried about you, that's all," Sheila said, hurt creeping into her voice.

"All right, all right! If you must know, I took the car through a car wash and the roof got stuck open."

Tony snickered as Sheila's eyes widened. "What did you do?" she asked.

"Well, there wasn't much I could do. So, that's why I look a little worse for the wear."

From inside the house, the phone started ringing. Sheila jumped up like a dog wearing an invisible leash and ran to answer it. *Saved by the bell,* I thought, but not quite. Tony Carlucci sat on the steps grinning.

"Nice save," he said. "Now what really happened?"

I glared at him. "What're you doing at my house talking to my daughter?"

"Somebody had to bring her home from work, especially with her Mama out gallivanting."

I took a step closer. "What?"

Tony leaned back and rested his elbows on the top step. He was enjoying every moment of this.

"Well, she called here looking for a ride home. They let her go early. I figured, since you weren't around, I'd better go get her."

"What were you doing in my house?" I shrieked.

"Waiting," he said calmly.

"It's my house! You can't just waltz inside anytime you want and answer my phone and eat my food. What's with you?"

Tony Carlucci just stared at me, his features darkening momentarily, then returning to their nonchalant mask. Something in that darkness terrified me, a streak of cruelty that might break loose and surface at any second, something perhaps not even within his control.

"I didn't answer your phone," he said. "I listened to your messages." He leaned forward and stared at me, his eyes hooded and dark, the raw anger returning. "I took care of your daughter because if I didn't, somebody else might. When are you going to get it? The other guys looking for Vernell are going to kill him. They're getting desperate now. They don't care how they get to him." He leaned back, his face completely cold and impassive. "They'd cut your daughter's heart out and show it to him, just to get what they want. So yeah, while you were out fooling around with the owner of that oversized shirt, I was watching your back."

"You don't need to watch my back, or Sheila's. I can take care of her. You've got no right to push your way into our lives. This is my home and you don't belong here. The next time I find you within a hundred yards of my property, I'll call the cops."

Tony shook his head like I was a slow learner. "I see how

much the cops have done for you so far. Honey, Greensboro's a small town. Your police haven't seen anything like what's headed your way if Vernell don't turn up."

I didn't know what to say, and fortunately I didn't have to say anything. Sheila walked back out onto the deck, the cordless phone in her hand, a stricken, colorless look replacing the carefree manner of a few moments before.

"Mama," she said, her voice small and childlike. "Somebody wants to kill Daddy."

I reached her as the sobs started, taking her into my arms. "What happened, baby?" I asked. Sheila was shaking.

"Somebody . . . somebody just said if Daddy didn't get the money back, people were gonna keep dying." Sheila pushed away from my shoulder and looked at me. "What did he mean, Mama? What's going on?"

Tony was standing up, his massive frame becoming a shield between us and the outside.

"Maggie, let's go inside. And for heaven's sake, turn off some of those damn lights and pull the curtains."

I didn't see the gun in his hand until we were in the house. He shoved it back into the back of his waistband, keeping it hidden by his black leather jacket. We both moved around the house, turning out some of the lights, pulling curtains and lowering blinds. The trouble with my house is, it's filled with windows—good for sunlight and good for target shooting, if you're the shooter, that is.

Tony led us into the narrow, windowless hallway between the kitchen and the dining room and prepared to hold council. Sheila was still crying, but softer now. She trembled as if she were cold, but I knew she was terrified. I was shaking for the same reason.

"All right," he said. "I'm gonna shoot straight with you, kid. Your dad's in a lot of trouble. Along about the time he disappeared, a lot of money vanished. Unfortunately, the man loaning your dad the cash is dead and your dad's the missing link. So people are looking for your pa, and as you just heard, they're not nice guys." Tony stopped and looked at Sheila, checking to see that she followed what he was saying.

Sheila looked up at him and nodded softly.

"I'm trying like hell to find him before they do," Tony said. "But I can't do that if I have two jobs to worry about."

Sheila looked puzzled. "What two jobs?" she asked.

Tony smiled gently, and for a moment all the menace was lost from his face. "I can't watch after you and find him. I'm going to have to ask you to help me out."

Sheila could only nod.

Tony looked at me. "Is there a safe place where you can go?" he asked.

I thought about Jack's and discarded it instantly. If Marshall Weathers could find me there, so could they. There was only one place for Sheila, back home with her Aunt Darlene and Uncle Earl. No one would find her there, and if they did, they'd sure be sorry. I thought of Earl's shotgun and his passel of guard dogs and smiled.

"Sure," I said, "I've got a place." But I wasn't stupid or foolish enough to tell him about it. Sure, he seemed like he only had our interests at heart, but I'd seen his eyes. And Tony was getting paid by someone to find Vernell. Until I knew more about that, I wouldn't trust Tony Carlucci with any information.

"I'm not going anywhere," Sheila said suddenly. "I'm gonna stay here and look for my dad."

"Sheila, there's nothing you can do. It's too dangerous." I'd figure out what to tell her about why I was coming back later. For now, I only needed to get her away from here.

"Sheila," Tony said, "I need you to help me by staying away." He was looking into her eyes, his hand resting on her shoulder. "If I'm not worried about you, I can work faster to find your dad. Besides," he added, "the quicker I find your dad, the quicker you and I can go back out cruising on my bike."

Sheila smiled.

"What? You took her on your motorcycle?"

Sheila and Carlucci both smiled at me indulgently. "Like, of course, Mama," Sheila said. "How else would I have gotten home? I mean, you did send him to get me, right?"

Behind her Tony smiled and shrugged his shoulders, as if saying "What else could I tell her?"

I sighed. They had me. "Well, that was just this once," I said. "I don't think you'll be riding on that thing anymore."

"Right," Sheila said, like she totally intended to follow my directions.

"Pack," I said. "You'll have to do it without turning on any lights. So do it fast and don't bring the entire universe with you."

"Where are we going?" she asked.

"Sheila, what does it matter? You'll be missing school and on vacation. I'll tell you all about it later."

Tony Carlucci wasn't fooled. He waited until she stalked off to her room before he started up again.

"You're staying there with her," he said.

"No I'm not." I tried to brush past him, but he grabbed my shoulders and spun me around, forcing me back against the wall.

"Let go of me," I said.

"Not until you listen," he said, his voice barely audible above the sound of Sheila's CD player. "You are worthless in this situation. This is what I do for a living. I find people. Just stay out of everybody's hair and let me do my job."

His fingers bit into my flesh, and when I glared back at him I was frightened by the intensity of the anger I saw there.

"All right, fine," I said. Let him think whatever he wanted. I just wanted to get away from him. Anybody can charm a schoolgirl, I thought, but it takes more than a cheap smile to put one over on Maggie Reid. I was coming back to town just as soon as I dropped Sheila off with her Aunt Darlene and Uncle Earl.

Carlucci could look for people all day long, but he didn't know Vernell like I did. I'd see the signs or read the clues far better than he or Weathers could do, and I cared far more about my ex-husband than outsiders ever could. I was coming back, all right, and Carlucci could just deal with it. That is, if he saw me before I saw him.

Thirteen

Sheila made the trip to Danville a living hell. She didn't want to ride in my car. She didn't want to leave without her CD player. She didn't think the towels I piled on the seats would keep her designer jeans dry. She complained about the smell, the drive, not having a cell phone like all her friends had, and not even owning a pager.

"Mama," she said, "if only I had a phone or a pager, then Daddy could've called me and told me where he was going."

So that was what was at the bottom of all this. "If onlys" were attacking Sheila. If only she'd been available; if only she'd stayed closer to home; if only she'd been the perfect child, her daddy wouldn't have left. I shook my head. I'd seen this same behavior when Vernell had left us for Jolene, the lovely Dish Girl.

"Baby," I said, reaching over to turn down the screaming radio, "if your daddy could've called you, he would've. If he's in trouble it's on account of not seeing what was coming, being blindsided." I patted her knee. "Sweetie, Daddy's a survivor. He'll be all right."

"Mama, my psychology teacher says what you're doing is called denial."

"And what your psychology teacher knows about the real world could be . . ." I bit my tongue. This would get us nowhere.

Sheila humphed and looked away. I tried again. "Baby, I know you're worried sick about him, but he'll turn up."

Sheila whipped back around. "Yeah," she said, "but will he be dead or alive?"

I was saved from answering her by our arrival at Darlene's trailer. We turned off the two-lane into a narrow dirt drive that was rutted with potholes. Darlene's husband, Earl, says he doesn't level it out more often on account of how it keeps trespassers away. What Earl isn't taking into account is the way it tears up a welcome visitor's car and shortens the life of Earl's own vehicles.

We bounced down the little lane, huge trees on either side reaching down with heavy limbs to almost touch the roof of my car. Sheila was gripping the door handle with feverish intensity and moaning about the water that ran from side to side on the floorboards. I was just trying to keep the car headed in the general direction of the bright yellow light that shone down on Darlene's doublewide.

By the time we stopped, Earl's vicious-looking yard dogs had run around to snarl at the intruders and Earl was standing on the back stoop with his shotgun in hand and Darlene right behind him.

"Mama," Sheila said, "you can't really be thinking we're going to stay here."

"Who's 'we,' kemosabe?" I said, under my breath.

When she recognized the car, Darlene whacked Earl's arm. "Fool, I told you that was them!"

Earl, a tall skinny man in a white undershirt and blue jeans, slowly lowered the gun and started to grin. He was a right handsome, dark-haired man, who'd been totally devoted to Darlene since high school, when he was a football player and she was a tiny cheerleader.

"I know it's them," he said. "But I didn't know until she

drove up. According to her, we can't be too cautious."

Darlene stepped out from behind the shelter of Earl. "Baby!" she cried, running down the steps for Sheila.

Sheila dwarfed Darlene by a good six inches. Darlene could be five foot two on a good day, and couldn't weigh more than ninety pounds. She's two years older than me, two sizes smaller than me, and still looks like a freshman cheerleader. When we were born, I got the voice, but she got all the coordination.

Earl had passed us, walking over to my car to pull out Sheila's suitcase and CD player.

"What choo do?" he grunted, "bring all of Greensboro up with you? Thought Sheila was the only one staying?"

"What?" Sheila's voice squeaked out into the darkness. She broke away from Darlene, walked over to the trunk and looked inside.

"Mama, where's your stuff?"

I ran my hand through my hair and prepared for the holy war. "I'm not staying, baby."

"Mama!" Sheila's tone said it all, and Earl and Darlene missed none of it.

"Sheila," Earl said, "come on out to the barn with me. I gotta show you someone."

Sheila didn't want to go—that much was obvious in the way her shoulders stiffened and the slow way she turned to face him. But I did not raise a disrespectful daughter. She followed him slowly, looking back over her shoulder at me, her expression saying that she wasn't through with the discussion.

"Hell," Darlene said, as she watched. "If I were you, I'd hop in that little bug and haul on outta here before that young'un gets back. Jeez," she sighed, "where'd our little Sheila go, and who's this creature?"

"Teenagers," I said. "That's what it is, a social disease. I reckon she'll be a complete and total idiot for another couple of years and then she'll return back to normal, if there ever was a normal."

Darlene watched Sheila's retreating back. "Well," she

said, turning back to me, "it ain't gonna matter much in another minute. You just wait. Here, listen."

We stood in the darkened yard, listening as the barn door swung open and Earl fumbled around for the light. There was total silence and then: "Oh Uncle Earl!" This was then followed by: "Really? He's mine?"

"Darlene," I said, turning back to her, "you didn't. You know that young'un can't keep track of a dog!"

Darlene stuck her hands on her hips and gave me one of her looks. "Well, maybe you'd better think about something. If that young'un's keeping up with a puppy, and tending to its every need, she might be less tempted to produce a litter of her own just yet." The rest of her sentence hung between us, unspoken . . . "like you did." Maybe it's just my sensitivity, because Darlene's never said one disapproving word to me, but still I thought it. Vernell and I were so young when we had Sheila.

"Hey," Darlene said, "why aren't you staying?"

I shrugged my shoulders. "All right, I'll give it a shot, but I truly don't expect you to get this because I don't fully understand it myself." Darlene and I walked up the steps to her trailer. She waited until we were inside, sitting at stools pulled up to the breakfast bar, before she urged me to go on.

"You know Vernell about as well as I do," I said. "He's lying pond scum on a good day and an alcoholic on a bad one. But all of his sorry little life, I've been looking for the good in that man. And you know it's there." Darlene nodded, but she didn't seem as convinced as I was.

"He loves me and Sheila. I don't doubt that. But something inside that man won't let him be the husband and father he wants to be. Now, he's a right good daddy."

Darlene interrupted. "Yeah, if you don't count him running off and leaving you and Sheila for a bimbo, he's a peach of a father."

She kind of had me there. "But he supports her. He took her in when I was having trouble with her. He loves her, Darlene, even you know that."

Darlene shrugged her shoulders in a grudging admission.

"And when Jolene ran off, hell, even before that, when his brother, Jimmy, died, who'd he come to first? Me."

Darlene raised up and glared at me. "You're not thinking of taking him back, are you?"

I smiled. "Darlene, pity is one thing, foolishness is another. I care for him. Somehow I see him as, well, like a kid that can't grow up. And he's Sheila's daddy. I've gotta help him whenever I can."

Darlene was still frowning. "I saw an *Oprah* show on that," she said. "What you got is a bad case of codependency."

"Well, what else I've got is a bad case of that man ran off with all the money in his business accounts and payroll's due and I'm half-owner and I can't cover it!"

"That," Darlene pronounced with satisfaction, "is a reason I can get behind."

"Just hang on to Sheila," I said. "She's right shook up about this, but of course it comes out as obnoxious behavior."

Darlene laughed. "She won't be obnoxious with me. I'm gonna put her to work. She'll be mucking out stalls and training that puppy. When she's done with that I'm gonna make her come teach the little ones with me down at the dance studio."

"So you figure she'll be too tired to be obnoxious? I wouldn't bet on it."

Darlene laughed. "Quit worrying!" Then she looked serious for a moment. "You are going to have protection, right? You're not just going to go bumbling around without someone or something to deal with trouble, are you?"

"Sure," I lied. "I'm covered over in protection. I've got a private eye and a police detective to watch out for me. I'm just going to lay low and help them out with information when I can."

Darlene didn't look like she believed me. When I walked down to the barn to kiss Sheila good-bye, she didn't believe me either.

"I know whose shirt that is," she said.

What could I say? I hadn't had time to change. I'd been in a hurry and hadn't given it a thought. So I went right on with my farewell instructions as if she hadn't said a word.

"And I'll run by the school and get your work, so don't worry about it." As if Sheila would give it a second thought.

"Mama," Sheila said, "if you're finally dating that detective, you don't have to hide it from me. After all," she said, tossing her long red hair back, "we are women. We can share these things. My psychology teacher says it is the hallmark of a self-actualized relationship."

I couldn't hold my tongue any longer. "And your grandma used to say that even a blind hog finds an acorn now and again. It just don't make him brilliant."

I hugged her neck and turned to go.

"Mama," she said, "don't let anything happen to you. Tell him I said to take care of you."

"He will, baby," I said, and turned away. I didn't want her to see my face. I didn't want her to know that I wasn't sure Marshall Weathers would look out for anything other than his own tough hide.

Fourteen

Greensboro was sleeping peacefully when I arrived back in town. I drove up Friendly Avenue, pacing myself to ride right through a string of green lights, winding around and turning onto Mendenhall, then slipping down the alley to my bungalow. There was no way I could stay there, but I needed enough clothes to last through the next few days. I could've kicked myself for not packing when I'd had the opportunity, but I'd been in too much of a hurry to get Sheila out of town and myself away from Carlucci.

I found myself flashing to the image of Carlucci, standing in my doorway, gun in hand, ready to take on the unseen threat to Vernell's family. I thought of the way he'd handled Sheila, easing her out of town, making her part of the solution, not another teenaged problem. And then I thought of him in a completely different manner. He was strong and attractive in a very different way from Marshall. Tony was there, in your face and ready. Marshall was more cautious, more reserved. I shook myself.

"Stop it," I whispered. "This ain't no time for thinking

about men." After all, it was better to be called foolish than to be called unprepared. I had to be ready. By the time I reached my street, I was all business.

The lights were all out, and there was no sign of Tony Carlucci. "Probably found a hole to crawl into somewhere," I muttered. But to be on the safe side, I parked at the far end of the alley and crept back. I walked around the back of the house, peering in the windows before I remembered we'd closed all the curtains and shades. There was nothing for it but to go inside.

I slipped the key into the back door lock, turned it, and entered into my bedroom, pausing for a moment as the light from the alleyway shone in across my bed. Nothing. No Carlucci. I breathed a sigh of relief, closed the door, and crossed the room headed for the tiny blinking red light of the answering machine. "The key is not to turn on any lights," I whispered.

I hit the play button and settled in to listen to the messages. There were at least four hang-ups, followed by Terrance Griswald, the manager at the Mobile Home Kingdom.

"Hey, Ms. Reid, listen, this here's Terry. Some of the guys are getting a little restless about their paychecks. I done like you said and had Becca make checks out for the ones that needed 'em, but the others are mouthin' off about it now." *Great,* I thought, *what else?* "Maybe you could get the bank to swing us a loan or something. Hey, the owner of VanScoy's Mobile Homes, Archer VanScoy, called again, too. Says Vernell was talking to him about selling, so now he wants to talk to you on account of he wants to buy us out. Is that true? Give me a call." The line went dead and I waited for the next message.

"Ms. Reid," a tired, female voice said, "it's Bess King. You're right, we gotta talk. The, um, funeral's tomorrow at eleven. The Holy Vine United Methodist Church, out on High Point Road. The family's gonna gather after that at my place. I'll just try to find a time. I don't know how, with everyone up under me, but we've got to talk." She hung up then and I sat on the edge of the bed, listening.

Three more hang-ups and then a hushed voice began to speak.

"Baby, izzat you? Come on now, honey, pick up. Maggie, pick up the damn phone, it's almost midnight. I know you're there!"

Vernell Spivey, alive and knee-walking drunk from the sounds of it. I looked at the red numbers on the digital clock. He'd called less than two hours ago.

"Oh hell, honey," he said, "I'm in deep dirt now. Maggie, come on, baby, talk to me." There was silence and then a loud clatter as Vernell tried to put the receiver back on the stand. In the background I could hear the whine of country music but nothing else. Where the hell was he?

"There are no more messages," my machine said.

"Figures," I said back.

I stood up and made my way over to the walk-in closet that stood in the tiny space between my bedroom and the kitchen. I stepped inside, pulled the door shut after me, and reached for the light switch.

"This is stupid. Vernell Spivey, you three-legged dog, why are you such a total idiot? After all this time, here I am, still at the mercy of your stupidity. I thought I'd come further, but a woman forced to pack up her belongings in the dead of night, with the closet door shut, can't have come too far."

I pulled a black sequined shirt off its hanger and stuffed it in a brown paper sack. The trouble with my closet was it took the spillover from all the junk that didn't fit in the kitchen. So there were shopping bags and cookie cutters jammed in next to cowgirl boots and fancy belts.

I grabbed a black broomstick skirt, and was just fingering a belt with a huge silver buckle when the lights went out.

"Carlucci," I yelled, "that's enough!"

I whipped around. The huge shape filled the doorway. I stepped right up to him and shoved as hard as I could, and that's when I realized it wasn't Carlucci. The man shoved me hard against the back wall of the closet, up against the shoe rack, then stepped up to me, grabbing my shoulders and slamming me into the wall again.

I screamed and tried to kick, but I couldn't get enough leverage to push off and lash out. His breath smelled of garlic and stale alcohol.

"Shut up," he said, his voice cold and even. In the dark I heard a tiny click, and then felt the needle-sharp point of a knife touch my neck.

"Where is he?" the voice asked. He had me pinned with one beefy arm, his hand pressed to my chest, the fingers curving in a claw at my neck. The knifepoint jabbed a little harder, and I knew he'd cut me.

"I don't know!"

He wasn't satisfied. The knife moved a little down my neck, biting into my skin, scratching a thin line as it cut.

"Then I guess I'll have to leave him a message," he said. "This'll hurt you a lot more than it'll hurt me." He laughed softly.

His fingers curled around the neck of my shirt, ripping the buttons as he tore it open. My hand tightened around the big belt buckle in my hand, and I brought it up, smashing it into his face with every ounce of strength I could find. He howled, pulled back briefly, and I tried to duck under him. He grabbed for me, then seemed to fall backward.

"Get off her!"

My attacker, surprised from behind, turned away from me, lunging out of the closet, his attention turned toward the new arrival.

"He's got a knife," I screamed.

"Get out of the way, Maggie!" Carlucci's voice thundered through the darkness. My attacker roared and jumped forward. All I could see was a tangled blur of black forms, wrestling. Then there was the sharp retort of a gun, echoing in the tiny space, muffled somewhat by the body in front of it.

There was complete silence. When the lights came on in the kitchen, Tony Carlucci stood over the still form of a man I'd never seen before. Tall, thickset, and balding, with short black hair, and a gunshot wound that was quickly turning his chest red and his face a pasty gray color.

"Call nine-one-one," Tony said, his voice dull and removed.

Within five minutes my house was a sea of black uniforms and guns, all standing over the body of one very dead man. Tony still leaned against the wall of the kitchen, but his gun was in a clean, plastic evidence bag.

In the minutes between my call to the police and their arrival, after we knew for sure that Tony had killed my attacker, he'd only said one thing to me:

"See what happens when you think you know better than everybody else?"

I wanted to think he meant the words for the intruder, but he didn't. I was wrong. I should've stayed away.

Marshall Weathers arrived about thirty minutes into the process. He stepped across the threshold of the back door, his eyes searching for me, then turning to the scene. He moved across the room, nodding to the other officers, listening to the squawk of the walkie-talkie he held close to his ear. He'd changed from camouflage to jeans, his shield clipped to his waistband, along with his gun.

"Are you all right?" he asked. There was no hint of how he felt about me in those words, and at that point, I really wasn't looking for one. His hand reached out, involuntarily, to touch the thin line of blood that ran along my neck. "He do that?" he asked, his jaw muscle twitching.

"Yes."

"Okay." He turned away, studied Carlucci for a moment, and then looked back at me. "I'm gonna have to catch this call, it's mine and it'll take half the night doing the paperwork. Where are you staying?" It was obvious to both of us that I wouldn't be staying at my place.

"I guess with Jack." The jaw muscle twitched again, but I didn't hear him offer to take me back to the sanctuary of the Blessed Saint Wanda. I was out of options, and Jack was the only person I could think to turn to.

"All right, I'll get up with you in the morning then." He looked at the officer in charge. "We have your preliminary statement. I'll probably have a few questions."

Carlucci watched us now, his face still a neutral mask of resignation and indifference. As if he felt Carlucci, Weathers turned and walked toward him, his hand extended.

"Detective Weathers," he said. "Let's go on downtown and sort this out."

Carlucci pushed off the wall and stood looking at Weathers, his legs slightly apart, like a boxer, on his toes, waiting for a thrown punch. He was a good three or four inches taller than Marshall, and probably outweighed him by fifty pounds, but Marshall was all coiled strength and readiness. Neither man looked away. Carlucci's eyes were hooded, black pools that studied Weathers as if he were considering the invitation.

"All right," he said, finally, "let's get this over with."

He turned and walked toward the back door, with Marshall following him. Both men left without turning around, leaving me in a kitchen filled with the coppery scent of death.

Fifteen

They buried Nosmo King in a mausoleum. To Mama's way of thinking, that was all wrong. The way we were raised up, you couldn't get to heaven if you didn't go six feet under ground first. "Ashes to ashes, dust to dust," Mama said. "That don't mean sticking a body in a closet, like you're coming right back. It just ain't right. Dead," she said, "is dead, and let no man put that asunder by filing a body away in a drawer."

I stood on the edge of the crowd that had gathered and watched the entire proceeding before following the mile-long train of vehicles back to Nosmo King's farm out in Brown Summit.

Mama would've disapproved of the farm, too. It was a rich man's attempt to appear earnest, and Mama didn't like the foolishness of false pride. Nosmo King had crammed a riding ring, a huge barn, and an obviously manmade pond onto five acres of white-fenced property on the edge of a subdivision. His gleaming-new, green John Deere tractor sat parked beside the riding ring. Probably didn't even have gas in the tank.

Cadillacs, Mercedes, and an assortment of other vehicles lined the drive up to the house. Up where I came from, if it'd been a true farmer's funeral, you would've at least seen an old tractor or two, and it would've been pickup trucks lining that driveway, not leather-cushioned luxury cars.

I pulled the bug in behind a BMW and started making my way up the smooth, black asphalt driveway. That's when I began to hear the music. The closer I came to the house, the clearer it was. Fiddle, banjo, guitar, and mandolin. The musician in me started picking out notes, looking for the tune. They were playing Fisher's "Hornpipe," not at all the somber "Crossing Over Jordan" you might've expected. In fact, any music at all was pushing the borders of respectability.

Nosmo's brick two-story colonial had a black wreath on the door, along with an arrow that pointed toward the barn. Up ahead of me, ladies carried covered dishes, and a few of the men toted instrument cases. If I hadn't known this was a funeral reception, I would've figured it for a party.

By the time I reached the barn, I'd given up all pretense of appearing to be a mourner. The place was packed. People were everywhere, and not a sad face among them. I walked inside and looked around. Nosmo King's barn had never known a horse, or hay, or any farm equipment. Nosmo King's barn was an entertainment haven. Gleaming wood floor, wet bar along one side, kitchen along the other. Rows of tables set out here and there, and a sound system that made the Golden Stallion Country and Western Palace seem antiquated and small.

Bess King sat at a round table, surrounded by people who seemed to be expressing condolences. She looked wan and tired. I couldn't see any way to get to talk to her about Vernell, at least not now. I turned away from her and started toward the huge buffet table of food. When in doubt, I find it useful to eat. A person standing around with a plate of food looks harmless and approachable. I figured with a full plate,

I could sit down at a table and observe without difficulty. No polite person questions someone when they're chewing. And what better than the homemade brownies I saw in the middle of the table?

Nosmo King's family had put on one hell of a spread. Mama still wouldn't have given it her stamp of approval, though—too many happy faces, and music. At a true southern funeral gathering there would've been just as many people and just as much food, but the voices would be hushed and respectful. If we laughed, it was because of a funny story told about the deceased, not because we were really having a good time. But all around me, people were laughing, and worst of all, they were drinking.

I stood there with my plate, watching, half looking for a place to sit and half amazed that there was a keg of beer sitting right out at a funeral luncheon. I looked over at Bess and saw that her mother had joined her. The two of them seemed to be the only ones in the room not enjoying the party.

"Makes you wonder, don't it?" a soft voice whispered.

I turned. Behind me stood Vernell Spivey, dressed in a cheap gray suit and sporting an even cheaper gray beard and hairpiece.

"Vernell!" I was so relieved to see him that I almost overlooked the getup and forgot the reason for his disappearance.

"Hush!" he commanded. He looked furtively from side to side. "Step over here."

He walked quickly to a deserted spot along the wall, in the shadow of all the activity, and turned his back on the crowd of partyers.

"Vernell, where the hell have you been?" I reached out and touched him, as if maybe he were an apparition.

He took a swig of beer from his cup and squared his shoulders. "Well, if you were thinking I run off and left you hanging, you're wrong. I'm gonna handle this, it's just that—"

"Vernell, put that beer down and talk straight! Do you know how much trouble you're in?"

He stood like a lanky scarecrow in front of me, and he did what he always does when he's dead wrong, he hung his head and looked sheepish. He was a little boy in a bad Abe Lincoln costume. He made it awfully hard to ride herd on him when he seemed so vulnerable.

"Aw now, Maggie," he said, "it ain't as bad as all that."

I hardened my heart, looked right past him, back out at the crowd and over to the big barn door. "Isn't it?" I said. "Then tell me this: If I was to tell you that Detective Marshall Weathers of the Greensboro Police Department had just stepped through that door over yonder, would you stick around to talk to him?"

Vernell's thin, pressed rat face drained of all color and his eyes widened. "You're kidding me, right?"

I looked back at Marshall, standing like a Texas Ranger, dressed in his charcoal-gray suit, and shook my head.

"Nope, I don't kid, Vernell. And as soon as his eyes adjust to the light in here, he's gonna be on you like a fat man at a pig pickin'."

"Catch you later," Vernell said, and started walking toward a side door.

"Vernell," I said, "you wait one minute! We've gotta talk! You've got some explaining to do!"

Vernell looked back at me for one brief second, shoving his beer into my empty hand. "I'll find your car, and I'll wait for you there. Now, go get rid of him!"

Vernell was as scared as I've ever seen him, and for a man who spent most of his teenaged years tangling with the law, I was impressed. But then, Vernell knew Marshall Weathers, and he'd seen what he was capable of doing when he put his mind to it. We'd both seen that, and Vernell was divorced on account of it.

I gripped my plate in one hand and Vernell's beer in the other. The best thing I could do was find a spot at an empty table and try to blend in before Marshall saw me standing in the shadows looking guilty.

He was looking in Bess's direction when I sat down at the closest table. I didn't give so much as a second thought to my new tablemates, only noticing that they were two women about my age. I kept my head down and started in on the food.

My companions didn't seem to care that I'd joined them; in fact, they seemed oblivious. It didn't take long to follow that piece of information up with another one. The women across from me were knee-walking, about to be bowl-hugging drunk, and one was crying.

"I tole you thish was a bad idea," one girl said.

"I know, I know," the crier said, "but I just wanted to be near his spirit."

I looked up then. The crier was a large, dark-haired girl, her hair permed into long kinky curls that fell halfway down her back in a frizzy halo. She could've been anywhere between twenty-two and thirty, wearing fifty pounds of mascara that ran as she cried, leaving fat black trails down her cheeks.

Her companion was a frosted blonde, with the same frizzy hairstyle and thick pancake makeup that couldn't hide an accumulation of bad acne scars.

I put my head back down and concentrated on my plate. This was gonna be good.

"Oh, Nosmo," the black-haired girl said, the words coming out in a long moan of anguish.

"Shush up!" her friend said. "People will know."

"Who cares now? He's dead," she wailed, "and it's all her fault! She killed him! He would've left, he told me so, but she killed him!"

Her voice rose and her friend, drunk as she was, smelled trouble. "Shut up! We'll take care of this, but not now!"

There was a brief pause and I figured they'd noticed me and were nudging each other. Still I didn't move or look up.

"Will you look at that guy," the blonde said softly.

"What guy?"

I knew what guy. There was only one guy in the room that deserved that tone, in my opinion.

"Oh my God, he's gorgeous!"

"And he's coming right over here! Wipe your face!"

There was a mad scramble as the girls fumbled for lip-
stick and I tried to sink lower into my chair. I turned my
head to the side and stared at the door that Vernell had gone
through, wishing I could be anywhere else. Still, when he
put his hand on my shoulder, a thrill went coursing through
my stomach, and I couldn't quite work up the cold indifference I'd sworn to show him.

"Well," he said, "fancy this."

I looked up and tried to smile. He stared down at me, his
eyes like lie detectors, looking right through me.

"This is right interesting," he said, pulling out a chair and
sitting next to me. He looked across the table, saw the two
women watching us, and smiled. "Ladies," he said.

They each raised a hand, wiggling their fingers and gig-
gling. Weathers gave them the 200-watt treatment and
turned back to me.

"This ain't like you, Maggie," he said, picking up Vernell's cup and staring into it.

"What? Drinking beer? I do it all the time."

Weathers smiled. "No you don't. And what are you doing
here? I thought you didn't know Nosmo King?"

He spoke softly, so his words didn't carry across the table
to his two admirers. I'm sure to them we seemed to be having an extremely intimate conversation.

I grabbed the half-full cup of beer, stared down into it.
"Well, shucks," I said, "this beer's about gone. How's about
filling it up when you get your plate?"

Weathers cocked an eyebrow. "Finish it," he said, "and
I'll run right up there."

But he knew me. He knew I didn't drink beer. I hated it.
In fact, I don't recall that Marshall Weathers had ever known
me to drink anything. And other than a frozen strawberry
margarita once or twice a year, I guess I didn't really drink.
But this was a showdown. This was to protect Vernell's un-
worthy hide. So I picked up the cup, held my breath, and
drank it down as quickly as I could.

"Go girl!" the drunken blonde said.

"Well," Marshall said, the smirk firmly in place. "Looks

like you need another." And with that he got up and crossed the room to the keg.

In the minute he was gone, I tried to leave. But there's something about alcohol on an empty stomach that makes thinking and acting difficult to do at the same time. So, instead I wolfed down my brownie and wished I was walking out the back door.

"Here you go," he said, plopping the full cup down in front of me. "Enjoy!"

"Well, I just will," I said. "I love beer. Don't know why I never told you that before." I took a huge swallow and looked up at him. "What're you doing here?"

He looked right back at me. "I got business here. Question really is, what're you doing here? You don't know Nosmo King." He pushed the beer a little closer to my hand, daring me, and I wasted seconds taking a huge swig.

"My that is good," I said. "Nothing like a fresh keg." Across the table, my drinking buddies giggled.

"I'd need a drink too, if he was gonna look at me˙like that!" the blonde said.

Marshall Weathers put his hand down on the table, right next to mine. He leaned in closer, his eyes never leaving my face.

"I've been thinking about you," he whispered.

My entire body started to respond. My heart started racing, my stomach did a little flip, and every place he'd touched the day before remembered the feel of his fingers. But my brain was on override. I tried to picture him with Tracy the cadet, but when he was staring like that, all I could think of was him.

"I've been thinking about you too," I said, but it came out kind of squeaky and high-pitched.

Marshall leaned back a little and stared at me. "You're up to something, Maggie Reid."

"No, I'm not. I'm just, um, glad to see you, surprised, that's all."

"Drink a little more of that beer, Maggie. You don't want it to go flat on you."

I picked up the cup, never broke eye contact, and drained it dry. It was all I could do not to spit it out. That's when I remembered Tracy.

"Don't you have a job to do?" I straightened up in my chair and frowned at him. Truth of the matter was, if he stuck around much longer, I was going to melt into a little puddle of desire, right at his feet.

"Yeah, way I see it, you're part of my job. You wouldn't be here if you didn't have something up your sleeve. After last night, I'd think you'd get a clue that this is dangerous business, but no, here you are in the thick of it. A good detective oughta be asking himself why."

"Way I see it," I said, "is I've gotta go." I started to get up, but he grabbed my arm and pulled me back down into my seat.

"I'd have to arrest you if you did that," he murmured.

"Arrest me! Why?"

My drinking buddies giggled.

"On account of drinking and driving being against the law and dangerous." He smiled, but it was a dangerous smile. He was licking his lips, enjoying the bind he now had me in, knowing he owned this particular situation.

"Way I see it, I'm gonna have to take you home." One of the girls sighed and he smiled over at her, then looked back at me. "You stay right here. I've gotta talk to a couple of people, then I'll be back and we can go."

While he spoke, the beer snuck up and whopped me between the eyes. I'd only had two, but they were king-sized cups, and on an empty stomach at that.

"All right," I said, "I'll wait. But if you take too long, and I sober up, I'm out of here." Then the beer took over and did the talking for me. "You know," I said, "I don't need you. And I don't even drive a van, so if you're looking for some backseat boogie queen, well, buddy, you'd better roll on."

Weathers raised his eyebrow, frowned for a second, and then laughed out loud.

"Backseat boogie queen?" he said. "That's good. No, honey, you're not the backseat boogie queen type."

I watched him turn around and walk away, still formulating my comeback. What did he mean I wasn't the backseat boogie queen type? I was just as wild as stupid Tracy. I had half a nerve to show him just how wild I was. Stupid men.

My drinking buddies were watching Weathers walk away, moon-eyed. The blonde took another swallow of beer, wiped her mouth with the back of her hand, and belched softly.

"You just don't see an ass like that every day."

"You got that right," I said. "Asses like that only come along once in a blue moon." Idiot.

The three of us watched him walk away, straight over to Bess King's table. I waited until he was deep in conversation and then reached for my little beaded purse. I pushed my chair back and got to my feet carefully. The beer buzz hummed around my head and left me feeling a little woozy.

"You're not leaving?" Nosmo's girlfriend asked.

I looked at my drinking buddies and smiled. "Like a silver bullet."

"But he told you to stay right there!" the blonde exclaimed.

"He can tell me all he likes, but I've got a mind of my own. I'm not sitting around waiting on some man to finish his business and come after me."

The dark-haired girl sighed. "I waited on Nosmo, and where did it get me?" The water faucet started up, and it was crying time again.

The blonde looked at me and rolled her eyes.

I couldn't help it. I truly was on my way out the door, but opportunity is not a lengthy visitor. I pulled a tissue from my purse, handed it to the dark-haired girl, and sank back down in my chair.

"You must've been very close to Nosmo," I said. And that was all it took.

"He loved me," the dark-haired girl said, sobbing. "She wouldn't let him go!"

The blonde's head dropped down into her hands.

"Yeah," I prompted. "She looks like the type to hang on, just like a rat terrier."

The dark-haired girl favored Bess with a malicious glare.

"Nosmo said she'd ruin him, take half of everything they owned! She's a money-hungry, greedy bitch, and there's not a person in town would disagree with that."

"Surely you don't think she really killed him, do you?"

"Aw, Pauline, let it go, honey," the blonde said.

Pauline drew herself up in her chair and stared at me, her eyes wide and raccoon-ringed with mascara.

"She did. I know she did. I don't know how she got away with it, but she killed him all right, even if she had to hire it out!"

"Pauline," the blonde sighed. "Look at her, she don't look like a killer. More'n likely, it was business."

Pauline grabbed her beer cup, knocked it over, and went for her friend's cup.

"All right then, Christine, then you tell me this. Why'd she have him followed? And when we got caught, why didn't she do anything about it? Huh? Answer me that! And a week later, he's dead." Her voice broke off in a hiccuping sob. "Oh, Nosmo!"

Christine rolled her eyes again. "It's always like this," she said. "When somebody dies young, everybody thinks it's a conspiracy. Well, this time it's just a plain old killin'. Nosmo had a lot of enemies, Pauline. You can't work for . . ." She broke off then and looked over at me.

I cut my head from side to side, then looked back at Christine. "It's okay," I said, "I know who he worked for."

"Well then," Christine said, "you understand. It was business."

I looked at Christine, checking out her tight black satin dress with the little rhinestones that ran around the low-cut neckline. She looked like the type to know. She looked like a gangster's girlfriend. Maybe she'd heard enough to know. Whatever she knew, she certainly wasn't going to tell me. She hadn't even told Pauline.

I pushed my chair back again and stood up. Weathers was still talking to Bess and her mother. Her mother was frowning and sitting up ramrod-straight, as if she didn't like what Marshall was saying.

I took one last look at the back of his head, allowed myself one last little thought about the way it felt to run my fingers through that hair, and then turned away. I smiled at my companions, winked, and walked right out the side door into the midafternoon air.

Sixteen

It was closing in on three o'clock in the afternoon. The sun had warmed the autumn air to a right tolerable temperature, and everywhere I looked brightly colored leaves were falling, swirling down around my feet as I walked slowly down Nosmo King's driveway.

All in all, it might've been a lovely afternoon, had I not had Vernell Spivey to deal with and Marshall Weathers on my tail. My feet wouldn't quite land where I aimed them, and it was taking a lot of my concentration to walk in a straight line toward my car. It's not as if I were drunk exactly, just a tad wobbly. My head was as clear as could be, my feet were my only problem, or so I thought.

I got right up to the car and saw no sign of Vernell.

"Vernell Spivey, if you've run off like the low-crawlin' snake that you are, I'll have your hide before sunset!"

The bushes off to the side of the driveway rustled, and out stepped my ex-husband, a red and gold leaf clinging to his phony gray beard. His wig was askew and his clothes were rumpled. It didn't take long to realize that while I'd been sweating it out with Weathers, Vernell Spivey had been peacefully napping, as if he didn't have a problem in the world.

Vernell let out a long, slow whistle. "Maggie, you're a picture. Why, just look at you. With that emerald dress and them green eyes, baby, I don't know why I . . ."

"Vernell, shut up. Sweet talkin' don't work on me. Now tell me what's going on and be quick about it. It's only a matter of time before that detective comes hunting me up, and I'd like to know the truth before I have to face him down again."

"You know," Vernell said, "you are just like your mama made over. I swear, honey."

"Vernell. The truth."

Vernell sighed and fumbled in his pocket for a cigarette, found none, and frowned. "Come on back here, then," he said. He took two steps toward me, grabbed my hand, and pulled me into the bushes.

"Vernell!" This was vintage Vernell behavior.

"Maggie, it ain't what you're thinking. I just don't want that po-lice of yours to come waltzing down the lane and come up on me. We're just gonna sit on the other side of this bush and have us a heart to heart."

Vernell broke through the thick branches, pulling me with him, until we'd crossed through them. We came out in front of the bass pond.

"Now, see here, isn't this better?"

I took a look around and had to admit Vernell had found a tiny piece of heaven. The pond was still, autumn leaves from the hickories and maples that surrounded it were floating like tiny boats across the water. The ground was a thick cushion of reds and golds and the sun streamed through the break in the trees like waterfalls of bright light.

Vernell sat down and patted a spot right next to him. "Come here, Maggie. I'll tell you everything."

I sat down beside him. That was the trouble with Vernell. He was always going to tell me everything, but weeding out the truth from the way Vernell wished things to be took time and skill and years of living with a man who just wouldn't grow up.

"You 'member that time me and you went down to Lake Burton in Georgia?" he asked softly. I nodded and said nothing. It had been our honeymoon and I was three months along with Sheila.

"That sure was a good time, wasn't it?" I nodded again. It was back in the olden days, back when Vernell had stopped drinking for a time, and was taking his responsibilities as a future father seriously.

"I recollect sitting on the end of that dock by the boathouse," he murmured, "just a-swinging our feet, dippin' 'em in the water on account of it was still so warm from the summer, and jest a-holdin' your hand, all afternoon."

I remembered. I remembered so well it began to hurt, grabbing at my heart and squeezing it tight.

"Maggie," he said, his tone taking on a serious quality, "I'm sorry."

I looked up at him and sighed. "Sorry for what, Vernell?"

Vernell met my gaze and held it. "I'm sorry for every time I've ever hurt you. I'm sorry for being a dog, and drinking, and not being a husband to you. I'm sorry for breaking your heart and running off. I'm sorry for leaving you to pick up the pieces."

He reached over and took my hand. "Maggie, I'm sorry for losing the chance to be the one love of your life, 'cause it's too late now and I know it. It's too late to ever go back."

I felt the tears prick at my eyelids. "Let it go, Vernell."

"These past few days, I've been thinking a lot of things over. I've made a lot of mistakes, Maggie, and I can't make some of them right. There's water passed under the bridge and years gone that can't never be brought back." Vernell looked at me, reached out with his free hand, and tipped my chin up so that I had to look at him.

"I love you," he said. "I know that ain't what you want to hear now, but I do love you." He sighed and looked away for a second, then brought his attention back to me. "I just couldn't love you as a husband."

The pain in my heart intensified. He was slowly opening every old wound we had together and I couldn't stand it.

"Vernell, don't do this."

"Well dad gum it, I have to," he said. "Maggie, I know you don't want me back. I know we couldn't ever have what we had and it be right. But we've got to move on with our lives, and I can't until you forgive me."

A fish jumped out on the lake and I turned my head away. Forgiveness. It was easy as pie to tell Vernell I forgave him, but had I really? Could I look God in the eye and tell Her I had a pure heart? I shut my eyes and thought for a moment, really thought. I hated Vernell Spivey for the things he'd put me and Sheila through, but did I wish him evil? No. Trouble was, I understood Vernell completely, and I believed him. He did love me, but not in a way that could work for either of us.

"Vernell," I said softly, "I do forgive you."

Vernell sighed a big sigh of relief and dropped my hand. "Good," he said, "because I need to tell you I've done fallen in love, and it's the real and true thing this time, and I by God think I need to marry her and do this thing right for once!"

Vernell jumped to his feet, brushed himself off, and appeared ready to take flight. I sat there for one brief second before I, too, jumped up, but it was to grab Vernell Spivey by his polyester coat lapels and give him a solid shaking.

"Vernell Spivey, I have let you work me yet again! You are going nowhere. Nowhere, do you hear me?" I shook him and took great satisfaction in seeing the gray wig slide a little further to one side. I reached up with one hand and snatched off the fake beard.

"Ouch!"

"Vernell, your cheatin', lyin', stealin' days are over. You square up with me right now and tell me what's going on. Don't you try and lull me into some la-la land of past rights and wrongs. I want to know where you've been, and why there's a dead man in your vehicle and where your gun is, and what happened to all the money. And I intend to find that out right now, today, before you can turn and run."

The bushes rustled and parted. "My questions exactly," a deep voice said. Marshall Weathers had found us.

He stepped through the hedge and emerged in front of us. Vernell's jaw dropped and his eyes widened.

"Vernell," Marshall said, "I'm thinking it's time we went downtown and had a talk."

Vernell's eyes hardened and I knew he was about to become the obstinate cuss he could be when he didn't want to do something.

"Why?" Vernell asked. "I don't see we have anything to talk about. You want to talk to me, you can call my attorney. Make an appointment, detective."

I shook my head and closed my eyes. *Here we go.*

"Vernell, we can do this one easy, or we can do it hard. It don't make no difference to me."

I opened my eyes in time to see Vernell start to bluster. He waved his arms and was just about to launch into a tirade when Weathers stopped him.

"Vernell, is that a gun?"

Vernell dropped his arms to his sides, but it was too late. Strapped under his shoulder was a brown holster with a silver gun handle sticking out for all the world to see.

"Vernell, turn around and put your hands out where I can see them." Marshall's voice had hardened; he was all business now. Any hint of compromise had just evaporated at the sight of Vernell's pistol.

"You don't have a license to carry concealed," Marshall said. "Vernell Spivey, I am placing you under arrest." He reached into his pocket, pulled out a pair of cuffs, and slipped them onto Vernell's bony wrists.

"What are you doing?" I said. "You know Vernell. He would no more hurt you than fly to the moon! What are you doing?"

Weathers spun Vernell around and I caught a glimpse of the frightened boy that lived inside Vernell. This was too much. Granted, I was shocked to see him with a gun, but it had to be because he was scared, not because he was dangerous.

"Maggie, stay out of this, all right? It'll work out."

"Maggie, call me a lawyer, will you, honey?"

I just stood there, looking at them. The way I felt must've been written all over my face because both men stared at me with the same determined yet helpless-to-do-anything-else looks on their faces.

"I don't believe this," I said again. "Vernell, you could've made it easy. You know Marshall. You could've just talked to him. And you," I said, turning my attention to Marshall. "You don't need to treat him like a common criminal. Are you so full of yourself that you can't be human? Is that what policing is?"

"Maggie, I don't have time to explain this to you now," Weathers said, and started off through the bushes with my ex-husband.

"Marshall Weathers, there is no explanation, there is no excuse for this, so don't you bother ever trying to offer one!"

He didn't look back, but I could see the jaw muscle start to twitch. I wanted to hurt him. How cruel could he be to drag Vernell away like a stray dog? How could he not listen to me? Granted, Vernell was acting the fool, but to actually arrest him on a simple charge like carrying concealed without a permit?

I followed them through the bushes, steaming. Marshall's car was parked in front of mine, and closer to the barn. He'd found a spot I hadn't seen and had wedged his unmarked car right in between two pickups.

"Vernell, I'll follow you down and meet you at the station."

Both men whirled around and spoke in unison. "No!"

Vernell took the lead and said, "Maggie, just call me a good lawyer. I can take care of myself now, honey."

I stared at him and saw the determination square up in his shoulders. Vernell was turning a new leaf and I didn't need to be the tree he leaned against.

Marshall had to put his two cents' worth in behind Vernell. "And you can't drive drunk," he warned.

"I'm not drunk," I said, suddenly aware of just how sober I felt. Marshall turned away, marching Vernell up the drive.

As they rounded the corner, the side door to the barn swung open and Bess King emerged.

Marshall kept walking, oblivious to Bess, but Vernell froze, forcing Marshall to tug at his arm.

Bess stood absolutely still, her dress fluttering gently in the breeze, blowing back against her body and outlining her form. The sun hit at just the right angle, forming a halo around the crown of her hair. She stood staring at Vernell, her expression pained, as if she'd been struck. Her mouth opened, then closed, her head dropped into her hands, and her shoulders caved in and began to softly shake.

"Bess," Vernell cried out, as Weathers opened his car door.

She raised her tear-stained face and stared at him, but she still didn't move or say a word. She seemed frozen.

Weathers tucked Vernell's head and pushed him down into the car. This time he noticed Bess, staring at her, his eyes flinty and hard. Then he looked over at me.

"Maggie, catch a cab home. I'll call you later," he said.

"No, Marshall, you won't. I don't ever want to speak to you again."

I saw the words cut into him and hurt him, and still I turned away, because in that one moment I felt my heart snap right in half. Marshall Weathers was as lost to me as a summer breeze on a winter's night.

Seventeen

I cried the entire way back to my house. Kept on crying as I parked the car and walked up the back steps. I opened the back door into my bedroom and fell across my bed, still sobbing and still miserable. I lay there in the early evening darkness, my head in my pillow, crying for everything that now wasn't ever going to be.

"Does this mean you don't want dinner before you go to work? Because I was working on a pasta here that would knock your socks off."

I jerked upright. "What are you doing in my house again?"

"You know, Sparks called your machine, which I did not answer, and said he wants you at the Stallion early."

I rubbed at my eyes with the heels of my hands and stared harder. Tony Carlucci was leaning against the doorway to my bedroom, a big hulk of biker boots and black denim.

"Why can't you leave me alone?" I said. "Why are you following me around and making my life a living hell?"

"Well, the way I see it, you was crying when you got

here, so I don't take credit for your atmospheric environmental mood swings. And as for a living hell, well, if I hadn't come over when I did yesterday, you'd be dead, and where you spend your eternal rest would not be up to me. So living hell I figure is better than your alternative dead hell."

I just looked at him. He was such a Yankee.

"Now," he said, "it's five fifteen. Sparks wants you at the club by seven forty-five. I don't know about you, but I couldn't jump around and sing on a full stomach, so let's eat around six." Carlucci stared at me, his eyes doing a slow, thorough appraisal. "You know. I'm thinking you might want to take a shower or something. You've got leaves in your hair and you look a real mess. Them black eyes is fading, but now you made 'em all puffy."

He didn't ask why I was crying. Instead, he ignored the fact totally, even when I hiccuped.

"Did I have any other messages?" I asked.

Tony shrugged. "I try to keep up," he said, and pulled a small square of paper from his back pocket. "Archer VanScoy from VanScoy Mobile Homes called. Sounds like a serious sleaze to me. Your sister, Darlene. She said don't worry, Sheila's fine, but she's thinking of coming in town tomorrow night. And Jack from the band called, wants to know if you're sleeping at his place tonight." Carlucci peered at me over the top of the paper. "You get around, don't you?"

"It's not like that!" I said.

"Hey," he said, holding up one hand, "it ain't none of my personal concern who you sleep with. I'm just saying, be aware. In this day and age . . ."

"Shut up, Carlucci. For as much as you profess to know about my life, you really don't know anything at all."

Carlucci stared at me again, his eyes dark. "Maybe you'll have to educate me, Maggie." Then he shifted up off of the doorjamb. "But not until you sort out your love life. I don't do complicated."

With that, he turned around and stepped back into the kitchen. The man had some nerve. I jumped up off the bed, grabbed my thick white terrycloth bathrobe from its hook on the wall, and stomped past him into the bathroom. He chuckled to himself as I went past.

I stood in the shower until the water started to run cool. By the time I emerged from the bathroom, I felt more like myself and less like a tearful, dependent female. Like Mama always said, "Ain't nothing like a shower to wash away self-pity."

Carlucci had his back to me as I passed him. The aroma of chicken and lemon filled my tiny kitchen, and I was suddenly hungry.

"Five minutes until it's on the table," he said.

I reached into the closet and pulled out a sapphire-blue dress. It shimmered in the light of the closet and for an instant I was right back where I'd been before, the image of the dead intruder suddenly fresh in my mind.

"Who cleaned up?" I asked, whipping around and walking back out into the kitchen.

Carlucci kept his back to me. "I did. I didn't want you coming back and finding that."

I stood there, holding the dress up to my chest, staring at the spot on the floor where the body had been. I'd been so caught up in Vernell and Marshall that I hadn't even given it any thought until now. Two men had died in my home now: Vernell's brother, Jimmy, and an intruder who'd meant to scar me for life.

After Jimmy died, I came to feel as if his spirit still lingered around. It wasn't a sad or scary thing, it was oddly comforting, as if he still wandered through my life, keeping in touch. But this other person, this intruder, that was different and frightening. I stared at the floor and saw no trace of blood.

"Thank you for doing that," I said.

"It's all right," he muttered. As I watched, he lifted my big stockpot and poured the contents into a colander in the sink.

"Do you know who he was?" I asked. "Did they tell you?"

"I knew who it was." He still didn't look at me. "His name was Sammy Newton, but everybody called him Mouse." I waited, because I knew there was more. "He's Redneck Mafia, Maggie. I figure you know that."

I supposed I had, but I'd blocked it out, not wanted to think about it or face it. When Tony turned around, he was holding a steaming platter of pasta.

"Go put that down and come eat. Let's don't talk about trash right now." His face was a tight-set mask of control. Even looking into his eyes didn't tell me what emotion lived there, or how he felt about killing a man and then cleaning up the gory aftermath. It was a closed subject.

I turned away from him, laid the dress out across my bed and walked back through the kitchen and into my dining room. Carlucci was lighting candles, throwing the room into a milky yellow glaze of soft lighting and good smells. It was like entering another dimension, where violence had no place and death was kept at bay, held off by the sounds and smells of living.

Tony Carlucci's black hair gleamed in the candlelight. His strong shoulders rippled as he moved a heavy white bowl to the center of the table. His hands were a roughened contrast to the smooth white surface of the dish he held. I wondered about him for a moment. Who was he underneath that tough exterior? Where had he lived before he'd arrived in Greensboro? Who had he left behind? Did she miss him?

He looked up when I entered, then back down at the table.

"This is a recipe handed down from my great-grandmother, on to my grandma, to my mother, and now to me. Don't even try asking for the ingredients or anything else, because if I told you, I would be forced . . ."

He broke off, not wanting to finish the phrase, *to kill you.* I looked at my plate and back at him.

"Well, whatever you did, it smells wonderful. I'm starving." I smiled and made a big show of digging in, but all I could do was think. The events of the past few days ran through my head like a slide show. Vernell turning back up should've been the release I needed, but it only made matters worse, because as sure as I sat there eating lemon-cream pasta, I knew he'd be charged with murder by daybreak. That's just the way Vernell lives. If a storm is gonna come up, Vernell's gonna be stuck smack in the eye of the hurricane.

I looked back at Carlucci and found him watching me, his smoky eyes dark and impossible to read. When he reached for the pepper I found myself watching the muscles in his arms. I wondered what it would feel like to have them wrapped around me. Just as quickly, I shook the image off and swallowed. What in the world was I doing thinking like that?

As if he read my mind, Carlucci smiled.

"You should wear that robe to dinner more often," he said. "And let your hair go like that, so it just goes all curly. You ever think about not fixing it up, just leaving it be?"

"You know," I said, laying my fork down on my plate, "you and my ex-husband would get along."

"And how's that?" he asked.

I stared right back at him. "Whenever Vernell doesn't want to deal with something, he starts complimenting me. Here you are, in my house again, without my permission, making yourself at home, and I'm supposed to just take it and go on."

Carlucci licked his lips. "Exactly."

"Why?"

"Because you'll get yourself killed if I don't stick around. Besides," he added, "I think we've got some unfinished business."

I could feel my face flame up under his gaze, the heat spreading down my neck and into my chest. What did he mean, unfinished business? Who was I kidding? I knew exactly what unfinished business he meant.

I tossed my hair back over my shoulders and looked at him. "I have no idea what you're talking about."

Carlucci laughed. "You most certainly do. I can see it in the way you squirm when I look at you."

I jumped up, pushing my chair back behind me. I didn't want him to see it in my face, to read what we both knew I felt. I didn't want to deal with him. I couldn't face what I felt. Not now, maybe not even later. "I'm late. I've got to get ready."

Carlucci just stared at me, his eyes roving down the V of my robe, taking his time. "You do that, Maggie Reid, you get ready."

I turned away from him and stalked off to my room, closing the door and locking it behind me. Who did he think he was?

Eighteen

I left Tony Carlucci and a pile of dirty dishes, headed for the Golden Stallion. If there was one cure for trouble, it was music. It didn't matter how bad things got, or how screwed up my love life was, music was the cure. All I had to do was hear Sparks slide into the intro with his silky pedal steel guitar, and I was transported away from every worry I'd ever known.

The Golden Stallion club is my home away from home. It sits in a pitted gravel parking lot looking like a derelict, A-framed warehouse just back off busy High Point Road. It isn't a thing to look at, inside or out, but it's where I feel the most like myself of anywhere next to my house or Mama's.

Of course, just stepping through the doorway makes me sick. The stage fright overwhelms me, right up until the band starts playing my song and I run up the steps, out onto the stage and take the mike in my hands. It was no different tonight than it is any other night. I stepped into the front door, hugged Cletus, the bull-necked bouncer, and ran for the ladies' room.

But as soon as Sparks launched into "Your Cheatin' Heart," I was out the door and walking up on stage, my heart pounding, my palms sweating, and a huge smile on my face.

Sparks looked up from the pedal steel, his huge white cowboy hat sparkling under the lights. His mustache takes up half of his face, and when he smiles, he'll melt your heart, but Sparks doesn't give himself away easy. He holds on to that smile and only lets it out when he's assured that he's in charge and things are going his way. I figure it's on account of him being short. He has to set the tone with you, let you know his bite is just as strong as his bark. Tonight he wasn't smiling. I'd missed early rehearsal. I hadn't even remembered it, until I saw the scowl. Oh well, this was just not the day for perfection.

Harmonica Jack saw me and danced across the stage, the harmonica up to his lips and his eyebrows wiggling with the exertion of playing the melody line.

I strolled up to him, rubbed up against his shoulder and began to sing. Behind me, Sugar Bear, the rhythm guitar player, stood like a massive dark-haired, bearded mountain man.

Chris, the lead guitar player, picked out a harmony lead and laid it right down under my vocals.

We were good, my boys and me, and there ain't nothing like a tune well done to draw a crowd out onto the dance floor.

"When tears fall down, like falling rain," I sang, and looked out at the dancers. For a moment my mind replayed the image of Bess King, standing outside her barn door, watching Weathers lead Vernell away. And in that same instant I realized who Tony Carlucci worked for. It was as plain as the nose on my face. Bess had hired Tony to find Vernell before her husband or anyone else could.

I was startled to hear Sugar Bear's strong baritone come in behind me, and realized that I'd stopped singing. Sparks was giving me the evil eye and Jack looked plain worried. I shrugged my shoulders and grinned, like maybe I'd suddenly forgotten the words, but nobody seemed fooled. I sang that song every single night, and I'd never messed up, not once.

"You all right?" Jack murmured, dancing right up to my shoulder.

"Yeah, fine, just a little distracted." Behind us, Sparks was playing his solo.

"You staying with me tonight or what?"

I held the mike down at my side and looked at him. "It might get dangerous, Jack. I don't want to jeopardize your safety. I could never forgive . . ."

"Maggie," he interrupted, "I'm younger than you, but I'm not a child. I know what's going on, and I think we can handle it. Now sing, you're up."

The words came automatically this time, and all the while I was looking at my friend. When everything else went to hell in a handcart, there he was. He didn't try and sweet-talk me or manipulate me or leave me in the dark. No, he was just himself, calm and steady. Just what I needed when my entire world was up in the air.

Bess King was at the top of my list for tomorrow, along with Vernell Spivey. Between the two of them, I knew I'd find the key to whatever was going on. I all of a sudden had a business to run. If Vernell was arrested or otherwise incapacitated, I had a 49 percent share of a mobile home lot that was going to one day send Sheila to college. I had to find the money Vernell had run off with and square things with the employees before the Mobile Home Kingdom folded. And if anyone was going to prove to Weathers that Sheila's father was not a murderer, it would have to be me. As for Marshall Weathers, well, it was best not to dwell on him. For a second I felt what it was like to let go of him, to know that he wasn't the one, and that was enough for me. All I needed was my music, and to forget.

I sang and sang. It wasn't until the third set, the last set of the night, that I noticed Tony Carlucci had come in and somehow gotten himself backstage to stand in the wings, watching.

He made the band nervous. They kept looking over at

him, and he made it worse by staring right back, no smile, no give to his expression. He stood with his muscular arms crossed, wearing a black motorcycle jacket, black jeans, and a very black attitude. When I made eye contact, his facial expression remained unchanged. His eyes flickered from me, to the band, to the house. This wasn't a social call. Carlucci was working, or whatever it was that he did.

Harmonica Jack edged closer. "You see that guy?"

I frowned at Carlucci. "Don't worry about him. He's an idiot."

Jack looked at Carlucci and ran the harmonica along his lips, then pulled it away and started talking. "Well, he sure seemed friendly with Cletus. Two of them were just a-laughin' and slappin' each other on the back awhile ago. Maybe he's a new hire."

I was watching the crowd. A silver-haired man in new jeans and boots was making his way closer to the stage. He looked out of place and ill at ease, like he was slumming.

"He's a private investigator," I said. "He wants to find Vernell."

Jack laughed. "Well, he ain't here!"

"I know. He thinks if he sticks to me like tape, Vernell will show up. Must not know Vernell's down at the jailhouse, entertaining a certain detective."

Jack played a line or two of the break and then danced toward me again. "That ain't necessarily stupid, Maggie." Then he broke off and stared at me. "What do you mean Vernell's in jail?"

But I was singing, looking at the young cowboys who danced below me and belting out "Feeling Single and Seeing Double." The silver-haired man was staring at me, his ice-blue eyes almost as pale as his hair.

"I need to talk to you," he mouthed.

I looked back at Carlucci, saw him watching, and felt covered. Whoever this guy was, he wouldn't get far if he intended to hurt me. When the song ended, we were done for the night. I looked at the newcomer and nodded him toward the edge of the stage.

Carlucci took it all in, and Harmonica Jack watched Carlucci, and over it all, Cletus the bouncer was watching. I couldn't have been safer.

"Archer VanScoy, Ms. Reid," the silver-haired man said. His voice was as cool and slippery as ice. "I tried to reach you at home, but you haven't returned my calls."

Something about him made me mad straight off. I didn't like him. Didn't like his tone, the way he seemed to be trying to make up to me. So I didn't apologize.

"What can I do for you, Mr. VanScoy?"

"Archer, honey, just call me Archer."

I said nothing. This one here was a snake.

He didn't seem to mind my obvious coolness toward him. He stared at my breasts and began to talk.

"Vernell and I were trying to set up a little deal," he said. "I wanted his mobile home lot and Vernell wanted to sell it." VanScoy smiled broadly. "Would've worked out right nice for the both of us. However . . ." Here he stopped smiling, easing his face into a Teflon-coated expression of sympathy. "I understand Vernell's in a bit of a bind. Now I know you're the other partner, and while we still need Vernell's John Hancock, I feel sure we can wrap this deal up and cut you a check. Money's what Vernell needs now, I'm sure."

I took another step lower on the stage stairway and stared at him.

"I'm not sure what bind you mean," I said.

VanScoy nodded, as if he understood why I might be leery of him. "Well, between us," he said, looking around like a co-conspirator, "Vernell's taking all the cash assets out of the bank, and then disappearing with a large sum given to him by what you call investors is a bit of a bind. Being arrested for Nosmo King's murder, on the other hand, is a legal emergency as well as a bind."

"I think you've got your facts wrong," I said. "Vernell is not under arrest."

He leaned back a little, his eyes flashing from my breasts to my face.

"Honey," he said, "you might want to call down to the police station. The eleven o'clock news was covered over with it. Vernell's been arrested for Nosmo King's murder. They got him locked up tighter than Houdini's trunk."

Archer VanScoy fished into his suit coat pocket and drew out an embossed business card.

"Why don't you get up with your husband and then call me? Vernell's gonna need all the help he can get." He hesitated, before he handed me the card. "Of course, some time's elapsed. My original terms have changed. It's one hundred thousand now."

I turned my back on him and walked up the stairs and onto the stage. All around people moved like ants, disassembling cables and equipment, packing up instruments, and closing up for the night. The house lights were on and the last few customers were clearing out. Tony Carlucci hadn't moved.

I walked over and stood in front of him, looking right into his eyes without flinching.

"Vernell's in jail," I said. "If you want him, go get him."

Carlucci was unreadable. "I know."

"Then why are you still here?"

"Vernell's in jail, but the money isn't. They're not going to ease up any with him in jail, they'll just come after you."

Jack walked around us, behind Carlucci, standing just out of Carlucci's sight, but where he knew I could see him.

"I can take care of myself," I said.

"Yeah, I've seen how well you do that." Carlucci pushed off from the wall and looked down at me. "People get right pissed about three million dollars," he said. He took a step closer and I felt the heat radiating from his body. "You don't know what they'll do to get their money back."

I shuddered involuntarily and Jack started toward us.

"Maggie, you ready to go?"

Carlucci stared at him, but Jack didn't move.

"In a couple of minutes," I said. "I'm just finishing something up."

Jack took the hint and moved back a few feet, still unwilling to let me be alone with Carlucci.

"So, you gonna let them kill him too?" he asked.

"Stop it!" I hissed.

"Stop acting like an idiot and I won't have to continue to bombard your small mind with the realities of your current situation."

"Jack's is the safest place I can think of," I said.

"You want to stay alive? Come with me and let me put you someplace safe."

He was too close. I had the sudden urge to turn and run, but didn't.

"I'm not playing with you, Maggie," Carlucci said. "Ditch your friend and let's go."

I looked at Jack, saw him watching, and smiled a tiny, tight smile.

"They'll kill him to get to you, Maggie, and he'll die trying to defend you. And don't think they won't hunt you down, because they will."

"What makes it any safer with you?"

Carlucci looked at Jack, then back to me. "Because I don't love you, Maggie. This is what I do for a living, straight up. I find people and I protect people. I'm trained and I'm objective. Your friend isn't any of those things. He'd defend you to the death; you can see that in his eyes. I won't have to."

I looked over at Jack and saw that Carlucci was right. I turned away and walked over to where Jack waited.

"He wants me to go with him," I said, "and I have to do it." I raised my fingers to his lips when he started to argue. "It's all right. This is what I want to do."

And I walked away, knowing I'd hurt him.

Nineteen

I woke up at five A.M. because I could feel him watching me. Tony Carlucci had played an elaborate shell game with my car and his motorcycle before putting me on the back of his bike and driving me in a zigzag pattern across Greensboro, south of town to the small village of Pleasant Garden. He stopped several times, waiting, watching, making sure no one followed us, and then proceeded to drive his Harley across a field and up onto the back of his property.

It was a long, narrow piece of land, rimmed on three sides by a tall, barbed-wire fence. Tony stopped the bike by a gate, unlocked it, and drove the Harley through before returning to lock it behind us.

"Do you live in a prison?" I asked. Floodlights spotted the backyard, which was filled with fruit trees.

"Nope, I'm the caretaker," he said. "It's a concrete factory. They let me live in the house that was here on the property. In return, I keep out the riffraff."

He drove across the yard, up to the deck that spanned the back of the tiny, brick ranch. The instant we pulled close, a

Doberman lunged out at us, his neck bound by a heavy collar that was attached to a thick chain. The muscles corded and strained against the collar and the dog drooled in his attempt to get to us.

"Popeye," Carlucci called. "It's me, bud."

Popeye growled, unwilling to accept that I was a guest. I was equally unwilling to accept that Popeye could ever be considered a pet. It was a standoff that only got better once Tony took me inside.

His house was a monument to cleanliness and order, almost military in its precise attention to detail. Everything had a place and there was no sign of clutter or the dust bunnies that called my house a home.

Carlucci supplied me with a toothbrush, a comb, even pajamas. But Carlucci was lacking in one essential: There was no guest bed.

"I'll take the couch," he said.

"I'm fine with a couch."

"Be that as it may," he said, "I'm still sleeping on it."

I stood looking around his room, staring at the pale blue walls, the blue plaid sheets on the bed, the matching pillows, the curtains that hung just so at the windows, and the dresser that had no personal belongings upon it.

The couch in the living room looked more comfortable than the hard mattress of Carlucci's bed, but beggars couldn't be choosers. I closed the door behind him and was asleep within minutes. How I ever awakened from my coma would remain a mystery, but I did. I felt him watching me, even in my dreamless sleep, and I rose up through the mire of unconsciousness to find him in a chair at the other end of the bedroom, his smoky eyes staring into mine.

I sat up, still startled and in between sleep and wakefulness. "What are you doing?"

"Thinking."

I tugged at the covers, pulling them tighter around me, suddenly cold.

"What?"

Carlucci looked at me for a slow moment. "About you."

He still wore his black jeans, shirt and boots, but the jacket was gone. The way he said *about you* made my skin tingle as little hairs rose up on the back of my arms.

"Not like that," he said, reading me again. "Well, maybe some of that, but I told you, I don't do complicated. You're complicated." He stretched and stood, walking slowly toward me. "I was thinking about your situation. I'm thinking you and Bess King oughta talk."

"So you had to come in here and watch me sleep?"

His eyes followed the outline of my body under the covers, moving slowly, like I was a consideration and he was biding his time.

"Yeah, something like that. That and I thought I heard something a little while ago, so I just thought I'd sit here, just in case."

I looked at him and didn't believe him.

"The dog didn't bark."

Carlucci laughed. "How would you know? You were snoring too loud to hear much of anything."

"I was not!"

At that moment, Popeye went crazy. His deep, excited barking filled the air, lights flicked on in the backyard, and a gun materialized in Tony's hand.

"Get out of bed and down on the floor," he commanded.

I jumped, hitting the cold wooden floor next to the bed with a sharp slam.

Tony walked to the window, stood to one side and pushed the curtain away with the barrel of his gun.

"It's probably nothing," he said. "A cat maybe, or a raccoon." And for the second time in as many minutes, I knew he was lying.

Popeye was hysterical. Carlucci let the curtain slip back into place. "Stay right where you are." He tossed me the cordless phone. "If I don't come back in five minutes, call nine-one-one."

"Wait! Don't go out there! That's stupid."

Popeye screamed, a dog howl of anguish and pain, and Carlucci was gone.

I heard the front door open softly, then close. Popeye was silent. There was no sound from the outside at all for a moment, then gunfire. Two or three blasts close together, then the sound of a car starting up in the distance and pulling away.

I hit the buttons on the phone and heard someone say "Nine-one-one, what is the nature of your emergency?"

"Someone's shooting at us," I said.

"Okay, ma'am. Just tell me where you are," she said.

And that's when I stopped. I didn't know where I was. I hesitated, looked up, and saw Tony step into the doorway. "It's all right," he said. "Tell them you're fine. Tell them never mind."

I looked at him, not believing that he was serious.

"It's fine. Tell them."

His voice was hard.

"I'm fine. I'm sorry. It was a mistake."

"Ma'am," the 911 operator said, "are you sure you're fine? All you have to do is say no and we can send a car."

I tried to calm my voice, to convince her. "I'm sorry," I said, "I guess I got a little frightened. It was just a car back-firing." I laughed apologetically. "It woke me up, and I guess I got carried away."

"All right then, ma'am," the woman said. "It's all right."

Tony walked into the bedroom and sank down on the floor beside the bed. His face was white and drawn, and when I looked I saw something that terrified me. His hands were covered with blood.

He stared at me, as if he were looking right through me. "They killed Popeye," he said. "They shot him with a high-powered bow. He's dead."

He looked down at his hands, as if they didn't belong to him, and then he stood up. "I'll be back."

He turned and walked away, his back stiff, his gait strangely uneven.

"Where are you going?"

He looked at me for a second then turned away. "To bury my dog."

I listened to his footsteps dying away, the sound of the back door deadbolt sliding as he unlocked it and stepped out onto the deck. The next sound I heard was that of a shovel ringing against the hardened ground as Tony dug a grave for Popeye.

When he came back inside, the sky was beginning to lighten. I could see it seeping through the edges of the curtains. Tony had walked past me, into the bathroom, and closed the door. I heard the sound of water running, then the broken sound of water hitting his hands and him washing, over and over. When he came out, he walked over to where I still sat on the floor. With one harsh movement he pulled the covers from the bed onto the floor, then reached for the pillows. Next he pulled his gun from his waistband and placed it on the floor next to the phone.

He started arranging the blankets, making a pallet, and as soon as I realized this, I began to help.

"We can't sleep on the bed," he said, his voice thick with fatigue. "It's not safe. And you're not sleeping alone."

He lay down on one side of the blanket and turned away from me, onto his side, his fingers inches from his gun. I watched him for a moment and then, finally, lay down beside him, wrapping myself in the blanket and turning away from him. Within moments, we slept.

Carlucci was up before I was, and the smell of coffee was what finally drove me out of the warm blanket and into his kitchen. Tony was standing by the window over the sink, staring out at the field behind his house, watching concrete trucks kick up clouds of white dust as they moved through the gate and into the plant. The look on his face frightened me. His eyes were hollow and rimmed with sleepless, dark circles. His hair was wiry and unkempt. But when he turned to face me, his expression took my breath away. He was more than angry; he was enraged.

"You should've called me when you found Vernell," he said. His voice escaped through clenched jaws, rasping at my sleep-drugged mind, forcing me into a sharp awakening.

"You had a million opportunities to let me know you'd found him, and you didn't. What's wrong with you? Didn't I tell you I had to know? Don't you think some of this could've been avoided if I'd had first crack at him and not your precious detective?"

He frightened me, but I wouldn't let him see it.

"What was I supposed to do, Tony, say "Excuse me," and step into a phone booth? I don't carry a cell phone. And what would I have said, huh? 'This P.I. is looking for you, he breaks into houses and waits, he drives your daughter home on his motorcycle without our permission, and he says he wants to get in touch with you before the other people looking for you kill him'?"

Tony's eyes narrowed. "Something like that."

I straightened my back, pushed the hair out of my face, and frowned. "First off, there wasn't time to call you. Second, Marshall Weathers found us, I didn't call him. And third, I don't really know a thing about you. What if you're looking to hurt Vernell, just like the others are looking to do?"

Tony folded his thick forearms and the frown on his face deepened. "So you're saying basically that you don't trust me."

"Something like that," I echoed.

"That's why you didn't tell me straight out when you got home?"

I walked past him to the coffeepot, grabbed a mug from the hooks that lined the underside of his cabinets, and poured myself a cup of steaming coffee.

"I didn't tell you because I wasn't ready to tell you. I wanted to talk to Vernell first, find out what's really going on. I have a history with him. I don't have one with you."

He'd talked to Bess. She'd told him. That much was easy to guess.

"You're playing it wrong, Maggie," he said. His eyes were narrow angry slits, and his face was set in cold, hard lines that sent a chill running through me.

"Take me home, please. Now."

"You can't go home."

That's when I lost my temper. "Yes, I can. Watch me, Mr. Carlucci. You can take me home, or I can call a cab or I can call a friend, or"—and I let the word dangle for a second— "I can call a cop. Somehow, I don't think you're exactly in favor of that idea, are you?"

He took a step toward me, and I braced myself, but I didn't move. I thought he was going to keep coming. I expected him to try and hurt me, but he didn't. He stopped himself, his fists clenched by his side, his face colored with a dusky red rage, and as I watched, he let it all go. He stared at me, never taking his eyes from my face. He inhaled, held it, and exhaled, visibly relaxing the muscles in his body.

"All right," he said at last, "I'll take you to your car. But it's not safe. I'm telling you they're looking for that money and they won't stop until they have it. Hurting you is just an amusement for them, Maggie."

I looked past him, out the window, staring at the barren fruit trees.

"They didn't have any trouble finding me here," I said. "You told me, the only way I can get out of this is to go see Vernell and get him to tell me where the money is. If they have their money, they'll leave me alone."

Tony reached for his jacket, pulling it off the back of one of the kitchen chairs.

"Then I'll take you," he said.

"I'll take myself."

Tony shook his head, a small smile tugging at the corner of his mouth. "You're a piece of work, Maggie Reid." He stepped closer to me, standing so close I could smell the leather and oil of his jacket. "Let me help you."

I wanted to tell him I didn't trust him, that I couldn't trust someone who carried that much excess anger around like spare luggage, but I couldn't say it.

"All right," I said finally. "Take me."

Twenty

Carlucci drove down Washington Street to the front of the Municipal Plaza, bumped his Harley up onto the sidewalk, and guided it across the concrete, almost to the broad steps that led to the police department. He stopped the bike in front of a statue of a policeman patting a little boy on the head.

"You're nuts," I said as I pulled off my helmet. "You're surrounded by cops and here you are begging for a ticket. What's wrong with you?"

He looked around the empty plaza. "I don't see anybody coming to take me in. They probably do it all the time themselves."

I shook my head, remembering how Weathers pulled up on the sidewalk exactly as Tony had, but the difference was that he was a police officer and Tony was definitely not one of *them*.

I handed him the helmet and walked away. Tony Carlucci was strange, and I didn't know that he was any of the things he said he was, or that I could trust him any further than I could throw him. But he was only one of my worries. Vernell and the Redneck Mafia were my main concerns.

By the time I'd worked my way up the stairs and into the lobby of the police department, I'd worked up a good head of steam. When I presented myself to the receptionist in the Criminal Investigation Department, I was almost shaking, I was so mad.

"Detective Weathers, someone's here to see you, says she's a Miss Reid."

I glared at her. "I am Ms. Reid," I snapped.

The receptionist looked startled.

"He'll be right out. Just have a seat over—"

"I'll stand right here," I said.

Weathers rounded the corner and found me waiting, my hands on my hips and a frown on my face.

"Where is he?" I asked.

"Across the street." He said it like maybe Vernell had stepped out for coffee, and not been locked up.

"Take me to him."

Weathers walked right on past me, opened the black door out into the corridor and held it open for me.

"Right this way."

I followed him, not trusting myself to look at his face. I stared at the wall as we walked, noting all the pictures of ex-chiefs and old police cars.

"Maggie, are you going to talk about this or not?"

I still couldn't look at him. "I'm listening."

Weathers opened the front door, led me around the corner of the building, and grabbed me by the shoulders.

"We have the gun, Maggie. It's registered in Vernell's name. He hadn't reported it missing or stolen. Maggie, you've got to face up to this. Vernell killed Nosmo King. He went over the edge. He's been headed this way his entire life."

I looked at the third button on his white oxford shirt.

"Maggie, look at me, damn it!"

I raised my eyes slowly, biting the inside of my cheek so I wouldn't give my feelings away.

"Vernell Spivey has as much as admitted that he killed Nosmo King. The man you put up with for all those years isn't who you thought he was. He tried, and I know you loved him for who you thought he might become, but Maggie, he killed Nosmo King."

"No, he didn't!" The tears welled up in my eyes and I couldn't see. Marshall Weathers began walking down a long outside corridor that led to a set of steps into the parking lot.

"Then I think you should talk to him. Let him explain it to you."

Weathers was calm, too calm. It was as if he trusted Vernell's reaction and I couldn't for the life of me see how. Vernell didn't kill Nosmo King.

We walked across the street, up a wide ramp to the glass doors leading into the sheriff's department and the city jail.

Weathers pulled open the front door, stepped inside, and turned left. He walked up to a small glass window, and spoke to the uniformed officer inside.

"We're here to interview Vernell Spivey," he said. He looked at me apologetically. "It's the only way I can get you inside," he said. "These aren't regular visiting hours. I have to go with you."

A buzzer sounded and Marshall pushed another door open, admitting us to a small room.

"Put your purse and anything in your pockets up on the counter," he said. He reached for his gun, put it in the tray that the jailer extended and then waited for me.

"Okay," Weathers said. "Here goes."

The heavy steel door in front of us swung open, revealing the jailer and a narrow, beige corridor. Weathers and the short, fat man exchanged pleasantries as we walked to the interview room, but I wasn't listening. The jail smelled of disinfectant. I could hear the clang of metal in the distance, the drone of a TV and the sounds of men's muffled voices.

We were led into a small room, just like the movies, with a Plexiglas shield, wooden chairs, and a scarred wooden counter between our side and the prisoner's.

How could Vernell Spivey have come to this?

The door swung open a few minutes later and Vernell stepped into the room, clad in a bright orange jumpsuit, a two-day growth of beard and a hangdog look on his face.

His eyes brightened when he saw me, then dulled as he took in Marshall Weathers. I picked up the handset and waited for him to do the same.

"Hello, darlin'," he said, just like George Jones sweet-talking Tammy Wynette.

"Vernell, why are you in jail?"

He smiled a weak, wishy-washy smile and shrugged his shoulders. "Aw, you know, honey, fate, I guess."

"Fate, you guess? What does that mean, Vernell?"

His eyes wandered over to Weathers then back to me. "Get me a real good lawyer, Maggie."

"That would take money, Vernell. Where is it?"

A thin sheen of sweat broke out on Vernell's forehead. "Use the dish business as collateral. Get a loan."

"You know we can't do that! Where's the money?"

Vernell switched the phone from one hand to the other, rubbing his sweaty palms on his thighs. What was the matter with him?

"Tell me the truth. What happened? It's all right, honey, the truth will set you free."

He gulped. "I don't think so, Maggie," he said. "Not this time."

A chill ran up my spine. "Sure it will, tell us what happened."

Vernell looked at me. He was pleading silently, but I wouldn't give.

"Maggie, the money's going to work out. I'm working on something." His gaze shifted to Marshall. "I'd rather not go into it just now."

"Honey, now is the only time you have. Nosmo King is dead, shot with your gun, in your truck, and you don't want to talk about it?"

Vernell smiled nervously. "Not really."

I pointed my finger at him. "This is your daughter's future we're talking about, Vernell Spivey! I have half a mind to go ahead and work that deal with Archer VanScoy and have done with it!"

That got a reaction. "Maggie, don't you dare! You can't sell without me! The lot's not for sale, not at any price. I told him that!"

I glared at him. "Oh yeah, well, when you're sitting in prison, I can do whatever I want! I'll take his hundred thousand dollars and run. At least that way I know Sheila will be taken care of!"

Vernell jumped to his feet, the receiver pressed to his ear. "I will take care of my family! I have a plan!" Then he paused, frowned, and stared straight at me. "VanScoy told you a hundred thousand? That business is worth hundreds of thousands more than that. See why I have to handle it?"

"VanScoy said you took too long, and now he knows you're in trouble, so it's one hundred thousand. See?"

Marshall Weathers was watching me, I could feel it, but I wouldn't look at him.

"Where's Nosmo King's money?" I demanded.

Vernell sighed. "I don't know nothing about that," he said. "I don't have it. I told him I didn't need it after all."

Now we were getting somewhere. I looked at Marshall. "Can you not step outside for a moment?" I said. "You'd have to leave if I was his lawyer."

Weathers shrugged, looked at the window, and motioned to the jailer. "I'll give you three minutes," he said, "then I'm back inside."

The second the door closed I was on Vernell like ugly on an ape. "All right, you low-life pond scum, this is for Sheila. You remember her, don't you, the daughter who thinks you walk on water?"

Vernell's eyes reddened and for a second I thought he might cry. "Maggie, I'm working for the higher good here. I didn't kill King. I didn't take his money. And I'm working on something with the money, so lay off! Get me a lawyer."

"Were you there when Nosmo got killed?" I asked.

Vernell shook his head. "Last thing I remember, me and Nosmo and his girlfriend were drinking. I woke up and it was dark and I was in a field and my truck was gone. I swear, baby, I wasn't working no deal with Nosmo."

"Then why didn't you come straight out and tell the police your truck was missing?"

Vernell wouldn't meet my gaze. "On account of I wasn't sure what happened. I had a bad feeling about Nosmo. I was waiting to find out if anything was wrong." He looked up for a second. "I've been drinking too much lately, Maggie. Sometimes I don't even know what day it is. By the time I came out of it, everybody was looking for me."

Vernell looked pitiful.

"Did you tell Detective Weathers?"

Vernell snorted. "Yeah, and what did that get me? Murder One, Maggie." He leaned in closer, raised his hand to touch the glass and stared straight at me. "I didn't kill him, Maggie. I went to see him to square a few things."

I could see Marshall standing out in the hall, entertaining the jailer.

"What were you trying to square, Vernell?"

Vernell looked down at his lap, then back at me. "I wanted to ask him to let go of Bess."

Oh great, give Vernell yet another motive to murder Nosmo King.

I shook my head and buried my face in my hands. The doorknob twisted and Marshall Weathers was back in the room with me.

"I'm sorry, Maggie," Vernell said. "I didn't mean for it to come out like this."

The door opened and the jailer appeared behind Vernell, motioning for him to come. I stared at Vernell, watching the way his jumpsuit hung on his bony frame, memorizing the way his eyes sought out mine, begging me to understand him.

"Baby, get me the best lawyer they got. I didn't do it."

Marshall Weathers waited until Vernell left the room before he spoke.

"See what I mean?" he said softly. "I didn't have another choice."

I stood up, squared my shoulders, and stared right into his eyes. What else was there left to say?

"Thank you for your time," I said. "I appreciate you getting me in to see him like this."

The jailer returned for us, opened the door, and led us back through the system of doors to the front of the building.

I stepped ahead of Weathers, who stopped when another deputy called his name, walked out the front door and down the ramp to the sidewalk. I didn't hear the motorcycle coming. Didn't track that Carlucci was there until he pulled right in front of me.

"Here," he called, handing me my helmet. "Let's go."

He didn't have to ask how it went. It was written all over my face.

As he pulled away from the curb and into traffic, I saw Marshall Weathers step out of the jail and walk toward the sidewalk. I looked in Carlucci's side-view mirror and watched him stand there and watch as we rode off. Then I closed my eyes and tried not to think of him at all.

Twenty-one

Dumping Carlucci wasn't easy. He took me to the side street where I'd hidden my car, took elaborate care to check it for bombs and whatever else he thought might be attached to it, and with great reluctance agreed that I could drive it. I wasn't in much of a mood for arguing or fussing over what my next move was going to be. Instead, I let him tell me what the plan was.

"Let's take your car back to my house," he said. "No one'll try and bother us in the daytime. It's too busy, what with the concrete trucks coming and going. We can eat a late breakfast and go from there."

I nodded and he took pity on me.

"It's gonna work out all right, Maggie," he said. "Weathers is all wrong."

I couldn't bring myself to talk much. I sighed, took the keys from his outstretched palm, and opened the driver's-side door. Let him think I was a half-zombie, completely devastated by what I'd learned about my ex-husband, and at the hands of my ex-boyfriend who'd never really been my boyfriend anyway. Let him think I was an overwhelmed female. That suited me just fine.

I slid behind the driver's seat and cranked the engine. Inside a little kick of adrenaline flared up and I could feel the surface of my skin prickle.

"I'll follow you," I said, my voice a tired, hopeless monotone.

"Okay. I'll drive slow so I don't lose you."

I nodded and waited for him to put his helmet on and start off down the street. I waved one hand out the window and started off after him, content to let him wind me through the older neighborhood of homes, around the back of Greensboro College, and into downtown Greensboro.

I stayed right up behind him, until I knew for certain he was confident that I'd follow him all the way to Pleasant Garden. Then, as we drove down Eugene Street, moving away from the police station in a lazy zigzag, I cut off, did a U-turn across Battleground, and disappeared up Greene Street.

I knew I had mere seconds to escape, but I had one advantage my northern friend didn't—I knew Greensboro. I knew every little alley and more than that, I had a parking card to the BB&T bank building employee parking lot, courtesy of my lease with them for the Curly-Que Salon. While Tony would have to park, dismount, and begin his search, I could evaporate.

I slammed the VW into a basement-level parking slot, ran for the stairs and raced up two flights of steps to the Greene Street exit. I stood just inside the door, peering out for any evidence of Carlucci, and when I was sure he was still circling the garage, I lit out around the corner, past the Carolina Theater, and around the corner to the Curly-Que.

The bell tinkled as I ran inside and Bonnie looked up from her chair by the counter. Velmina was back at the shampoo station, carefully working on a little old lady. Rozetta, the receptionist, was making change for Bonnie's departing customer, an unlit cigarette dangling from her lips.

"Bonnie," I said, dashing over to her. "Help me quick!"

Bonnie's eyes widened. "Maggie, what's wrong?"

Unfortunately, everyone in the salon, with the exception of Velmina's customer, heard me. I had their complete and undivided attention.

"Hide me! A big guy, dressed in black, will probably come busting through that door in two minutes and he can't find me!"

Bonnie's customer turned around. She was a tall, slim woman with blunt-cut, strawberry-blond hair and freckles. When she moved I saw the gun clipped to her belt and the quick way her eyes moved to the door and back to me.

"I'm an intensive parole officer," she said. "You need help?"

Bonnie grabbed my hand and pulled me toward the shampoo station.

"Nah," she said, her voice like tumbling gravel, "this kinda crap goes on all the time. You might oughta hang around, though, just in case it gets interesting. Besides, he might be single." She laughed, choking it off into a smoker's cough.

"Sit down," she said, and threw a huge black cape over my body as she pushed my head back into the bowl of the sink.

"Hey," Velmina said, "he's gonna see her legs and know." Velmina sat her customer up, wrapped her head in towels, and walked over to my chair. "Here, do this." She knelt in front of me, pulled off my shoes and rolled the legs of my jeans up until they were tucked underneath the black vinyl cape. She grabbed a pedicure pan and quickly stuck my feet in the cold water.

"Oh God!" I shrieked. "It's freezing!"

"Can't help that now," Velmina said calmly. "It's all right, dear," she murmured to her now-anxious customer. "Foot problems. Had 'em all her life."

Bonnie dunked me under the warm water and began pouring shampoo onto my head.

Rozetta, not one to be left out, got up and grabbed a tube off the makeup counter.

"He'll see her face! Honestly!" She clacked up beside me in her four-inch stiletto heels and began slathering a thick cream on my face.

Bonnie cackled. "Oh, that's good," she said. "Green goop. Now she looks like a Martian!"

"Great!" I sighed.

"I think it's high time someone changed your look anyway," Bonnie said.

"Why don't we color her hair?" Velmina asked.

The parole officer was watching the door. "Big, black hair, black motorcycle jacket?" she yelled over the din in the salon.

"That's him!"

My heart began to dance up into my throat and my chest tightened. The bell tinkled, the door flew back against the wall, and everyone but Bonnie and Velmina's little old lady jumped.

"Well, son," Bonnie said slowly, "we can all tell you need a haircut, but don't bust the place down trying to get it!"

Rozetta slowly exhaled, placed the last dollop of goo on my face, and turned away. I kept my eyes tightly shut, afraid like the Indian legend that my soul might escape from my body if I inadvertently looked into his eyes.

"Do you have an appointment, baby?" she purred.

"No," Carlucci said, his voice as angry-sounding as I imagined he was. "I'm looking for Maggie Reid."

I heard him walking toward us, pacing and examining.

"You must not know, sugar," Bonnie said. "She don't work here on a day to day basis no more."

His steps drew closer, stopping a few feet away from the shampoo station. "Where is she?" he asked, but it wasn't really a question. It was a command. Produce her. Now.

"Now, honey, I know you were probably attached to her way of doing you, but really, put yourself in our hands, and you'll look every bit as good."

He moved a few steps, pulling open the door to the closet.

"Hey," Bonnie said, "what are you doing?"

His footsteps moved across the floor and I heard the bathroom door open. At the same time I heard the parole officer cross the floor, her flats making an authoritative slap as she walked up behind Carlucci.

"Excuse me, sir," she said.

I don't know because I couldn't see what she did, but I could only assume that she let him see her gun and her badge.

"If you're not here to get your hair cut, and if you don't have an appointment, well then I suggest you—"

"I was just leaving," Carlucci muttered. He crossed the floor, through the waiting area and over to the door. The women beside me held their breath, no one moving, except for Velmina's customer. Velmina's little old lady seemed to wake up out of her shampoo-induced stupor.

"Hey," she sang out, "was you looking for a little red-headed girl?"

Bonnie groaned under her breath.

Carlucci was sugar and spice. "Why, I sure was," he said. "Have you seen her?"

I held my breath, my toes curling in the frigid water.

"No," she said. "I just wondered. I used to have me a little redheaded girl what cut my hair, but she ran off with the circus. Ain't that some shit?"

Velmina laughed, a high-pitched, hysterical shriek of laughter. "No, Mrs. Watkiss, Maggie didn't join the circus. She's a singer."

Mrs. Watkiss belched. "I didn't mean her. I meant this girl I used to know, another redheaded girl. Why, I saw Maggie just—"

"Just last month," Bonnie interrupted. "She did your hair for Brian's wedding."

"That was it," Velmina cooed. "Now here, let me dry you off."

Whatever Mrs. Watkiss would've said was muffled by the thick white towel Velmina used to dry her hair, and Carlucci, sensing defeat, opened the door and stomped out.

For an entire thirty seconds, no one made a sound, until the parole officer called out "All clear!" As soon as she said that, we all screamed, jumping up to high-five each other and dance around the shampoo stand.

Only Bonnie seemed restrained. When I noticed this, I stopped and looked at her, our eyes locking. "Okay," she said, "what's all this about?"

The others stopped too, but Bonnie was having none of it. "Me and Maggie are going to have a little powwow," she said. "Velmina, you go on with your customer. And Charlene, I'll call you. Thanks for sticking around. The next cut's on me." Then she turned to Rozetta. "Good thinking with that face cream, but did you really have to crack open the hundred-dollar jar of Egyptian mud?"

Rozetta batted her long, fake lashes. "A crisis is a crisis. Besides, we get it wholesale for twenty bucks. Don't worry, I won't let it go to waste!"

Bonnie sighed as Rozetta walked away. "I got dogs smarter than that young'un," she said. "If she wasn't Mark's girlfriend, she'd be out of here."

"Now, Bon, you gotta admit that the cream idea was pretty darn slick." I pulled a tissue from its box and began wiping the gunk off of my face.

Bonnie sighed. "You know why I hired her?" Our eyes met in the mirror. Bonnie dropped her tone down to a whisper. "On account of Mark works nights. I figure with Rozetta here, she won't be over at my house sleeping with my eighteen-year-old son!"

Bonnie fumbled in her smock for a pack of cigarettes and motioned to me to follow her out the back door and onto the little covered stoop that overlooked the bail bond office.

We stepped outside and Bonnie lit up without hesitation.

"It's gonna kill you," I said, waving the smoke away.

"Yeah, maybe one day, but that fella that was just here looks like he'll be the death of you a lot sooner." Bonnie took a drag on her cigarette and squinted through the smoke. "So what's up? And why is Vernell in jail, really, because as much as I hate him for what he's done to you, he ain't no cold-blooded killer."

I leaned back against the hard, red brick wall and shut my eyes for a second. Then I told her everything.

"So, I don't know what Vernell's done with the money. If Vernell didn't kill Nosmo, then I've got to figure out who did."

Bonnie was listening, smoking her second cigarette. "Who's on the short list?"

I thought for a moment. "In no particular order, Nosmo's girlfriend was drinking with Vernell and Nosmo before Vernell passed out. Maybe she shot him and took the money."

"Huh," Bonnie said. "A woman killin' for greed. Now who'da thunk that?" Then she laughed. "Who else?"

"Maybe one of Nosmo's rivals. Maybe it was all a big setup. If Nosmo was in the Redneck Mafia, maybe one of them took him out. It happens all the time in the real Mafia."

Bonnie stubbed her cigarette out against a brick and tossed the butt into a far corner of the little courtyard.

"Listen," she said, "you know anything about the Redneck Mafia?" I shook my head. "Well I do," she said. "They're a loose-knit bunch of men who pull construction scams. If Nosmo was laundering money, or lending it, there'd be plenty of folks ready to rip him off or take over. Maybe that fits, what with Vernell set up to look like the shooter. Had to be someone who don't know Vernell well enough to know he's a big 'fraidy cat."

I shrugged. "Could be Bess King."

Bonnie's eyebrow shot up. "The dear widow?"

"Yeah, think of it. She loses an abusive husband, she gains three million dollars, plus Nosmo's insurance money, and if Vernell's been ripped off, she could've taken his money, too."

Bonnie shook her head. "You know," she said, "Vernell's got a brain the size of two BBs rattling around loose in a freight car. When it comes to women, Vernell lets the little head do the thinking, and look where it's got him." She stopped herself, looked over at me, and shrugged. "You were his only exception. And what did he do? Run away from his one shot at normalcy. I'll just never understand that. Rodney was the same exact way . . ."

And she was off. Bonnie'd be talking about Rodney for the next half hour, and given the least encouragement by her next customer, she'd talk about him for the next hour. Some things just die hard, I reckon, and the marriage of Bonnie and Rodney Miller was certainly a weed that wouldn't die easy in Bonnie's memory.

As for my situation, I had a murder to investigate, without the help of two particularly irritating men. That would take some doing. I just needed an afternoon alone to work. Surely I could escape the watchful eye of Tony Carlucci for that long.

Twenty-two

Bonnie's car was an aging Toyota van that had seen better days a few years before she bought it. It was reliable and unobtrusive. In short, it was the perfect vehicle for an afternoon spent snooping.

I ducked out the back door of the salon, high-tailed it the few feet to the driver's-side door, and was freedom bound within seconds, turning off the tiny street where the Curly-Que sat and out onto Greene Street. The radio was blaring Reba's latest, and I was humming along, too busy concentrating on my next step to sing the harmony.

Nosmo King's girlfriend might hold the piece I needed to clear Vernell, but if she did then it probably meant she'd killed her beloved, or at least helped to plan it. I thought back to her behavior at the funeral reception and couldn't quite picture the sobbing, black-haired Pauline as a killer. And then I thought of her friend, the bleached-blond Christine. Now there was a cold-blooded vixen. Maybe the two of them together could've killed Nosmo King, but Pauline wasn't sharp enough or hard enough to do the job alone.

"You are just the last of the naive innocents, Maggie Reid," I said aloud. "Do you really think that all murderers have to look like the posters on the post office walls? Pauline could've pulled that trigger for two million dollars and been acting the grief-stricken girlfriend three days later if it meant saving herself."

But she'd seemed so certain that Bess King had killed Nosmo. Either way, Bess King was my starting point. If she'd hired Tony, maybe she knew about Nosmo's girlfriend. I turned the van toward the northeast and began the drive out toward Brown Summit. I looked into the rearview mirror, saw no one I recognized, and drove on, satisfied that Tony Carlucci was sitting on the hood of my car, fuming.

Just as quickly, I flashed to my last image of Marshall Weathers, standing outside the jail, watching me ride off with Carlucci. In that brief second, the pain overwhelmed me, taking my breath away.

"You weak-willed woman," I said. "What is wrong with you? You let a man see you naked for the first time in God knows how long, and the next thing you know, you think you're in love." I turned onto Route 29 and headed north. "Desperate and dependent, that's what you are." I merged into the early afternoon traffic. "You weren't this way last week. What's wrong with you, getting all upset over another stupid man? He told you he wasn't looking for a relationship." But that was it. He wasn't looking to get hooked up and here I was seeing that as a challenge.

It was the raw hurt in his eyes. It was the way he smiled when he took me into his arms, the way he held me as I fell asleep. It was all too much. I hadn't ever felt like that. It only made sense I magnified it into meaning more to him than it really did.

"Can't make a soufflé out of turnips and hog jowls," I said, quoting Mama. The car chirped in agreement, and then chirped again.

I looked at the console. What was that noise? It was insistent and regular, and quite loud. I listened and heard it again, coming from Bonnie's tape holder. Bonnie, ever technologically aware, had a cell phone, the better to keep tabs on her six kids and the errant, estranged Rodney.

I picked it up out of a tape slot and opened the receiver. "Hello?" I said cautiously.

Bonnie's voice crackled to life inside the van. "Sugar, how're you doing?"

"How'm I doing? You just saw me ten minutes ago. What do you mean, how am I doing? What's wrong? Is somebody there with you?"

A cautious "Yes."

"Is it Carlucci?" If he was there threatening her . . .

"Nope, babe, can't say it is."

"Male?"

"Oh Lord, yes!"

Damn him! "Weathers?"

"Well bless my soul," Bonnie exclaimed.

"Does he know you're talking to me?"

"Well, sweetie, I just called to see if you were on your way home from school."

"I see. Put him on."

"I was hoping it might go that way," she said, and sighed. "It's always worth a good listen, especially if you've got a past history."

I was pulling off of 29 and onto the exit to the King ranch. What did it matter if I talked to him? He didn't know where I was.

"Bonnie, he's an idiot, just like they all are. When you look at him, I want you to think Rodney."

Bonnie laughed. "Nah, I ain't never seen this one flash his butt in the back of a pickup. Somehow I don't think it's the same."

She handed the phone to Weathers. I heard her speak to him first. "I had to see did she want to talk to you, but being as how you think it's urgent, I guess she will."

His deep voice rumbled in my ear. "Maggie, where are you?"

"Weathers, state your business or move on."

"I need to see you." *Beg me,* I thought.

I pulled off to the side of the road, across from the King farm, and sat staring at the bass pond.

"I don't see that we have anything to say. I think we've covered it all."

"Sheila called me after you left." And with that one statement, my heart froze and he had my complete attention.

"What did she want?" I kept my tone casual, as if it didn't shock me that she'd call him.

"She knew we'd arrested Vernell. She was upset."

"Well, do you blame her?"

My face flamed up and I could feel my neck flush. Could he have no feeling for what she had to be going through? Did he not know she'd be devastated?

"She said she's coming to talk to me. I just thought you might want to know, maybe even be here with her."

"What? What do you mean, she's coming to see you? She can't come see you!"

Marshall chuckled. "Maggie, since when does anybody stop Sheila from doing anything she wants to do?"

"Do you not get it?" I screamed. "Nosmo King's money is missing. It's Redneck Mafia money, Marshall. They want it back. Don't you see that as a danger to Sheila?"

"Maggie, calm down. She couldn't be safer once she's here. She's probably driving over from school or your house. I'll send a couple of cars out to watch out for her. She'll be fine."

"No, Marshall, she won't be fine. She's with my sister in Virginia. How's she going to get to you? I had her safe. You shouldn't have let her come."

"Maggie, I didn't know. I just wanted to help her out, and that's what I intend to do."

The trees surrounding the back side of the bass pond began to sway gently with a breeze that gusted up. Clouds skittered across the sky, gray and white, signaling an approaching front. What had been a beautiful fall day was beginning to turn into something far more ominous.

"Someone killed Carlucci's dog last night. I was there. I think they were trying to get to me. You can't tell me

Sheila's safe. Now I've gotta go. I'm gonna call my sister and tell her to hang on to Sheila."

I hung up on him, dialing Darlene's number as fast as I could.

"Hey." Darlene's husband, Earl, never fooled with social niceties.

"Earl, where's Sheila?"

Earl paused for a second and I nearly went through the tiny phone after him.

"Well," he said slowly, "I reckon she's still at the drugstore, but it has been awhile. Said she was going after some feminine products. Guess that takes some time to figure on what you want and all."

"Earl! Did she go with Darlene?"

I was beating my hand on the steering wheel, trying to keep from screaming and making matters way worse.

"Nah, Darlene's down to the studio. Sheila didn't go with her on account of she didn't feel good and she needed to go to town. She borrowed my pickup."

"Earl, listen to me. I think Sheila's run off."

"Not without her puppy," he said. "Sheila don't go nowhere without that thing. And he's right out here in his . . ." I heard the trailer door swing open and Earl step out onto the stoop. "Aw shoot! Dadgummit!"

"The dog's gone, isn't he, Earl?"

"Uh-huh."

"All right, listen here, I'm going to call you every hour. Don't you leave that phone. You hear me, Earl?"

Earl sounded miserable. "I'm sorry, honey," he said.

I couldn't help him out. Instead I hung up, jammed the phone in my pocket and sat in the van, thinking. If I was calm enough about it, I could realize that Sheila was in an unfamiliar pickup, headed directly to the Greensboro Police Department and Detective Marshall Weathers. That in itself should keep her safe. I had to focus on removing the source of our danger. I had to find the money.

I put the van in gear, crossed the two-lane, and started up Nosmo King's driveway. As I pulled to a stop, Bess King emerged from the door of the barn, a red bandanna tied around her head, kerchief style, wearing faded jeans and an oversized denim shirt. She was wearing white tap shoes.

As I drew closer, I realized she was sweating, red-faced from the exertion of dancing.

"I tried to call you again a little while ago," she said.

I just stared at her. How could she be dancing with Nosmo dead and Vernell in jail charged with his murder?

"I can't go home," I said. "Someone thinks I might know where Nosmo's missing money is." And I began to wonder if Bess King might be that someone.

Bess wiped her brow with the tail of her shirt, and held the barn door open. "Come on in," she said. "Let's talk." She saw me staring at her and put it together. "I dance because it's the only thing that keeps me going. If I couldn't dance, I'd go crazy with it all." She walked across the room, grabbed a plastic cup left over from Nosmo's funeral, and ran tap water into it. She stood with her back to me, drinking, until the cup was drained dry. When she turned and walked back toward me, she was all business.

"Tony said you went to see Vernell this morning," she said, and for the first time her expression changed, a spasm of pain moving quickly across her features. "I'm going tonight, when they have visiting hours."

She led me over to a round table and sank down in a chair. I sat across from her and put my hands out on the table, palms down.

"I'm just going to lay this straight out," I said. "I'm not much for dancing around a subject when the best way in the house is through the front door." Bess nodded, watching me.

"I won't ask if you killed your husband. I don't reckon you'd tell me if you did, because if you're the killing kind, then you're the lying kind, the kind to let Vernell Spivey take the fall over something he didn't do. So I won't ask you about that. Same way I won't ask you about the money."

Bess's face got redder and her eyes sparkled with anger, but I didn't give a rat's tail about what she was feeling.

"Vernell didn't kill your husband. I'm going to prove that

one way or the other. What I need to know from you is how long you've been seeing Vernell and what you know about Nosmo's girlfriend."

Bess blinked, pulled the kerchief off her head and ran her fingers through her curls.

"Just for the record," she said, her voice taut and angry, "I love Vernell Spivey and we intend to spend the rest of our lives together. And if you think I'm just sitting back twiddling my thumbs while Vernell goes to jail, I'm not. Tony Carlucci is working for me, and if he wasn't so busy covering your tail, he might be a lot closer to finding Nosmo's killer."

Well, if she wasn't a little fireball. I raised one eyebrow and cocked my head to the left.

"You haven't answered my questions."

Bess King never looked away, and I had to give her grudging credit for that. "I started seeing Vernell two months ago. He was here talking to Nosmo and I invited him to stay for dinner."

Bess's eyes grew damp and she stared off beyond me. "He was such a kind man," she whispered. "I couldn't see why he was talking to Nosmo, but that was before I knew about Nosmo and the men he worked for."

"What about his girlfriend?"

Bess focused back on me. "Pauline Conrad?" Bess snorted. "She was nothing but a cheap plaything to Nosmo. He likes them young and pretty and stupid. So Pauline was just perfect. He'd had her for about two years, kept her in a little condo on Elm Street. Two years is usually his limit. That's about when they get difficult and he gets rid of them."

She must've seen the look on my face because she jumped in with an explanation. "No, not like that. He doesn't get rid of them like that. He buys them out and cuts them off." She frowned. "You look surprised, like why would I stick around if I knew all that? Well, I'll tell you why. Nosmo wouldn't let me leave. He said he'd find me and kill me if I ever tried to walk away."

Bess tapped the table with the tips of her long acrylic nails.

"And baby, Nosmo King was one to make good on a threat."

She lifted a curl away from the side of her forehead, exposing an ugly pink scar. "You see that?" she asked. "That's what happened the only time I ever asked him for a divorce. He hit me with the butt end of his pistol and I wound up with thirty-two stitches." The curls fell back in place. "And yes," she said caustically, "he said the only way I'd leave was over his dead body."

"Where were you last Friday?" I asked.

Bess King laughed. "At the Twilight Motel, waiting on Vernell. He never showed."

And that's when I caught her. Bess King was lying.

"Bess, I've got a witness says they saw you go into the Twilight Motel with Vernell."

Her face changed, for a second there was a flicker of uncertainty, and then nothing. "I mean later. I went in with Vernell early, but then he left, said he had something to take care of and for me to wait."

I sat back in my chair and just stared at her for a long moment. I tried to rock my chair back on two legs like Weathers does, but I couldn't do it and look tough. I wanted to look hard, and like I'd made her for a liar.

"Bess," I said, "a cop taught me that when a person lies, their eyes cut up and to the left." Actually, I couldn't remember which direction it was, but I figured I had a fifty-fifty shot at being right anyhow. "You are telling me a whopper."

"I am not!" she cried.

I just looked at her, like Mama would if I'd been fibbing to her.

"Then make me believe you," I said.

I watched her wrestle with it, tossing and turning her options over and over in her head. While she stewed, I looked around the barn again. Every bit of the reception had been cleared away. Even the trashcans stood empty.

At last Bess made a decision, raising her head and placing her hands on the table in front of her, folding them together like a child in church. I figured she wanted me to believe her.

"Vernell was the one who told me about Nosmo," she said, her voice hushed and soft, so soft I had to lean in to hear her. "I'm so stupid, I actually thought the gas station was his only business. Then I found out he was a banker for the Redneck Mafia." Her face twisted with contempt. "That's how come he had so many friends. I couldn't see why anyone would like him at all, but Vernell set me straight. They don't like him, they need him."

I said nothing, just sat there watching her twist her hands together, over and over, as if washing them clean.

"Vernell needed money. He thought Nosmo was his only option. He was in big-time trouble." She looked up at me and frowned. "He said he didn't want to tell you about it. He figured he'd messed things up enough."

So he told her. Well, it figured. I was more of a mother to Vernell than a confidante. And that was how it had to be.

"We didn't mean to fall in love," she said. "What woman in her right mind does?" A quick smile flashed across her face, then vanished. "But he was so kind, and he just listened and listened. I guess it just sort of happened. Next thing you knew, I was no better than Nosmo, sneaking off to motels and hiding lingerie."

She rubbed her hands across the surface of the table, back and forth as if soothing herself.

"I didn't know he was going to ask Nosmo to give me a divorce. All I knew was that Vernell was going to meet Nosmo and tell him he didn't need the money after all. He said the price was too high. Nosmo would want Vernell in his pocket. Vernell don't do that. But Nosmo was expecting to give him three million dollars."

Three million dollars? Vernell Spivey and three million dollars? The idea blew me away. Maybe the mobile home lot and the satellite dish business together were worth a million, but not three. How would Vernell have paid it back?

Bess looked up at me. "It would've worked out fine," she said, "but then Nosmo got himself killed and now we're all in a mess."

Bonnie's cell phone rang, startling both of us. I fished

into the pocket of my jacket, drew out the phone, and flipped open the lid.

"Just thought I'd let you know she's here," Weathers said.

"Good." The relief was clear in my voice and Weathers picked up on it.

"It's all right," he murmured. "I'm not going to let a thing happen to her."

"Well, I would appreciate it if you would not start in with her until I get there." I looked at my watch. "Give me fifteen minutes."

I didn't wait for an answer; instead I flipped the phone closed and hung up on him. For the briefest second I wondered if Tracy the cadet was giving my daughter hot chocolate and making nice.

Bess looked at the phone. "Guess you need to go, huh?"

I stood up, pushed the phone back into my jacket pocket, and scowled at her. "Maybe this is something you and Vernell need to discuss tonight when you go to see him. When three million dollars is missing, people get angry. Nosmo's boss is looking to get his money back. Since he can't get to Vernell to convince him, he's threatening his family. If Nosmo didn't know about you, then his boss probably didn't know about you. That leaves me and Sheila on the front line. Vernell is jeopardizing his daughter's life in an attempt to make money."

"That's not fair!" Bess said. "It's not like that at all. He's trying to give Sheila a future. We don't know where Nosmo's money is. Hell, for two days I didn't even know where Vernell was!"

I seized on that. "Where was he for two days?"

Bess shook her head. "He can't remember. He started drinking with Nosmo. He'd been sober for a month, but the strain of facing Nosmo down was too much, I reckon. He tied one on good."

Bess had the earnest face of a do-gooder, an I-know-he'll-change-with-enough-love face. I'd been the same way with Vernell when I was twenty, but years of him letting me down had hardened me to reality. I didn't think Vernell would ever change, not enough. This latest foolishness seemed to prove it.

I left Bess sitting at the table and walked back out to Bonnie's van. I was no better off for talking to Bess than I had been before, except that I knew who Nosmo's girlfriend was and I had an idea about where to find her. But why wasn't Marshall Weathers interested in Bess as a suspect? And why wasn't the Redneck Mafia going to her for answers? And where had Vernell been for two days? What if he'd taken the money in an alcohol-induced blackout, and then lost it? What if he'd killed Nosmo and couldn't remember?

I started up the van and began to move down the driveway. I couldn't think about it all anymore. I had one thing on my mind: getting to Sheila and making sure she was safe. I had to make Weathers believe that we were in danger, and I had to figure out how to protect my daughter. I reached for the radio, hit the button, and was immediately rewarded with Patty Loveless.

"I just hate country music."

I screamed and swerved, almost throwing the van into the path of a car out on the two-lane. Carlucci was right behind me, his voice in my ear.

"Why did you run off, Maggie?"

"Listen," I said, my eyes on the road as I pulled out onto the two-lane. "You are not my father. I can take care of myself. And frankly, I can get to the bottom of things easier if I don't have some overgrown biker following me around!"

"Now, that's just stupid," he said. "What you could do is get yourself killed a whole lot easier. I was trying to help you out, and you're fighting me at every turn. What is that?"

I accelerated and turned off onto Route 29, headed for downtown Greensboro and the police department.

"Carlucci, I'm sure you mean well, but face it, your job was to find Vernell and you've done that, so why are you still hanging around?"

He was silent for a moment.

"There is the matter of the missing money," he said. "And then, there's you and Sheila."

"What?" I jerked around to look at him, almost ran off the road, and had to pull hard to avoid going into a ditch.

"Watch the road, Maggie!"

"If you'd come up here where I can see you, and not slink back there in the shadows, I might not be running off the road. And furthermore," I added as he moved up beside me, "what are you doing hiding in my vehicle anyway?"

"It wasn't hard to figure where you'd go," he said. "Nothing about you is hard. In fact, I have come to the conclusion that you are probably too stupid to take care of yourself." He was just warming up. "Obviously, being attacked in your own home hasn't scared you off, so I doubt anything else will either. But you're gonna die if I don't watch out for you."

"Why don't you look for the money your way, and I'll look mine?"

Carlucci turned in his seat. "Maggie, I'm going out on a limb here, and if I'm wrong, well, I'll apologize later, but I'm saying it anyway. I think you're putting yourself in danger to avoid looking at what's really going on."

"What?"

Carlucci shrugged. "Yeah, that's what I think. We both know you can't find that missing money any better than me or the cops or Nosmo's people. You could be somewhere safe, taking care of your little girl, but no, you're out here, and any smart person's gotta wonder why."

I was almost on Eugene Street, a short hop to the police department. Five minutes from now I'd be sitting with my daughter, listening to Weathers try and worm his way out of having arrested Vernell Spivey.

"And I suppose you're so smart you've got it all figured," I said.

"Maybe not that smart, but I've got ideas. Look at what just happened here," he said. "I tell you that one of my reasons for being around is to look after you and Sheila, and what do you do? You start in on me. You change the subject. You're scared of me, Maggie. I frighten you 'cause there's nothing holding me back. I am completely available, and I like you, and you know it. So go on, Maggie, run away. Just don't get your kid killed over it, okay?"

I stopped the van, pulling it over against the curb into a tow-away zone. I couldn't think. I couldn't hear for the roar of blood that thundered in my ears. I wanted to kill him.

"That is so totally unfair!" I yelled.

Carlucci just looked at me.

"I would not jeopardize my daughter's life! That is not true! I can't believe you'd even say something like that!"

I wanted to tear him apart. I wanted to scream and scream and scream until he went away or said he was wrong and I was right, but he just sat there, waiting.

"Vernell needs me," I said. "No one believes he's innocent."

Tony raised an eyebrow. "Bess King does. He doesn't need you. You need him. You need to be needed. You wouldn't know what to do if someone wanted you just for you and not for what you can do for them."

"Shut up!"

"Marshall Weathers," he said, "another prime example. I didn't have to spend thirty minutes with the man to see what a piece of work he is. You can still see the pale spot on his ring finger, Maggie. He's just another wounded bird."

I lashed out at him then, swinging my hand up to hit his face, stopped by his hand grabbing my arm.

"Let me go!" I jerked my arm back, but he wouldn't release me. He pulled me closer, leaning across until I felt myself backing away.

"See," he whispered, "you're afraid of me."

"No I'm not," I said, my voice even through clenched teeth. But my heart was racing, and the van was suddenly too close and confining.

Carlucci reached over and hit the button that held my seatbelt in place. He moved, grabbed my legs, and turned me to face him.

I froze, knowing what was coming, remembering the last time he'd kissed me and called me scared. I was not going to back away. I'd show him it didn't matter. And when he reached out to cup my chin, I went to him. His kiss was gentle, but mine was not. I pushed. I kissed him hard, ignoring his attempt to be tender, until he at last responded as I had, giving in to some force that ran between us like a current.

"There," I said, pushing away and wiping my mouth with the back of my hand. "Still think I'm so frightened?" I looked at him and hated him.

I saw the hurt flare up then pass away and the inky blackness return to his eyes. "You are really terrified," he said. "Whoever hurt you cut deep, didn't he?"

I reached for my seatbelt and snapped it back in place. "If I need a therapist, I'll pay one," I said, and pulled back out into traffic.

Twenty-three

I didn't need to worry about Sheila Lynn Spivey. It was Detective Marshall J. Weathers who needed prayers and divine intervention. By the time I dumped Tony Carlucci out of Bonnie's van, returned it to her, and scooted over to the police department, half an hour had passed and Weathers was firmly roasting on the skewer of Sheila's rapierlike anger. There is nothing like a scornful adolescent to rattle the cage of your self-assurance. And Miss Sheila was one dynamite cage shaker.

Weathers led me to her. He had not isolated her in an interview room, knowing that this would not be appropriate, but the price he paid was that every detective and support staff member of C.I.D. had full access to the exact extent of Sheila's wrath.

"She's been giving me hell," he said when he came for me.

"Uh-huh," I answered.

"I can't seem to get her to calm down. She just goes on and on. I told her we're looking at all the evidence. I told her that I didn't want to arrest her daddy, but I had no choice. Why won't she listen?"

He seemed genuinely perplexed. I said nothing, just followed silently behind him, thankful that my little girl was indeed all right.

When we rounded the corner into his cubicle, I saw her. She sat across from his desk in a battered metal chair with a vinyl seat cushion that had ripped and spilled a thin crumble of ancient, spongy filling.

Her legs were sprawled out in front of her, crossed at the ankles, and she slouched in the chair with her arms crossed and a giant wad of bubble gum stuck in her mouth. On her lap was a puppy of indistinguishable heritage. Despite her attempts to dress otherwise, Sheila looked five years old.

"Hey, babe," I said, stroking her hair as I pulled up a chair next to her.

Sheila looked over at me with the same frown she'd been reserving for Weathers. "Whatever," she said softly. Then, sensing a probable ally, she straightened up, glared at Weathers and turned to face me.

"Mama," she said, "you're, like, over him, right?"

I groaned silently and felt myself melt under the intensity of her gaze.

"Sheila, let's focus on what's going on here. I thought I told you to stay on Darlene and Earl's farm. They are worried sick. And technically, you stole your uncle's truck."

Sheila sighed impatiently. "Whatever, Mama," she said. "But somebody had to take care of Daddy."

And the awful realization hit. I was raising her to be just like me.

"No, honey, Daddy can take care of himself."

"From a freaking jail cell? Oh, I think not." She turned her attention back to Weathers. "All right. You've got Daddy's gun as the murder weapon. But there was no gunpowder residue on his hands, was there?"

Sheila tossed her hair like she'd just played a trump card and Marshall hid a smile.

"Too much time had elapsed, Sheila," he said. "The test wouldn't have shown anything."

"So, like, what would be his motive?"

"There's three million dollars missing."

"Oh well, like, duh. My dad is so stupid he'd shoot someone when everyone knew he was going off with the guy? My dad is not that stupid."

Before Weathers could answer, I stopped the process. "Baby, this won't get you anywhere. I've called in Roth Carruthers. He'll try and get Daddy out on bail tomorrow."

Sheila drew her long legs up and stood, cradling the sleeping puppy in her arms. She looked at each of us. "So, this is being adult, huh? You call a big-shot lawyer and try to act all civil about it." Her voice dripped with rage and contempt. "Well," she said, looking at Weathers, "I don't think that's honest. I say you're a big, stupid jerk. And I say, if you come near me and my mom, I'll . . ."

"Sheila, stop."

Weathers looked sad. "I'm sorry about this, Sheila. I can understand why you need to be angry with me."

"Oh, bite me, cop!" she said, and took off.

"I'm sorry," I said. Marshall Weathers had done a terrible thing. For the first time I found myself doubting Vernell's innocence, and that felt horrible.

"Maggie," Weathers said, "I heard what you said about being worried for your safety. I'm going to put someone on your house, or wherever it is you go. If you take Sheila back to Virginia, I'll call up there and get some coverage too."

The moment might've turned, could've gone any one of a number of ways, I was so confused, but I didn't have to worry about that. Tracy the cadet chose that moment to make a well-timed entrance into Marshall's cubicle. I didn't doubt for one second that she'd been listening to our conversation.

"Mama," Sheila called from somewhere out in the corridor, "let's get out of this place!"

I couldn't have agreed with her more or moved any faster.

"Hey, Marsh," Tracy said, "can you pick me up tonight? My car's in the shop."

Yeah, probably busted from all the rolling around they'd done in it the night before, I figured. And then I found myself staring at the third finger of Marshall's left hand, looking for the pale indentation. I caught myself, caught Marshall watching me, and spun around.

"Mama!" Sheila called.

I tore out of the cubicle like the *Queen Mary* headed for England, sailing past Sheila and right on down the hallway toward the exit. Sheila followed me, her heavy shoes making loud clomping noises that echoed off the walls of the police department corridors. I waited until we were out in the parking lot to take on my hell-raising daughter.

"Sheila, I know you're mad about your dad, but there's something you need to understand. He's in big trouble and it's very dangerous for you to be around right now."

Sheila's puppy woke up and stared at me with huge, liquid brown eyes. Sheila was staring too, but her stare was hard and unfriendly.

"I'll be eighteen next year," she said. "According to the law, I could be declared an emancipated minor right now. I know how to shoot a gun. Daddy taught me. I took two self-defense classes and knocked Mr. Gray right on his butt, not just once, but every single time we sparred."

She patted her puppy's head absently and continued her lecture.

"My psychology teacher says that my reaction time and my cognitive thinking skills are peaking. So, I think I'm gonna stay right here and help you."

"Your reaction time may be peaking, but your judgment skills are nowhere near functional." I squared off, my hands on my hips and a frown on my face.

"Mama, you are starting a power struggle, a control battle. That is, like, so totally unnecessary. We should work together on the problem, not let it come between us."

What kind of Martian was her psychology teacher?

"I'm not going back," Sheila warned. "And if you take

me, I'll just run back here and not tell you where I am."

Now what? It was one of those mother-daughter crisis moments where you wish your own mama was around to clue you in. I looked at Sheila, I looked at her mangy dog, and I sighed.

"Good!" Sheila cried. "I knew you'd see it my way. Now, where are we going?"

I shook my head and started walking off toward my car, then stopped. Why take my car when everybody knew it was mine?

"Let's take the pickup," I said. "I'll drive."

"Mama," Sheila started, then for some reason let it go and handed me the keys.

We climbed up into the cab of Earl's old Ford pickup. He'd had a run-in with a fence post or something because you had to pull hard to close the door, and when you did, the hinges screamed in agony. It was a clunker, but when I stuck the key in the ignition and turned, it roared to life with all of its V-8 power.

We bounced out of the lot onto Washington Street and headed for Elm. There was only one set of condominiums large enough to hide a well-kept bimbo, and I headed right for it.

"What did you name him?" I asked.

Sheila looked down at her puppy, stroked its head, and was rewarded by a frenzy of licking.

"Wombat."

I laughed in spite of myself. "You named a dog Wombat? Why?"

Sheila hitched him up in her arms like a baby. "I don't know, on account of he's so strange looking, I guess. I mean, he's got black hair, and brown and gray and white and yellow. It's curly up front and straight in the back. His legs are long and he doesn't have a tail. Mama, when he's happy, he wags his little stump so hard it knocks him over! Isn't he cute?"

I looked over at Wombat. Wombat's eyelashes were longer than Rozetta's fakes, and his eyes were a whole lot prettier.

"I guess he does have a way about him."

We pulled into the lot of the ten-story condo building and stared up at it.

"Now what?" she asked. "Which one is it?"

I leaned on the steering wheel. "I don't know."

"Mama!" Sheila said. "There's gotta be ten gazillion apartments in there." She sighed. "Wait a minute, I'll go find out. What's the name?"

"Pauline Conrad, but the apartment may be in Nosmo King's name."

Sheila had the door open and was almost gone before I could stop her.

"Sheila, they won't tell you where she lives. It's part of their security system."

Sheila jumped out of the truck, handed me the puppy, and straightened her camisole top.

"Well, like, duh. Of course not. I'm not going to ask them like that. I'm going to ask them like a stupid harmless kid would ask them. Just wait here."

She started out, stopped, and walked back up to the passenger-side window.

"So, like, if I'm not back in, like, five minutes . . ." She paused for effect. "Call the freakin' cops!"

As I watched, Sheila walked across the parking lot, hitching her school backpack up on her shoulder and slouching. She walked up to the entrance, opened the door, and disappeared inside. Within two minutes she was back, a triumphant smile on her face.

"Ten A," she said.

"How did you do that?"

Sheila sighed, as if the explanation was too much for her. "I just told them that I was supposed to stay with my aunt after school, but I couldn't remember the apartment number."

Sheila smirked. "That is sooo adolescent, don't you think? Teenagers just never listen. And then, after he told me, he went right off upstairs to help some little old lady move a chair. That is, like, so dumb. What if I was a criminal or something?"

I handed Wombat to her. "You might oughta walk him," I said. "I'll be back in fifteen minutes."

"I'm coming with you," she said.

I shot her a look that said, don't even try me.

"All right, you don't need to take on an attitude!"

I walked away and left her standing there, her ridiculous puppy in her arms. This was going to be a hell of an investigation.

I swept past the empty doorman's stand, hit the elevator, and rode up to the tenth floor. "A" was the first door on the left. I walked across the thickly carpeted hallway and punched the doorbell. It rang like a high-class doorbell, a deep dinging that sounded nothing like a shrill apartment buzzer.

I waited, heard footsteps cross the foyer, and then waited some more as I was checked out through the peephole and a decision made.

Finally the door swung open, just wide enough to stretch the security chain. It was not Pauline Conrad who answered the door; it was her blonde friend, Christine.

"Hey," she said, her voice wary. "You're that girl from the funeral. What're you doing here?"

She did not seem at all pleased to see me.

"I need to talk to Pauline, please." I smiled and tried to look harmless, like I'd dropped by for a glass of tea.

"She's not here," Christine said, but she was lying. I could hear water running in the background and someone was humming.

"I really do need to talk to her," I insisted.

"About what?" Christine's expression looked skeptical. Her eyes were narrowed and her mouth was a flat line of displeasure with what she was hearing.

"Nosmo King," I said. "She and my ex-husband were probably the last two people to see him alive. I just wanted to talk to her about—"

Christine cut me off. "You're Vernell Spivey's wife? Well, we for sure don't want to talk to you."

"Fine," I said, "then I'll just talk to the police about it."

It always works on TV, but Christine wasn't buying it.

"Fine then," she said. "Talk to them." And closed the door.

I stood out in the hall listening to her footsteps dying away, hoping to hear her talking to Pauline, but there was not a sound.

"Great," I muttered. "Some detective I am."

I rode the elevator back downstairs, walked outside, and found Sheila and Wombat deep in conversation with a young guy with long stringy hair and a goatee. Sheila had a knack for attracting oddballs.

I walked to the truck, pulled open the squeaky door, and climbed up inside. Sheila noticed me, waved me off, and continued talking. I watched her through the rearview mirror, watching her toss her head and laugh at something the boy said. She was so young, and despite her façade, so vulnerable.

After a few moments, Sheila stood, gathering Wombat up into her arms and saying her good-byes. The kid watched her walk away and I watched them both in the mirror. Young love.

I cranked the truck as she stepped up into the cab.

"I believe you could find a boy to talk to in an all-girls school, Sheila."

Sheila smiled and tried to speak without moving her lips. "Mama, just wait until he can't see us."

I shrugged and pulled back out onto Elm Street. I debated for a moment about where to go and then figured my house was best, even though it was broad daylight.

Sheila startled me when she started talking again. "Mama, that was no boy, as in attractive, go-out-with type boy. He works as a maintenance guy at the condos."

"Nothing's wrong with a service profession," I started.

"Mama, get a grip! That's not what I'm saying. I'm saying he's worked on that girl's apartment and he was telling me all about her." Sheila took a deep breath. "Mama, she is, like, totally shallow, you know what I'm saying? Like totally not authentic. She was Nosmo King's, like, woman. He paid for everything. The apartment and all is in his name. Did you know that?"

I sighed. "Yes."

"Well, so, like, did you know that Nosmo was cheating on his girlfriend with her own girlfriend?"

Now she had me. I looked over at her. "What do you mean?"

Sheila sighed. "What do I mean? I mean, Todd said that once, when Pauline was out, he had to go in and do something to, like, her toilet or something. And guess what? That King guy was there, and so was this friend of Pauline's, some blonde girl that's always around. Well," she said, "the blonde girl was topless. See, they didn't know Todd was coming. And when he opened the door . . ."

Sheila started laughing. "The old fart was in his boxers and the blonde was like on his lap. The old guy jumps up and the blonde falls over and Todd said he was, like, too freaked to move." Wombat shifted in Sheila's lap, unable to get comfortable with the amount of wiggling Sheila was doing to tell the story.

"What happened?"

"What happened?" Sheila echoed. "The old guy, King, goes ballistic. He freaking screams at Todd for, like, five minutes before it dawns on him that Todd could dime him out to his girlfriend."

"Then what?"

"Todd just like stood there, grinning, until the old guy gives him, get this, a one hundred dollar bill, and tells him to forget about it, or else." Sheila shook her head. "Todd was, like, about to wet his pants then on account of he sees a gun out on the table. Todd is like a vegan. He's, like, totally nonviolent." She sighed. "I'm thinking he won't remember my number because he didn't have a pen."

I thought about Todd, the mental image of him burned into my memory, and hoped he wouldn't remember her number. On the other hand, Todd certainly was full of information about Pauline Conrad and her friends.

"So what else?" I asked.

"Mother," Sheila said, "like, isn't that enough!"

"Yeah, baby," I laughed. "That is actually a gracious plenty."

"Thank you," she said.

We drove on to the house, each lost in her thoughts. I had to figure out where to put Sheila so she'd feel a part of things and yet be safe. I had only two hours left before I was due at the Golden Stallion and something had to be done. I thought about Carlucci for a second, but just as quickly discarded him. No way was I subjecting us to him again. And then I thought about Marshall Weathers.

What Carlucci said wasn't true. Weathers and I had an understanding. He didn't want a relationship. Well, neither did I. I'd thought about it. My life was fine without a man in it. I had a great job, a great daughter, and lots of wonderful friends. If I wanted a relationship, I could have one any time at all. I just didn't want one. And of course I was feeling a little needy right now. Who wouldn't, with someone trying to kill you and get money from you that you don't have and with your ex in jail for murder?

"Humph!" I said, forgetting Sheila was there.

"So who are you thinking about, Mama?"

I shook my head. "Just life in general, babe."

We turned onto our street and were headed for the drive back into the alley when I spotted the patrol car.

"Oh great!" Sheila said. "Now he's having us staked out! If he's so worried why doesn't he let Daddy out?"

We swung around to the back, pulled up in the backyard, and climbed the stairs to the door.

Wombat, new to the situation, stepped over the threshold and sniffed. He trotted past us and walked right up to the spot where my intruder had died at Tony Carlucci's hands. Wombat sniffed, then yipped, and then without warning, urinated all over the floor.

"Oh gross!" Sheila cried.

I walked past her into the kitchen, picked up a roll of paper towels and a bottle of disinfectant, then handed them to my wrinkle-nosed daughter.

"Welcome to parenthood, baby," I said. "It's tough, but ultimately rewarding."

Sheila sighed. "Whatever."

Twenty-four

While Sheila cleaned up after Wombat, I listened to my messages. There were the usual assortment of hang-ups and solicitations, then Terry Griswald from the Mobile Home Kingdom came on.

"Ms. Reid," he said, his voice thin with anxiety. "The fellas heard about Vernell being arrested. I'm sorry, but done all of 'em walked out. I'm still here, though. Are you gonna be coming down anytime soon? I reckon we oughta talk. That VanScoy fella stopped by again. Said to tell you and Vernell it's seventy-five now. Well, all right, I guess. Call me."

He sounded desperate. I figured he was, too. Christmas would be coming up in six weeks. I knew he had a wife and new baby to think about. What was I going to do?

The next message was from Vernell himself. "Hey, baby," he said. "Listen, you've gotta take care of a couple of things for me." Yeah, right, like returning three million dollars to the Redneck Mafia. "Call Brenda McCoy at Cornerstone Realty and tell her to just hold on. I'll be ready to sign the contract in a couple of days. The same with the house, too. Tell her I want a full-price offer."

Then Vernell cleared his throat and hesitated. "Baby, listen, I don't want you to think nothing about this, but if she says anything about the Satellite Kingdom being up for sale, don't worry. I'm just selling off the land and the office. It's no big thing. I talked to the lawyer and all after you left. It don't look like I'll be leaving here for a little while, so I'm gonna need you to kinda step in and help me out." There was a pause and then Vernell spoke again, so softly I could almost not make out the two familiar words. "I'm sorry."

Sheila was standing in the doorway, listening, her eyes wide and red-rimmed.

"Why is Daddy in so much trouble?" she asked.

I shook my head. "I don't know, baby."

Wombat skittered into the room, sliding across the slick wooden floor, unable to stop himself before he crashed into the bed and fell backward. Sheila smiled and picked him up, snuggling him in her arms and burying her face in his soft fur.

The roar of a motorcycle running up into the backyard distracted the three of us. Tony Carlucci was back. How he'd managed to get back out to Bess King's farm, retrieve his bike, and return to Greensboro in such a short amount of time was beyond me, but I didn't care.

Sheila was past me, over to the door, outside, and down the steps. Tony smiled when he saw her, removed his helmet and pointed to little Wombat. As I watched from the doorway, she held the dog up to him and he slowly shook his head. He reached over and shut off the bike.

"What in the hell is that?" he said.

"Like, a dog," Sheila answered. "I think he looks like you." They laughed like old friends, until he looked up and saw me in the doorway.

"I suppose you're planning on working tonight," he said.

"Yep."

He looked at Sheila, watching her run after Wombat, her back to the two of us.

"How about I take her with me?"

"Not on that thing."

Sheila turned around, listening. "We can take the truck," she said. "That way Wombat won't be here alone. You know I can't leave him, don't you?" She turned to Tony, her face open and vulnerable. But he had gone dark on her. He stared past her, looking first at Wombat and then off down the alley. He was seeing Popeye. He was remembering and he was hurting.

It frightened Sheila. She didn't know and couldn't understand the rapid change that had come over Tony.

"He won't make a mess," she said, mistaking his hesitation.

Tony didn't answer her. Instead he rubbed his hands across his face and shook his head.

"Yeah, all right. We'll take the truck and drop your mama off at the club." The smile came back and the look he gave her reassured her. "But I'm gonna drag your ass out at two A.M. to go get her. This isn't some slumber party where you hang around painting your toenails and looking pretty. We've got some things to do. I can't be babysitting no kid, you got me?"

Sheila puffed up and gave him her best womanly look. "I'm not a kid. I can take care of myself, like, totally."

"Yeah, right," he said. "Whatever."

He'd done it. He'd worked her and she'd fallen for it.

"I've gotta take a shower and get changed," I said. "Why don't you two go pick up a pizza or something?"

Tony shook his head. "I'm not leaving you alone."

"You didn't see the patrol car in front of the house? I'll be fine. Go pick up a pizza and bring it back. You can drive the truck."

I reached into my pocket to fish out money, but Tony wouldn't take it.

"Wombat likes meat pizza," Sheila announced.

"Dogs don't get pizza. Dogs eat dog food."

Sheila was right back at him. "Wombat eats whatever I say he eats."

They argued all the way to the truck and were still fighting as they drove off. I watched them until they were out of sight, standing on my porch as the late afternoon sun dipped below the horizon. In the early evening dusk, the world seemed more sinister than it had a mere thirty minutes before. For a moment I felt as if someone were watching me, standing just outside my line of vision, following my every movement.

I shook it off, turned, and went inside, switching on every light I came to. The shades were still pulled down, the blinds and curtains closed. No one could see inside. No one could watch me here, but still I felt ill at ease. I walked through the house, into the living room and opened the front door. The cop car was gone.

"Okay," I muttered. "You were just here a minute ago. Where are you?"

It couldn't matter. I couldn't let this matter. Wherever he was, he'd be back. "It's probably just shift change," I said. "There'll be a new guy here any second. Go on, take your shower. Tony's picking up a pizza, but his bike's here. People will think he's here and I'm not."

But I couldn't shake the feeling of being watched. I closed the front door, locked it, and leaned against it. It was five fifteen by my watch. Outside people would be returning home from work or their classes at the college. Lights would start to pop on all over the neighborhood. No one would bother me now. It would be stupid to make a move now.

I walked into the bathroom, turned on the shower, and left to take my clothes off and grab my robe. I opened the closet door and felt the panic hit. I remembered him coming up behind me, throwing me against the far wall, his knife biting into my neck.

I raised my fingers up to touch the thin scab and felt myself begin to lose it. I froze, trembling, and crossed my arms to grab at my stomach.

"No, no, no," I moaned, rocking back and forth. "No. Stop this. It's okay. He's gone. It's okay." But nothing I said helped. I sank down onto the floor, aware of the sound of the shower, knowing that it ran on and on and I was powerless to stand up and go turn it off. The fear swept over me in wave after wave of icy nausea. I couldn't breathe.

As I sat, trying to regain some control, the back doorknob rattled, twisting slowly back and forth.

I screamed, drawing air deep into my lungs and pushing the sound out like a wall to keep the intruder away. I barely heard him call my name. I stood up, grabbed a knife from the butcher block in the kitchen, and turned back to face the door, and as I did so, I realized it was Weathers calling to me, shaking the door in his attempt to reach me.

I dropped the knife and half-ran across my bedroom to turn the lock and let him in. His face was raw with concern, his hand resting on the butt of his gun.

"Maggie, what is it? Did I scare you? I knocked first but I wasn't sure if you were here. Didn't you hear me?"

I shook my head numbly. "No. I was . . . I went . . . and then I . . ." But I couldn't form the words that went with the thoughts.

He stepped inside the room and held me, his arms wrapping around my shoulders, pulling me into him and just standing there. After a minute or two he pushed back enough to look into my face.

"Is that your shower?"

I nodded and the panic began to subside, ebbing as quickly as it had surged.

"Yeah." I tried to laugh, but it was a hollow attempt. "I, um, I was going to get ready for work, you know, but I looked out the window and the patrol car was gone. And then I came in here and, I guess that was that." My voice drifted off and I just stood there for a moment before I remembered the shower. "I'd better go turn that off."

"Go take your shower," he said. "I'll be right here."

Part of me wanted to send him away, to tell him that I was fine now and didn't need anyone watching out for me. But the rest of me shook inside and my nerves felt like Jell-O.

I wound up not saying a word, just grabbing my robe off its hook in the closet and walking into the bathroom. What was wrong with me? I'd been home since the shooting. I'd been inside the closet. I hadn't panicked then, why now? Probably because it was my first time alone. It would be better now. I wouldn't panic the next time. But when I stepped into the bathroom and closed the door, the feeling returned. The steam covered the mirror and thickened the air so I couldn't breathe. The window, tiny and shuttered, seemed an open portal for intruders.

I had to step over to the door, open it, and look out into the hallway. Weathers was right there, his arms folded across his chest, an easy smile on his face.

"You were thinking maybe I'd join you?" he asked.

That took the panic away. I took a deep breath and tried to smile. "No, actually, it's just a little bit close in here, I was just going to let some cool air in."

I didn't fool him. His eyes softened, but the smirk remained. He wasn't going to baby me.

"Well," he drawled, "maybe while you're in there, you might compare your shower to mine. You didn't seem to mind the steam over at my place."

"I didn't mind it at all," I said, before I could stop myself. He'd done it again, charmed me into forgetting that he was only in it for the game.

"Hey," I said, unknotting my bathrobe slowly and letting him watch. "Don't you have somewhere to be?" The robe started to slip open, just a little bit.

"No," he murmured. "I've got all the time in the world."

I smiled. "Oh, that's funny. I thought you had to run carpool for the junior police auxiliary."

His face reddened and I closed the bathroom door.

On the other side of the door I heard him chuckle. "Funny, Reid, real funny."

I jumped into the shower and pulled the curtain. It was my shower again, my bathroom, and my home.

I stood under the hot water until I felt it begin to cool off, reluctantly turning it off only when I knew I had to. I stood behind the curtain and reached out for my towel, feeling around on the rack and realizing that it was gone.

"Real funny," I yelled. "Bring my towel back."

I waited a second and was rewarded with the sound of the door opening. My towel flipped up over the shower curtain and I grabbed it, pulling it down and wrapping it around my body.

"So you had to resort to stealing my towel?"

I whipped open the curtain and came face to face with Tony Carlucci. He was standing there with a broad smile on his face and his finger to his lips.

"Shhh," he whispered. "Wouldn't want Sheila to hear you, would you? She and your friend are out on the front porch. I believe she's uninviting him to dinner."

"Oh no!"

Tony grinned. He was enjoying the situation. He stood there, staring at me, his eyes covering every inch of my body, slowly examining.

"Get out!"

"Looks like you missed a spot on your back," he whispered.

"Get out!"

Tony shrugged and held up his hands. "Whatever you say. I was just trying to help out." He slipped out of the room just as I heard the front door slam and Sheila come storming back through the dining room, her footsteps stopping just outside the bathroom door.

"Mama!" she cried. "How could you let that jerk inside our house?"

"Sheila, were you rude to him?"

"Well, I should hope so," she huffed. "And then I told him all about that girl and Nosmo King. You know, I think he actually was forced to listen to me. See, I told you I'd be a big help!"

I sighed into my towel and looked at myself in the mirror. "Whatever," I muttered.

"What did you say?" Sheila demanded.

"Nothing, honey, just go set the table."

"Whatever!" She clomped off into the kitchen and could be heard pulling open drawers and fumbling with silverware.

It was one of those days, one right after another, right after another.

Twenty-five

Tony and Sheila were thick as thieves by the time they dropped me off at the Golden Stallion club. Tony gunned the engine and the two took off for who knew where, not to return until closing time.

I walked inside knowing I had fences to mend. I'd hurt my friend and there was no way I could think of to make up for that. When I entered the club, Jack had his back to me, fiddling with the monitor in such an obvious way that I knew he'd seen me arrive and didn't want to face me.

He waited until I was right behind him to turn around, pretending to be surprised and happy to see me.

"I want to talk to you," I said.

"Sure, Maggie, sure, but not right now, okay? Sparks asked me to check this monitor and we're due to start any minute. How about later?" He smiled but he wouldn't hold my gaze. At the first opportunity he turned back to the sound system and wandered away. The others were all tuning up, oblivious to me. When Chris finally looked up and saw me, he reached for my guitar.

"I'll get it tuned up for you," he said. "You want to do that new one we were working on last week?"

I nodded, but my heart wasn't in it. I stepped up to my vocal mike and did a sound check, watching Homer back on the soundboard nod and give me the thumbs up. The lights were flickering, traveling across the stage in broad beams of red and gold as the techies adjusted them to focus on the band members. On any other night I would've been eating this up. It was my dream to sing and now here I was, on stage five nights a week, the lead singer in a house band, and I couldn't enjoy it.

I walked to the dead center of the stage and looked out at the house. It was almost nine o'clock. The regulars were beginning to file in. Brenda Lee was just finishing up with her line dance lessons, putting a bevy of overweight middle-aged women through their paces. I waited there, in the spot where I always stood, and closed my eyes, wishing like anything for the feeling to come. I wanted the adrenaline rush I always got before I sang, but it wasn't coming.

"Maggie! Maggie, my God, move!" Sparks screamed and my eyes flew open, but not in time. I turned around and saw nothing but Jack. Jack running and hurtling toward me, a fierce look of determination on his face, his arms outstretched as he flew into me, knocking me off my feet and sending me flying backward.

A speaker tower crashed to the ground, falling from its position high above the stage, landing on the spot where I had just been standing. It shattered, splitting open, spilling wires and shards of black plastic everywhere.

Jack had tackled me, the force of his body throwing me off balance, across the stage, the two of us landing in a heap on the hard wooden floor.

"Are you all right?" he gasped. He pushed up off of me, turning to look at the spot where the heavy piece of equipment had landed.

"I could be dead," I whispered.

"But you're not," he said, and then he smiled. "You're not."

Cletus and the other bouncer were running up onto the stage. Pandemonium had erupted among the techies and the roadies, with everyone looking for the cause of the accident. But I knew it wasn't an accident. Accidents like that didn't just happen.

I started to shake and suddenly it was freezing, even with the ultrahot lights and the heat from the equipment.

Jack looked back at me and smiled. "Son of a bitch!" he said. Then he was standing, reaching down to pull me up.

"Cletus," he called, "we need to look and see if anybody's been fooling with the equipment. See who's been hanging around this afternoon. This couldn't have happened without someone noticing something." Jack was stronger and taller than he had been minutes before, and more certain of himself. The easygoing, peace-loving boy was gone, replaced by a self-assured man.

Sparks was impatient with the entire process. "Come on, get the other tower in here," he called to the stagehands. "Get this mess cleaned up." When the others ignored him, he became even more controlling. "Let's get moving, people. We're on in five."

Cletus stooped down by the broken amplifier, stretched out a hand, and pulled the broken chain away from the bits of equipment and examined them.

"Yep," he said, his eyes meeting Jack's. "Somebody cut on it."

"No kidding!" Jack couldn't seem to decide whether to be amazed at this or pleased that he'd figured it all out. He turned to me. "Let's go ahead and call your detective friend. He's gonna want to see this."

When a stagehand moved in with a broom, Jack stopped him. "You can't touch this. It's a crime scene."

"Aw, for pity's sake," Sparks moaned. "We've got a show to do."

"Well, we can just work around it if we have to," I said. But I knew that wasn't the case. Once the police arrived, we'd be twiddling our thumbs for hours while they took pictures and scratched their heads.

Cletus handed me his cell phone. "You'd better call," he said. "You seem to know them better than we do." He winked at me and smiled. "Tell him we need the V.I.P. treatment."

I dialed the number, knowing Weathers wouldn't be there, listening to the familiar recording: "This is Detective Marshall J. Weathers of the Greensboro Police Department's Criminal Investigation Unit. I am unable to take your call at the moment, but if you would leave me a detailed message, including the time of your call and your number, I will return your call as soon as possible."

I waited for the tone and tried to be brief. "Marshall, it's Maggie. I'm at the club. There's been an accident here, but it probably wasn't an accident, so could you come down?"

I hung up, handed the phone to Cletus, and turned back to Sparks. "Let's do it. Let's start off and work around the mess."

Sparks was all white hat and mustache, a short man with big pointy-toed cowboy boots and no sense of humor.

"Good enough," he said, and headed for his pedal-steel guitar. The rest of the band followed suit, picking up their instruments and plugging them into their amps. A techie pushed a heavy backup amp out to the edge of the stage.

"It won't be perfect sound," he said to Sugar Bear, "but they'll hear you fine."

Sparks started the count and the others began playing. I took the mike the roadie handed me, walked around the near-fatal mess, and stood just in front of the broken amp. I closed my eyes and began to sing.

> *"I'm standing on the edge of a broken heart,*
> *I can't believe that we're falling apart.*
> *Your touch has grown as cold*
> *As the love that you stole*
> *When you walked away from me."*

Sparks brought the pedal-steel in under the melody, each note a sliding teardrop that broke just at the end of every syllable. The lights dimmed as couples moved together in a slow, steady circle around the dance floor.

Chris walked up to the mike right next to me, looked me in the eye and began the second verse of our duet.

> *"You're breaking my heart as you walk away,*
> *I can't believe I'm your yesterday.*
> *I tried for so long,*
> *But you tell me it's wrong,*
> *As you walk away from me."*

Jack stepped in between us, his harmonica sweetly moving through the break as Chris picked up his mandolin and added a harmony to it. For a moment I lost sight of the danger, forgot about everything but the music and the song. But only for a moment; Marshall Weathers was the only reminder I needed to know that things weren't right. He stepped into the club and stood by the doorway letting his eyes adjust. By the time Chris and I came back in to sing the third verse, he was standing in front of me, staring at the ruined amplifier.

When the song ended, he walked up the side steps onto the stage and over to the smashed tower.

"Folks getting a little careless around here?" he asked. His thick mustache barely moved when he spoke, but his eyes seemed to be taking everything in. He was wearing tight faded blue jeans, a white dress shirt, and his lizardskin boots. He could've passed for a customer if I hadn't caught a glimpse of the gun that rested securely on his hip, hidden by his jacket.

"Cletus thinks somebody cut the chain," I said.

"Uh-huh," he muttered, stooping as Cletus had to pick up the twisted metal links.

"Don't you want to wear gloves when you do that?" Sugar Bear asked, his curiosity overcoming him. Sugar Bear has a thing about the law. He avoids them at all costs, figuring that one of these days he'll get arrested for intent to possess illegal drugs.

Weathers looked up at him and seemed to stifle a grin. "Nah. If there were fingerprints on this bit of chain they'd be long gone by now, smudged off by all the people who've probably handled it since it fell. Besides, it's really hard to lift a print off a thing like this."

Sugar Bear looked disappointed, as did just about everyone else, including me.

"Y'all might want to clean up this mess," he said. "Somebody could get hurt." He turned and looked at Cletus, who was standing on the edge of the crowd. "How about you tell me what happened and we'll go from there," he said.

Cletus nodded and spoke into his walkie-talkie, giving instructions to the other security staff.

"All right," he said, his voice a thick, bull-like monotone. "I'll buy you a cup of coffee in my office."

Marshall started to follow, then stopped and returned to the spot where I stood. "Give us a couple of minutes, all right, Cletus?"

Cletus nodded. "You know where I am," he said, and stalked off.

Marshall took my elbow and leaned down to murmur in my ear. "Let's go outside a minute."

I walked away with him, feeling his comforting presence by my side and wishing I didn't want him to stay. I wanted to lean into him, to feel his arm slip around my waist. I wanted him to make it be all right.

As soon as the back door closed behind us, Marshall turned and kissed me. It was a long, slow, deep kiss, full of promise and expectation. His hands encircled my shoulders and slid down my arms, and then he pulled me closer, until I could do nothing but melt into him.

I kissed him right back. I felt our bodies join together and suddenly there was nothing I wanted more than him.

He pushed away and looked down at me, his eyes delving deep inside me, probing for confirmation of what we both felt.

"What was that for?" I whispered.

"What do you think, Maggie?" He tilted my chin up again

and brushed my lips with his. "Don't think I'm walking away from you," he whispered. He kissed me again, his hands moving to pull me closer again. "Now," he said, his voice soft against my ear, "I'm going to put a uniformed officer inside the club. I don't think anyone will try anything else tonight, not here at least, but I'd feel better with someone watching you. I'll be back to pick you up at closing time."

The alarm went off in my head and I panicked. He'd be back? So would Tony Carlucci. Now what was I going to do?

"You don't need to do that," I said. "I'll be okay."

"Maggie," Weathers said, his mustache tickling my ear as he whispered. "No arguments. I'll be back at two thirty."

He pulled his cell phone out of his jacket pocket and called to have a patrol officer watch the club and me. As he spoke I felt myself spiral further and further away. I couldn't tell him about Carlucci. He'd never understand that. And I couldn't call Carlucci. I didn't know his number. I had no idea how to find him. And even if I could, what would I say? Thanks for watching my daughter, but never mind? I'm going off with that man you say is a loser? And furthermore, what did I care what Tony Carlucci the Thug Private Investigator thought? And then, to top it all off, there was Jack. What was I going to do about him? He'd saved my life and all I'd done lately was hurt him. Tony Carlucci was right—Harmonica Jack did love me, or at least he thought he did, and I'd done a powerful job of ignoring that fact. But how long could that go on?

My ears were ringing. I was confused and frightened and living my life at the hands of others. I was going to have to do something, but what? I wandered away from Marshall, leaving him with his ear glued to the phone, issuing instructions and barking orders. I walked back inside, past the technicians and sound men, past the stagehands and backstage hangers-on, right up to Sparks.

"I'm leaving," I said. "I'll be back in time to finish the last set."

Sparks pushed his ten-gallon hat back on his head and favored me with a malevolent glare. "You can't do that," he said.

But I wasn't listening. I was walking away.

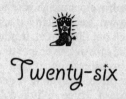

Twenty-six

I don't think anyone expected me to take a powder. Sparks didn't yell out after me. The boys in the band didn't say a word as I walked away, assuming that I was going to get a drink or stop by the ladies' room. When I stepped outside the front door and stood with my back against the wall, it was just like any one of a dozen or so nights that I'd come outside for a breath of fresh air and a glimpse at the traffic that raced up and down High Point Road.

"Ain't too busy tonight," the doorman drawled.

"Nope," I answered.

"You guys on break already?" He laughed. "Wish my job were as easy as yours!" He turned to make change for a trio of women and when he did, I spotted a regular customer making his way across the parking lot.

"Billy," I called, "will you do me a favor?"

Billy, a young farm boy in his early twenties, was only too happy to give me a ride downtown to my car. He laughed and flirted and never once asked why I needed a ride. When he dropped me off beside the BB&T Bank parking lot, I pecked him on the cheek and ran into the deck, my keys in hand.

I started up and drove out of the parking lot, onto the almost empty downtown streets. I circled around, past the police station and back out Elm Street, heading away from the business section and crossing over into the wealthy residential area of older Greensboro.

I was trying to piece everything together in my mind. Nosmo King was dead. Three million dollars was missing. Nosmo was shot with Vernell's gun, in Vernell's truck, and Vernell himself admitted he had no alibi, and all the motive in the world. In fact, the only reason for not believing Vernell had killed Nosmo was my own stubborn belief that he wouldn't do something like that.

But things kept circling around to Vernell. Everything pointed to Vernell and I had to wonder why. Why shoot Nosmo King with Vernell's gun? Wouldn't it be easier to use another gun, a gun not attached to Vernell's body? Why go to all the trouble to make it look like Vernell was the killer? Who would want Vernell and Nosmo out of the way?

I pondered on that one as I found myself winding around through Old Irving Park, approaching Vernell's concrete palace from the less obvious back entrance to New Irving Park.

Nosmo's girlfriend had motive and means and quite probably opportunity. She was next on my list, but first I wanted to look through Vernell's house one more time, without interruption. I glanced at my watch. It was ten thirty. I could do this and see Pauline before closing time. I could be back at the club before Tony and Marshall returned for me, and if my luck were running right, I'd figure some way out to deal with the two of them and avoid any painful consequences.

But who was I fooling? Three men would be waiting for me when I returned, and not one of them would be easy to handle.

I pulled up in Vernell's driveway, cut the lights, and

slipped around to the side entrance. When I came within five feet of the door, the security lights flicked on and a strange robotic voice barked "Key in your security code or ring the doorbell." I punched in Sheila's birth date and waited.

"Accepted," the robot said.

I stepped through the door, closing it firmly behind me and locking it. This time there would be no slip-ups, no unwanted intruders like Tony Carlucci.

I stood in the mud room, just off of the garage, waiting for my eyes to adjust to the dim light that shone in from the kitchen.

"If I were Vernell Spivey, and I was trying to hide something like my important papers or money, where would I put it?" There just had to be some way to figure out what the connection was between Nosmo and Vernell.

The stove in Vernell's kitchen glowed with the light from the hood overhead. I walked in and stood by the huge pine table, looking around at the excess Vernell had poured into his new home.

The range was a Viking, but Vernell couldn't cook. The refrigerator was a subzero, but when I opened it, all I found was beer and a shriveled lemon. The tiles on the backsplash were hand-painted. The window treatments were custom-made, something Vernell and I could never afford in all of our married life.

I looked around and realized that Vernell's palace was an interior designer's dream, and that there was not one personal item or picture from his life present in any of the rooms downstairs. Vernell and his second wife, the lovely nymphet, Jolene the Dish Girl, had bought and paid for their lives together, without so much as one idea of what true life really meant. I shook my head. Where had all of Vernell's money gone? Had he ever really had any money?

I looked across the hallway, into Vernell's darkened study. I remembered the stacks and stacks of bills that Vernell had left unpaid on his desk. At the time I'd assumed he was merely irresponsible, not unable to pay them.

I walked out into the huge marble foyer and began climbing the steps to the second floor of Vernell's home.

Vernell and I had started out poor, so poor we lived in a repossessed trailer that had been gutted by its former owners. Somehow, I remembered those days fondly. We were still in love then, puppy love, the kind where you can't see obstacles, only possibilities.

I was pregnant with Sheila, sick as a dog, and still I couldn't help but feather our nest. Vernell would drag in used bits of wood and Formica, rebuilding me a kitchen, hand-laying the tiles to form the floor. He worked for a mobile home lot as a repo man. The pay was terrible and the hours were long, but the promotions came quick. Before we knew it, Vernell was a salesman and the little bit of money he brought home bought the crib and curtains for Sheila's room.

I looked around Vernell's stone palace and shuddered. It was cold and loveless. The trailer in southeast Greensboro had been dog-ugly but filled to the brim with love. But that didn't last.

"I don't know what it's all about anyway," I muttered. I stopped at the top of the stairs and looked both ways up and down the hall. Vernell's master suite lay off to the right, the only room in the house that I'd never seen. Sheila's room and the guest rooms lay to the left.

When Sheila had lived with Vernell, he and Jolene had tried to give her all the love money could buy, and for a while it had worked, and I'd lost her. But those things have a way of showing themselves to be just what they are, and Sheila came back to me. Poor Vernell couldn't understand why she left, but then, he hadn't understood Jolene either.

I shook myself and turned to the right. Might as well step into the lion's den. It couldn't hurt me now anyway. But I was wrong. My feet sank into the thick white carpeting as I walked into his room. But when I crossed over the threshold, I stepped onto a hard wood floor. The room was dark. Dark hulks of furniture stood out, casting dark shadows in the reflection of the streetlight outside.

I reached for the light switch, deciding to take the risk. I had to be able to search his room. What I saw took my breath away. Vernell's room was a huge expanse that took up the entire end of the house, but that wasn't what stopped me.

Vernell had pulled up the carpeting that covered the rest of the upstairs and laid hardwood floors. The carpet was shoved into one of the two walk-in closets, the closet with all of Jolene's clothing. Along with the carpeting, Vernell had torn the curtains from the windows and torn the bedding from the king-sized bed, throwing it all in on top of the carpet. What he had done next broke my heart.

The yellow wedding ring quilt Mama had made as a gift for us on our wedding day covered the bed. Vernell had pulled out all of the pictures he had of Sheila, from infancy until last year, slipped them into plain wooden frames, and hung or placed them with care around the room. Against the far wall he had hung a picture from our first home, a cheap watercolor print of a forest scene. His mother's green velvet rocker stood against the window, with an ancient floor lamp beside it, and on the floor lay a bible and an empty Jack Daniel's bottle.

Vernell Spivey had done his best to come home. I stepped into the room and looked around some more. Vienna sausage cans filled the trash can, along with an empty bottle of hot sauce and an empty saltine cracker box. It was obvious that Vernell lived alone in his palace, in one solitary room, grieving his roots. No wonder Bess King had seemed like such a miracle. She was a home girl, just like I had been, just like Vernell's mama and her mama before her.

I walked over to the rocker and sat down, reaching over to pick up the heavy family Bible. The underlined words on the page blurred as my eyes filled up with tears. Vernell had been highlighting his favorite passages, reading them over and over. My curiosity overwhelmed me and I wiped the tears away and began to read.

"The righteousness of the upright saves them, but the treacherous are taken captive by their schemes . . . Whoever is steadfast in righteousness will live, but whoever pursues evil will die." I flipped through the pages of Proverbs, reading the passages Vernell had carefully underlined in yellow. "Misfortune pursues sinners, but prosperity rewards the righteous. The good leave an inheritance to their children's children, but the sinner's wealth is laid up for the righteous." Then the last passage, underlined twice, read "Some pretend to be rich, yet have nothing; others pretend to be poor yet have great wealth. Wealth is a ransom for a person's life but the poor get no threats."

Poor Vernell. If it were possible, he seemed to be changing his ways, or at least considering it. A piece of paper fluttered out of the Bible as I turned the pages, falling into my lap. It was scrap paper, and on it Vernell had written "The Satellite Kingdom," then scratched that out. "The Mobile Home Kingdom," and scratched that out. This was followed by a series of names: "Vernell's Palace of the Future," "Millennium World," "Divine Accommodations," and "Seek and Ye Shall Find It All World," all scratched out. Finally Vernell had arrived at something that worked for him. "The Promised Land Kingdom of Earthly Transportation and Accommodation."

I shook my head and looked away. What scheme had Vernell concocted now? I looked across the room at the bed and saw a piece of wood sticking out from underneath the dust ruffle.

When I pulled the dust ruffle aside and looked, I found Vernell's master plan. It was a balsa wood model, carefully constructed and delicately laid out, a two-foot-by-two-foot square. Vernell's "Promised Land Kingdom." There, in miniature, was his plan to take over Greensboro's transportation and accommodation needs. An entire village of mobile homes, satellite dishes, and used cars that would sit on a huge plot of land just beyond the water park on South Holden Road.

I picked up the miniature mobile homes and saw crosses carefully engraved on the rear panels of the trailers. Each used car bore a tiny cross. Each satellite dish was carefully painted in black, with an image of Jesus, stretching out his hands to better receive the signal.

"Oh, Vernell," I sighed. "What have you done now?"

I had to admit, Greensboro had nothing like it. One-stop shopping for those of us living paycheck to paycheck. The used car lot was huge, bigger than any I'd ever seen. I'd heard tell of used car superstores in Atlanta, but Greensboro had nothing of this magnitude. And Vernell had plans to more than double his mobile home inventory. How had he intended to pull it all off?

Nosmo King. That's why Vernell had been talking to Nosmo. So what stopped him? What had changed his mind? I looked back at the Bible. "Wealth is a ransom for a person's life, but the poor get no threats." What was that all about?

"Okay," I whispered, "let's get to the bottom of all this."

I turned out Vernell's bedroom light and left the room, closing the door behind me. It was time to find Pauline Conrad and make her talk to me. I looked at my watch. It was almost eleven thirty. In three more hours I had to be back at the Golden Stallion, ready to face down three men and one angry teenager.

I walked back through the darkened house, mulling it all over. Vernell always seemed to have money, but the piles of bills on his desk seemed to say otherwise. The fact that he'd put together another outrageous business scheme didn't surprise me at all. Vernell always had something up his sleeve. But going to illegal ends to get the money, now that surprised me. What would make him do a thing like that? And what would make him decide against it?

I walked into the kitchen, headed for the back door and stopped as I was walking by the wall phone. I could hear Tony Carlucci's voice in my head. "He's got someone who cares about him. He's got Bess."

I looked at the pad of numbers Vernell kept beside the phone, mounted on a tacky little floral pad that had to be a Jolene leftover. Bess King's number was sitting right there.

"Why not?" I murmured. "Maybe two heads would be better than one."

I dialed the number and waited. After three rings I heard her voice, tired but not sleepy.

"Hello?" she said.

"Bess, it's Maggie. Listen, you want to help me get Vernell out of this mess?"

"What do you mean?" She sounded suspicious.

"I'm about half out of my mind trying to figure out what all's going on here. Maybe, since you've been with him lately, you can puzzle out some of the pieces that I can't figure. Maybe we'll get to this quicker if we both work on it."

She was thinking about it. She was quiet for a minute and then strong. "All right, let's do it."

I made it from Vernell's house to hers in fifteen minutes. She was waiting at the foot of the driveway, dressed in black jeans and a black leather jacket, a female version of Tony Carlucci.

"I'm thinking we should drop in on Pauline Conrad," I said. "I'm thinking seeing you might shake her up a little."

Bess smiled softly and looked out the window. "Now that's a conversation I might enjoy having. The widow and the girlfriend, together at last."

"Precisely," I said. "What do you know about the Promised Land?"

Bess looked startled, glanced at me then away. She knew everything.

"The Promised Land? Why, I guess I know no more than the next person," she said, but her voice cracked.

"Look," I said, speeding up and flying down the back road into town, "if you're with me on this, you've gotta be honest, no matter what you think Vernell would want you to do. I'm his ex-wife, Bess, not his enemy. I don't want him back, I just want him out of jail."

Bess sat with that for a minute, thinking and mulling it over.

"You know, I've been jealous of you a long time, Maggie. Vernell just can't seem to turn loose of trying to do it right for you." Her voice had a bitter edge to it. "He's got you up on some pedestal, just like he does his mother. You're the saint, the one who can never do any wrong, and he's your bad boy."

I started to say something and stopped. Let her say her piece.

"He's spent most of his life trying to fit in and be successful. He's been so busy impressing others, he's forgotten about living right. He wants everybody to think he's Mr. Greensboro, and to do that, he created a castle and married a trophy wife, and built up a mountain of debt."

She turned in her seat and I could feel her staring at me. "You didn't even know that, did you?"

"Bess, Vernell's money was of no consequence to me. All I wanted was for Sheila to be able to go to college. When her Uncle Jimmy died, I figured she was set on the half of the Mobile Home Kingdom he left her. I let Vernell do his thing and I tried to stay out of it, until he made it to where I had to become involved."

Bess sighed. "Vernell's been fighting the banks and just about everybody else trying to stay afloat long enough to make the businesses pay off. He was fighting a hostile takeover by VanScoy Mobile Homes on account of they smelled blood and were looking to clean him out. The Promised Land is Vernell's only hope."

I was back in town, rolling down Elm Street, two blocks away from Pauline Conrad's condominium.

"So, he was looking to borrow the money to finance the Promised Land from Nosmo?"

Bess shook her head. "No, not at first. When I met him, all he was looking to do was buy out Archer VanScoy, kind of a reverse takeover. But he didn't want to lose anything to do it. He wanted his image and the power of being the mobile home king. Do you know what a stupid thing it would've been to borrow three million from Nosmo? Twenty percent interest rate, impossible terms, and Nosmo just waiting to repo the whole deal."

"Why didn't he go through with it?" I pulled up into the

condominium parking lot, killed the engine, and turned to face Bess.

She looked me right in the eye. "Because we fell in love," she said simply. "And Vernell decided to walk in the path of righteousness."

"But he was still drinking!"

Bess shrugged. "I didn't say he was walking in the path of perfection. Vernell was new to doing things the right way. Every now and then, he fell back. But Maggie, he kept trying. That's what was new about Vernell."

Part of me wanted to set her straight, and part of me wanted to believe her. Was it possible that Vernell Spivey had found what I hadn't been able to provide? Was it true that he was growing up at last? I looked up at the tenth floor of the condo building and shuddered. Maybe Pauline Conrad had taken it all away from him. And if she hadn't, maybe she held the key to figuring it all out.

"Okay," I said, "let's go. There's the small matter of the doorman, and then we're in and up the elevator."

Bess stepped out of the car, her lips tightened into a firm, straight line. "Don't worry about him," she said. "I can get us inside."

Bess squared her shoulders and walked across the parking lot. I followed her, doing my best to match her long strides to my own shorter ones. When she reached the front door, Bess fumbled in her purse, produced a flat, plastic card, and stuck it into a slot by the doorway.

When she saw my mouth gape open, she smiled. "I hired a private detective to find out all about Nosmo. Like I said, I've known about his little love nest for years. He kept his passkey right out on his dresser. I guess he thought I was stupid."

She breezed inside, walked right up to the elevator and punched the button.

"Excuse me," the doorman said, "I don't believe I know you."

Bess favored him with a regal glare. "No, I don't believe you do," she said, and sailed into the open elevator. I stepped in behind her, my heart pounding, and watched as she hit the button for the tenth floor and then the button to close the doors.

"All you do," she said, "is act as if you belong and they don't. Another little trick my husband taught me. I'm not saying it's right, I'm just saying I learned it from him."

We rode up in silence. I had no idea what she was thinking, but I was trying to figure out the best way to get to Pauline Conrad. When the elevator stopped and the doors opened, Bess King was across the hall and ringing the doorbell without me having to direct her. Her eyes were hard and her entire manner had changed. Gone was the country girl, and in her place, a hard-nosed, all-business woman.

Footsteps scuffed across the foyer on the other side of the door. Someone peered out through the peephole, and then the door swung open on its chain.

Pauline Conrad wore bunny slippers and flannel pajamas. Her hair was pulled back from her face by a soft pink headband, and all the makeup had been carefully scrubbed away. She looked ten years old, with an early onset case of acne.

"Bess," she said, stuttering slightly and obviously startled.

"Hello, Pauline. Mind if we come in? I need to talk to you." Bess spoke softly, but like my old school principal, with authority and strength that simmered just below the genuine warmth and kindness. I didn't know how she was pulling it off. This was the latest in a string of women who'd slept with her husband on a regular basis, eroding her marriage into the sham it had become when she met Vernell.

Pauline closed the door, removed the chain and then swung it wide to admit her late-night visitors. As Bess stepped through the door, Pauline started offering her tea and coffee and all manner of drinks and hospitality, but Bess shook her head and waved her away.

"Let's go sit in your living room and have us a little talk," she said. She smiled, but I was reminded of the old tale Mama used to tell about the mongoose and the snake. I was willing to bet that the smile on Bess King's face matched the smile the mongoose gave the snake, right before it killed it.

Bess sat down on a white overstuffed sofa and glanced around the elegantly appointed room. It was all done in shades of white and cream, with rich textures and fabrics that screamed of money. A beautiful oil painting of a naked woman hung over the marble edged fireplace. The frame was thick with gold leaf covering its ornate scrollwork.

"My," Bess said, looking around. "Nosmo did have taste. Or did he hire a decorator?"

Pauline turned bright red, then began to pale. "Bess, it isn't . . ."

"Shut up, honey," Bess said. "It is exactly what it looks like. And don't think I'm especially offended by you. You're just the latest in a string of women that Nosmo installed here in his little love nest. I've known about it for years, so don't feel special."

Pauline started to cry and this only irritated Bess.

"Now listen," she said. "Don't waste your little crocodile tears on us, we really don't have time for them. I want you to start by telling me what happened to my husband."

Pauline choked off a sob and started to cough.

"Get her a glass of water," Bess said to me. As I headed for the kitchen, Bess continued. "I know you were with Nosmo at breakfast the morning he disappeared. I know you went off with him and Vernell Spivey. I know Vernell was drinking. Now, when you can pull yourself together, I want to know how my husband died."

I walked back into the room with the glass of water a minute later and found Pauline blowing her nose and Bess staring at her with an unrelenting gaze that would've made me confess to any manner of sins.

Pauline took the glass from me with a hand that shook so hard it threatened to spill the water over the edge.

"All right," she said. "Here it is, but you're not gonna like it." She tried to look spiteful, but it came off more like she had something stuck in her eyes.

"I know about them other girls," she said, "but Nosmo loved me. We were gonna get married."

Bess snorted. "I could care less about that. Tell me the facts, not your dreams."

Pauline tossed her hair back over her shoulders and went on. "That morning we had breakfast at Tex and Shirley's, just like always. We sat at a big old round table in the back, Nosmo's table they call it, on account of he sits there every morning, with me, and whoever else shows up. It's tradition. Vernell Spivey was there because he was due to get some money from Nosmo."

Bess leaned forward slightly. "Then what happened?"

Pauline cocked her head and closed her eyes for a second. "Well, a bunch of other folks stopped by and we ate."

"Who?"

Pauline frowned. "Um, Christine Razuki and her boyfriend, Archer. Um, Bill Leon and his 'friend,' Robbie. I guess that's it. I mean, the table was full, we were all packed in there. I guess some other people stopped by, but they were just saying hello. You know, like the city manager, a town council guy, Nosmo's barber. I don't know! What does it matter, anyway?" Pauline looked like she was getting impatient with all the interruptions. "So where was I?" she asked.

"Wait," I said, "I have a question. Where was everybody sitting?"

Even Bess looked puzzled by that question.

"Okay, it's a big circular table with chairs around one half of it, and like a half-circle, booth-seat-type thing around the other half, so it's built into the wall. Nosmo sits in the smack dead center against the wall. I sit to his right. Vernell was on his left." She closed her eyes, thinking again. "Christine's boyfriend sat next to Vernell 'cause they knew each other. Christine sat next to him. When Bill and Robbie came, they took the chairs that were left, across from Nosmo. Okay? Can I go on now?"

Bess and I nodded. But anything that came after this was going to be gravy. I had what I needed. I knew who took Vernell's gun.

"So anyway, after breakfast, Nosmo and Vernell had business to do, so they dropped me off at the condo. Nosmo was getting his oil changed and he said he wanted to look at some property with Vernell, so they took his truck."

"Was Vernell drinking?" Bess asked.

Pauline shrugged. "Well, he told Nosmo he was on the wagon, but Nosmo said they needed to celebrate. We were all sitting in the front seat of Vernell's truck. Nosmo brought out a bottle of Jack and said Vernell should take just one hit, you know, to signify their friendship."

I was having an awful feeling. I was beginning to see all the pieces of the puzzle fall into place and I didn't like it at all.

"So then what happened?" Bess asked.

Pauline shrugged. "I don't know. Nosmo told me to leave so him and Vernell could talk. I came home." She began to cry, real tears this time, that rolled down her face and dripped off her chin in big fat drops. "That was the last time I ever saw him," she sobbed. "The very last time!"

"Would you like to see him again?" a cool voice whispered. "Because I think it can be arranged."

The three of us turned, our heads whipping toward the sound of the voice. Christine Razuki, Pauline's guard dog, stood at the entrance to the living room, an ugly silver gun in her hand.

"I thought I told you not to talk to her," Christine said, her voice hard and angry. "I go out for cigarettes and this is what I find when I come back?"

Bess didn't miss a beat. She looked up, looked Christine straight in the eye and said, "Chris, don't go cutting the fool. You know me. Sit down and talk with us, that's all we're doing, talking about Nosmo."

Christine stepped into the room and walked across to a chair by the fireplace, but the gun stayed in her hand, out where it could easily kill any one of the three of us.

"We go way back, Chris," Bess said. "You and Nosmo are part of the business, the Family, if that's what you want to call it. I think the Family owes me a little respect."

Christine inclined her head, nodding slightly. "The Family lost a good man in your husband," she said, "but it was business. It was time to move on, and I can say this to you, Bess, because I know you didn't love Nosmo." Bess started to say something, but Christine held up her hand to silence her. "Respect? Were you going to say respect? Because you didn't respect him either, Bess. Not when you were screwing Vernell Spivey. That's not respect."

The gun came up a little higher, aimed more directly at Bess's chest.

"So what are you trying to tell me, Christine, that you've gotten a promotion? You no longer book the jobs, now you run the bank?"

Christine smiled slightly and Bess had her confirmation. Christine reached into her jacket pocket, pulled out a tiny cell phone, and hit a button.

"Come over to the condo," she said. "We've got some unfinished business." She flipped the phone shut and smiled at Bess.

"You killed Nosmo so you could run the money? You did that?" Pauline shook her head like she'd been hit and was trying to clear it. She couldn't grasp the concept.

Christine frowned, looked at her friend, and waved the gun a little as she spoke. "No, I didn't do that! That's ridiculous. I just took advantage of a situation, that's all."

Pauline wasn't through. "But you're talking so mean about him, Christine. He was nice to you. He was good to us. You shouldn't talk that way about the dead."

Christine looked at Pauline and laughed. "Nosmo King was the biggest asshole in Greensboro, maybe even in North Carolina. What did you think you had with him, a marriage?" Her laugh rang out like a harsh bark that bounced off the walls and echoed in my head. Pauline covered her ears, tears rolling down her cheeks.

"He loved me," she said softly. "And I loved him."

"Pauline, wake up! I was screwing him whenever he was here and you weren't. That's how it was, honey. Business, through and through. I paid the price, I got my promotions, and finally, I got what I wanted, everything. The three million was just a little extra something that fell into my lap."

A thick, guttural scream of pure rage came from Pauline, as she lunged from her chair, across the room toward her former best friend.

Christine's face never moved. Her finger tightened on the trigger, the gun went off, and Pauline dropped to the ground. Bess had jumped up, moving toward Christine, but stopped when Christine turned the gun back on her.

"You want to be next?" she asked. "I have no problem with making you next."

Before she could answer, the front door opened and Archer VanScoy stepped into the room. His hand was in his coat pocket, wrapped around a bulge that had to be a gun.

"Hey," he said. "I'm just in time, huh?"

"Well, it's about damned time!" I said. "I'd almost given up on you!"

"Huh?" Archer VanScoy turned and stared at me as if I was a crazy woman.

"What is she talking about?" Christine said.

I stood up and walked toward Archer, a big smile on my face and my arms open wide, blocking his view of Christine. "Tell her, sug," I said.

"Tell her what?" he said.

"Yeah, tell me what?" Christine asked. She stood slowly, looking at Archer with one eyebrow raised.

Pauline moaned and in that same moment I heard a sound behind me as Bess flew off the couch and into Christine. Christine grunted and flew sideways with Bess on top of her. The gun skittered out of her hand, flying across the floor. I rammed VanScoy, knocking him off balance momentarily, and grabbed a large white marble stone that looked like a bowling ball as he struggled to regain his balance.

I lifted it up over my head, bringing it down sharply on the side of his neck. VanScoy dropped like a load of bricks and shots rang out behind me. A woman screamed and I turned to look, the smooth stone still in my hands.

Pauline Conrad sat on the floor, Christine's gun in her hand. Christine lay sprawled backward on the floor, an ugly red stain blooming across her chest. But it was Bess who most concerned me. She was leaning against the wall behind Christine, her shoulder covered in blood, and the color completely drained from her face. Her eyes were closed and she appeared to be unconscious.

I dropped to my knees, reached into VanScoy's pocket, and pulled his hand away from the gun that I'd known was there. With it in my hand, I turned back to Pauline.

"Honey," I said, "put the gun down."

Pauline didn't even look at me. She was staring at her dead friend, tears rolling down her face, blood staining the right side of her pale pink pajamas. She lay the gun down on the floor at her side, and closed her eyes.

The room was completely silent for a minute. I sat there, holding Archer VanScoy's gun and trying to make my brain work. Then Bess moaned and I moved to her side, pulling her shirt aside and looking at the wound which seemed to bubble up with blood.

"Nine-one-one," I said. Bess's eyes opened.

"Good plan," she whispered. "Better call them. They don't read minds."

Pauline had collapsed onto the floor again. I grabbed Christine's gun and stepped over to the white cordless phone that was lying on an end table.

Bess sighed and touched her shoulder.

"Blood is so damn hard to get out of a white carpet," she murmured.

Twenty-seven

*M*arshall Weathers arrived with the ambulances. I saw him walking through the EMTs and police officers, weaving his way over to where I stood. At first he just stared at me, looking at me as if he'd maybe never seen me before, as if I were a stranger, and then he smiled. But it wasn't a happy smile, it was tight and controlled, as if he were making an effort. He looked at his watch and then back at me.

"This isn't exactly how I expected to meet up with you," he said. "If you'd maybe clued me in, I could've saved you some trouble."

I pushed my hair out of my face and looked up at him. "You could've saved me some trouble?"

"I've had a tail on Christine Razuki for three days now. When I saw her with VanScoy, I was beginning to put it together. I knew Christine was taking over for Nosmo. I knew Archer VanScoy was talking about expanding his business. They would've both benefited with King out of the way. I was very close." He sighed.

"I went back and talked to Vernell some more," he said.

"He told me about his new business plan, how he'd pulled all of his money out of the bank to do this one big deal. That's when it started coming together for me. VanScoy set him up. If Vernell had succeeded, VanScoy would've been ruined."

"Why didn't you tell me?"

Marshall had his cop face on. "I didn't get Vernell to talk until tonight. Before that I didn't want to get your hopes up. I wanted to be sure."

"Well, I guess we're sure."

Marshall sighed and looked around the devastated living room. "Well, it was a hell of a way to find out," he said. "I thought you were safe."

"I am safe, Marshall."

Weathers couldn't hold it in any longer. "They would've killed you, Maggie. They would've killed all three of you. Don't you understand that Christine Razuki has been working with the Redneck Mafia for years? That she grew up in this organization? It's not just some little ragtag gang of construction scam artists anymore, Mag, they're bigger than that now." He sighed and looked at me.

"It was nothing for Christine to order VanScoy to kill Nosmo King. She owned VanScoy. She had the money and the power to make or break VanScoy. Nosmo King was all set to back Vernell. What else could VanScoy do but play ball with Christine? And this was her big opportunity to take over."

"So it got a little out of hand."

Weathers shook his head and reached out for me, pulling me close to him and sighing. "Maggie, what am I going to do about you?"

"Marshall?" Tracy the cadet had materialized out of thin air to stand beside us and come between us.

Instantly, Marshall was all cop. "Yes?"

"The captain's here. She wants a report."

Weathers let go of me and looked from Tracy to me. "I'll be right back," he said. "I need to take care of this." He turned, took a step, and looked back. "Don't go anywhere," he said.

I smiled and watched him walk away before I noticed Tracy the Nose Basher studying my every move.

"He feels sorry for you," she said.

"What?" Marshall Weathers felt sorry for me? No way.

"Uh-huh," she said. She looked right at me, her face full of concern. "He told me that you're a single mom and that he tries to help you out because there's no one else to look out for you. You know, kind of like a big brother."

I couldn't believe what I was hearing. I stared at her, trying to gauge her honesty, and all I saw was pity.

"If there's ever anything I can do to help out, let me know," she said, and reached into her pocket for a business card. "Marsh and I really care about the people we work for. It's not just nine to five with us. It's a calling."

I looked across the room. He stood with his back to me, talking to his captain. As if he felt my eyes upon him, he turned, but he was looking for Tracy. He beckoned her and she put a hand out to touch my shoulder.

"I'll be right back," she said. "Will you be okay?"

"I'm fine," I said, shaking her off. "I'm going into the kitchen and get a glass of water."

"Okie-doke," she said, her voice overly cheery. I watched her cross the room and place her hand on Marshall's arm. That's when I turned away.

"What is it?" I muttered. "Do I just misread the world? Are my picker genes so bad that I find loser men on every street corner?"

I wandered into the kitchen, reached for a glass, and turned on the tap. It would all be in the paper tomorrow, how my alcoholic ex-husband got his gun stolen while he ate breakfast with a known criminal. How Vernell's rival shot Nosmo King and made it look like Vernell was the murderer and how Vernell was too blind drunk to know or even remember.

But what wouldn't be in the paper was how big a fool I'd been, traipsing all over trying to prove Vernell an innocent man, falling for a cop who only felt sorry for me, and bumbling in on a police investigation that might've eventually led to Vernell's release anyway.

I drained my glass dry and placed it carefully in the sink, looked over at the back door, and then back into the living room. Weathers was blocked from view by other police officers and crime scene technicians. I checked my watch and found it closing in on one A.M.

Mama used to quote her own passage from Proverbs when I was a young girl. "Like a gold ring in a pig's snout is a beautiful woman without good sense." Well, what kind of sense did it make for me to hang around mooning up after Marshall Weathers, or anyone else for that matter?

"Bye," I whispered, as I walked to the back door, unlocked it, and let myself out into a narrow hallway that led to the service elevator. In three minutes I had left the building, skirted the police vehicles, and driven out of the parking lot on my way to High Point Road and the Golden Stallion.

As soon as I hit Elm Street I started to have regrets. What was I doing running away? I remembered the way Marshall had kissed me on the steps at the Stallion Club and felt stupid all over again. Was that the kiss of someone who feels pity? No, it couldn't be.

Just as quickly I remembered the way Tony Carlucci had kissed me, and the things he'd said about me and about Marshall Weathers. Where was the truth in all of this? Was I just scared? Or was Carlucci wrong and Weathers right?

I was so confused. The VW seemed to find its own way back to the club while I steered on autopilot. I pulled into the parking lot, weaving my way around pickups and vans, until I reached the spot where the employees parked. I guided my car into a slot right next to Jack's restored Karmen Ghia, put on the brake, and leaned back against my headrest.

I closed my eyes and tried to envision the old home place as it had been years ago when I was a child and life was so much simpler.

"I thought you said I'd know when it was right, Mama," I whispered, and felt a tear slide down my cheek. "Why aren't you here to help me?"

The passenger-side door opened, startling me, and I

looked over to see Harmonica Jack sliding into the seat beside me.

"Hey," he said, reaching over and wiping the tear away with his index finger. "What's so terrible you gotta sit out here in your car crying?"

I couldn't answer him. The tears choked my voice, and before I could say much of anything, I was sobbing on his shoulder, and he was wrapping his arm around me and chuckling to himself.

"Why are you laughing at me?" I muttered, my voice muffled by his warm flannel shirt.

"Maggie, you are such a bundle of nerves and energy. It just amuses me, that's all." He handed me a handkerchief from his pocket and sat with me while I snuffled to a stop. He didn't say another word until I finally sat up, blew my nose, and looked at him.

"I hate men," I said.

Jack threw back his head and laughed. "No, you don't. That's your whole problem, Magpie, you don't hate them at all. You just put too much stock in 'em and not enough in yourself."

Jack looked away then, out the window at the few customers who straggled out looking for their cars.

I wanted to say something, something that would come right to the heart of things, something that would make it all right between us, but I didn't have the first clue.

"Thank you for being here," I said, finally.

He looked back at me and smiled. "Maggie, it's just not our time. That's not to say there won't be a time, or that I'm not just as much here for you as I always am. It's just not now for us, you know? And you don't need to feel bad about it or explain it or apologize for it. Some things are the way they are. Let it go, Magpie. Breathe."

I stretched out my hand and he slipped his into mine and we sat there, breathing, for a long time, until I knew we could sit there no longer.

"Sheila's due here any minute," I said.

"Mummm . . ." he said, deep into his relaxed state of

New Age meditation. He sighed. "Guess we should go inside then."

I reached over and opened my door. The cold night air blew in and brought Jack back to the present reality.

"Okay, let's go."

We walked in through the back door with five minutes to spare, but it didn't really matter, because at that exact moment Tony Carlucci, Sheila, and Marshall Weathers all arrived at the front door, their eyes locking on me like homing pigeons sensing their home roost.

"Jeez," Jack whistled softly. "Better you than me."

I stood there, watching and waiting, as they walked toward me. My heart was in my throat, my mouth was dry, and my palms were starting to sweat. It was decision time, and there was no doubt about that.

"You ready?" Tony asked.

"Maggie, I need to talk to you," Marshall said. "Why did you leave?"

"Mama!" Sheila said. "What's going on?"

"Breathe," I heard Jack saying in my head. *"You're terrified, aren't you?"* I heard Tony ask. And then Marshall: *"Don't think I'm walking away from you."*

My heart pounded louder and louder, filling my head, and rushing through my ears.

I stepped up to them, stretched out my hand and reached for my daughter, pulling her close to me.

"It's late," I said. "Really, really late, and I need to sleep." I looked at Tony and Marshall, and then over at Jack, who stood just behind me, listening.

"Mama always said a tired mind makes for foolish decisions. So how about you call me sometime tomorrow morning, late, and we'll talk."

Tony and Marshall stared at each other, frowning.

"Who, Maggie?" Tony asked. "Who do you want to call?"

I looked at them and smiled.

I turned around, gripping Sheila's hand, and walked out the door, my heart fairly bursting with the uncertainty and tension of it all. What if no one called me? What if they thought I was just too far above my raisings to deserve a call from either one?

We made it all the way to the car and halfway out of the parking lot before Sheila decided to put in her two cents' worth.

"Mama," she said, "do you, like, get what you just did back there?"

"Sheila," I said, "I think, like, totally. I, like, totally get it."

"Awesome," she sighed. "Damn, I wish I could do that with the guys I know! That is, like, so totally evolved."

I turned onto High Point Road and headed home.

"Whatever," I said.

I made it home, so tired I could barely remove my clothes before my head hit the pillow, and I fell into a deep and dreamless sleep that seemed to go on and on and on—right up until the bright sunlight of late morning streamed through the curtains of my bedroom window and the phone began to ring.

Discover Murder and Mayhem with

Southern Sisters Mysteries

by

ANNE GEORGE

MURDER ON A GIRLS' NIGHT OUT

0-380-78086-0/$6.50 US/$8.99 Can

Agatha Award winner for Best First Mystery Novel

MURDER ON A BAD HAIR DAY

0-380-78087-9/$6.50 US/$8.99 Can

MURDER RUNS IN THE FAMILY

0-380-78449-1/$6.50 US/$8.99 Can

MURDER MAKES WAVES

0-380-78450-5/$6.50 US/$8.99 Can

MURDER GETS A LIFE

0-380-79366-0/$6.50 US/$8.99 Can

MURDER SHOOTS THE BULL

0-380-80149-3/$6.50 US/$8.99 Can

And in hardcover

MURDER CARRIES A TORCH

0-380-97810-5/$23.00 US/$34.95 Can

Murder Is on the Menu
at the Hillside Manor Inn
Bed-and-Breakfast Mysteries by
MARY DAHEIM
featuring Judith McMonigle Flynn